MW01138281

YOUR
ONE-WAY TICKET
TO THE

GOOD TIME

Andy!
    I hope you enjoy this!

Thank you!!

BY

JUD WIDING

HIGHWAY STAR

"OH, no way!"

"What?"

Delmer Lippincott twisted and strained against his seatbelt, reaching into the well of the backseat. "Is your mom secretly awesome?"

Patch, best friend and bandmate, glanced into the rearview mirror, rising an inch in his seat before settling back down. "Almost definitely not."

Delmer rooted around in the rear of Patch's mom's '75 Buick Century, conjuring the unmistakable, almost *sensual* chunk-a-clunking of cassette tapes. "There's so much good shit back here!"

"What?" Patch rose in his seat once again, using the wheel as a lever. The car jerked slightly to the right. Onto the rumble strips. Patch corrected with a counter-jerk.

Inertia tugged Delmer halfway back into his seat. He made an *rrrr* noise high in his throat which, in that intuitive language that develops between lifelong friends, meant *eyes on the fucking road, dude.*

Patch grunted his assent in the same patois.

"This is nuts," Delmer chuckled in dumb old English as he plunged headlong back into the rear well. *Chunk-a-clunk* "Queen, Floyd…" *clunk-a-chunk* "Zeppelin…fucking *Sabbath*, are you kidding me?!"

Patch stole quick glimpses through the rearview, bouncing eagerly as though he'd spotted a clown car of naked ladies in pursuit. "Seriously?!"

Rrrr said the tires on the roadside rumble strips, and so too said Delmer.

"Bad steering," Patch mumbled as he straightened out the car.

Chunk clunk chunk. Delmer laughed. "Deep Purple and Nugent! AC/DC!" He swung himself back to the front and regained what he passed off as proper posture, cassette tape in hand. "I think your mom is fucking rock 'n roll, dude."

"No *way*. Moms can't be rock."

"I know. But there's some serious heavy metal down there."

"Were those just, like…"

"It looked like she'd tried to tuck 'em under the driver seat."

6

Patch looked at the seat beneath him. "Woah. So, I guess-"

Rrrr.

"The steering is bad, it's not my fault. *Also,* if I stayed in the lines all the time, I might not have shaken things up enough down there, and you wouldn't have seen the tapes."

"You don't know how I saw the tapes."

"I feel like there aren't that many ways you could have seen them."

That was a fair point, so Delmer didn't say anything. Instead he flipped open one of the little plastic cases and removed a cassette. With yearning confidence like he'd heard in the movies, he said "some day these are gonna be *our* fuckin' tapes, man. Some guys are gonna be discovering *our* music in their mom's car, and they're gonna be like, *fuck,* that's a cool mom."

"I don't want moms to listen to our music."

"*Cool* moms, though."

"Oh, that's okay, I guess. If they're cool with guitar solos and, uh, discussions of the devil and titties, and stuff." Patch glanced at the tape in Delmer's hand. "What'd you grab?"

"Wait, you'll see." Delmer pushed the tape through the little garage door of the tape deck.

It *thunk*ed against something already loaded in.

Delmer frowned. "Where's the eject button?"

"It's the triangle one."

"Gotcha." He pulled the current tape out, shook his head, and gave a condescending chuckle. "Doobie Brothers."

Patch laughed. "Fucking Doobie Brothers!"

"So fucking lame."

"Yeah. And it's McDonald-era, not even Johnston!"

"Ugh. Who even likes McDonald better?"

"Right? I mean, they definitely have some good songs from him."

"Oh, for sure."

"Just why would you *choose* him?" Delmer studied the tracklist on the tape. "This is actually a solid album."

"Nice. I do kinda like The Doobie Brothers."

"Yeah, me too. Just not as much as…" he slid the cassette he'd fished out of the backseat into the now-empty tape deck.

The offering was enthusiastically received, with a *clnk* and a *vvvvv* and a *k-CHNK.*

"Who'd you pick?" Patch asked.

"Just wait f-"

"-BUNGO PONY," the stereo system insisted, *"I DOGSLED ON IIII-"*

Patch pounded the ceiling of the car and howled like a wolf. "BLUE ÖYST-"

Delmer thumped the eject button. The music stopped. "That wasn't what I wanted."

"Oh."

"She's got these in the wrong cases."

"That *was* a good choice, though."

"It wasn't what I wanted."

"What'd you want?"

"Hang on," Delmer said, before diving back into the

well of miscased cassettes.

"You know what's crazy," Patch said to fill the sonic space that for one bright, shining moment had belonged to Blue Öyster Cult, "is she turned off 'The Red And The Black' halfway through. If it picked up halfway into the song like that. That's crazy." He glanced into the mirror, to the back of Delmer's head and shoulders, rising and falling in time with the *chunk-a-clunks* and *clunk-a-chunks* of his quest. "Like, even if I had a wife and she was giving birth, and I finally got to the hospital, if that song was playing I would just sit in the car and wait until the end."

Delmer swung back into his seat. "Are you saying like she's giving birth in the hospital and they called you, or she's in your backseat and you're driving her there?"

Patch laughed. "I was thinking the first one, but that'd be really funny if she was in the backseat."

"Hold on sweetheart!" Delmer called over his shoulder, chuckling as he did. "We gotta get to the end of this song!"

"Huh huh," said Patch.

Delmer pushed the new tape into the deck.

"Is it Sabbath?" Patch asked.

"Just wait."

"I do kinda wanna listen to my mom's Sabbath tape. It'd be like…seeing her naked."

"…"

"…"

"Do you want to s-"

"No," Patch snapped.

"duh-duh-duh-duh-duh-duh-duh-duh-" the stereo interven-

ed. It continued, *"duh-duh-duh-duh-duh-duh-duh-duh-"*

"OKAY!" Patch shouted, his voice cracking. "YES! DEEP *PURPLE!*"

Delmer made Elvis lips and banged his head as Ian Gillan's war cry warbled up from the depths. For no discernible reason, he flinched and slapped Patch's arm. "DUDE!"

"WHAT?" Patch shouted over (more accurately, *under)* the music.

"WE SHOULD GO ON THE HIGHWAY!"

"WHY?"

"…BECAUSE THE SONG IS CALLED 'HIGH-WAY STAR'!"

"OH!"

"DO YOU EVEN LISTEN TO ROCK 'N ROLL?"

"NO, I KNEW THAT WAS WHAT THE SONG WAS CALLED, I JUST, I GOT DISTRACTED BEC-AUSE I'M DRIVING."

"DO YOU KNOW WHAT ROCK 'N ROLL IS?!"

Patch laughed. "FUCK YOU!"

"LET'S GO!"

Patch reached out and turned the music down. "I've never driven on the highway though. I don't think my mom would be okay with that."

"Dude, the tape was in the car. You don't put Deep Purple in your car if you aren't gonna make it go fast." Delmer turned in his seat to fully face Patch. *"She* knows what rock 'n roll is. And she's a *girl."*

"Hey, no. My mom is a *woman."*

"…y-"

10

"Rock 'n roll," Patch interrupted, "is about breaking the rules."

"Right."

"It's about partying hard, and being up all night, and, and, gettin' laid."

"Fuck yeah!"

"It's about…not doing what…not doing what you're told…doing what you *aren't* told. Not to do. It's about breaking the rules."

"Great! So let's go on the highway!"

"But," Patch replied, "I also don't have my license yet."

"…then why are you driving?"

"It's my mom's car."

"…you still have to have a license though."

Keeping his eyes on the road this time, Patch grumbled "it's my *mom's* car."

"But…you still have to have a license to drive a car. Any car."

"That doesn't make *any* sense."

Delmer opened his mouth, closed it, then held his hands up in surrender. "I was just gonna say, do you know why they call this car the Century?"

Patch shook his head.

Delmer leaned towards his friend. "Because it can go *a hundred miles an hour.*"

"…seriously?"

"Yeah. TJ told me." Still tilted forward, Delmer cranked the volume back up. It would have been nice if he'd caught the song right when Gillan was singing about being a highway star. Instead he turned it up in time to hear *'SLOW ME DOWN'*. Bummer. "LET'S GO! DON'T BE A FUCKING PUSSY!"

"OKAY!" Patch shouted. "BREAKING A HUN-DRED TO 'HIGHWAY STAR'! ON THE HIGH-WAY! FUCK YEAH! LET'S DO IT!"

"ROCK 'N ROLL!"

"YEAH!"

Delmer pounded on the dashboard and made *boof boof boof* noises, like a big, jowly dog out of a cartoon.

They didn't get to the I-76 onramp until 'Pictures of Home.' As soon as Delmer saw the turn, he jammed his thumb onto the *rewind* button to queue 'Highway Star' back up.

"I'm gonna try to wait to gun it until the first chorus," Patch announced.

Delmer's brow fell. "Oh what? No, do it earlier. Once it gets into the first verse. When all the drums come in."

"All the drums?" Patch teased.

Delmer chuckled. "Oh alright dude, let's talk about guitars then, I'll laugh at *you* for not knowing how to play."

"I'm not laughing at you not knowing how to play," Patch cackled as he guided the car onto the ramp, "I'm laughing at you not knowing how to *talk.*"

"Well…" When no ferocious comebacks presented themselves, Delmer made a weird face and bobbled his head back and forth.

The car hit a bump.

The *vrrrrr* of the rewinding tape stopped.

12

JUD WIDING

Delmer frowned at the deck, and jabbed at the rewind button. "Fuck." He hit play. Nothing. "Fuck!"

"What's wrong?"

"The fucking tape jammed!"

"Oh, what?"

Eject proved as useless as the other buttons. "Yeah. It's...*shit.*"

"Shit."

Delmer thumbed the eject button a few more times, then gave up. "Piece of shit."

Patch glanced nervously from the road to the tape deck. "You gotta get that tape out, my mom's gonna be pissed if we busted her deck."

"Forget about the deck, we're almost on the highway and we don't have any tunes!"

"Uh," Patch offered, "maybe that's okay, because...I don't think we're gonna be getting up to a hundred."

Delmer looked out the windshield. Bumper to fucking bumper on I-76. "Goddamnit." He slumped back into his seat and plopped his head into his hand.

"Can you try to get the tape out again?"

Delmer did as asked, poking at the eject button a few more times before giving up once more. He sighed, returning his head to his hand. "Fuck this," he declared.

"Yeah."

"No. Not just this." Delmer gestured to the traffic jam. "I mean fuck this whole thing. Sitting around getting stewed up about it should be *our* cassettes that cool kids' cool moms are hiding in their cars."

"We were stewing about that?"

"Yeah." Delmer stewed.

Patch kept his eyes on the road.

A slow smile burbled up from Delmer's broth. "You wanna go?"

"If I could I would, man."

"No," Delmer laughed, "just forget the traffic for a second!"

Patch shrugged hard. "If I could I definitely w-"

"I'm saying, do you wanna *go* go. Like we've been talking about. All of us. Go make it happen."

"Oh…uh…sure. I guess."

"…I mean like let's get ou-"

"I know what you mean. I'm saying yeah, sure. Let's do it."

"…really?"

"Yeah!"

Fear seized Delmer by the belly, and kneaded his stomach like pizza dough. He despaired of holding on until the next available restroom. "Seriously?"

"Yes!"

"Shit. Fuck yeah. Oh my god, *fuck* yeah. Do you think the other guys'll be down?"

"Probably. If not, fuck em."

"Holy shit!" Delmer clapped his hands, which was *not* rock and roll, so then he pounded on the dashboard again, which *was*. "We're doing it!"

Patch howled like a wolf. "OW-OW-AR-OOOO-OOOO!"

"LA's not gonna know what hit it!"

Patch let his arm, primed and ready to pound the

ceiling, fall into his lap. The smile melted from his face.

Delmer noticed. "That's what we were talking abo-"

"Yeah, I know."

"Gotta go where the metal is."

"Yeah, I know. Just…saying it out loud is kind of…"

"…kind of *badass?*"

Patch cleared his throat. "Yeah."

"You know what?"

"What?"

"It's a long way to the top…"

Patch laughed.

Delmer leaned forward and chopped his hands through the air between them. "No, listen. Seriously. I'm not kidding. It's a *long* way to the top, if you wanna rock and roll."

"You're right."

"That's from the Bible, Patch. Stone fucking tablets."

Patch slapped his forehead. "How'd I forget?"

"I don't know."

Their smiles faded. Silence descended. Patch inched forward as the traffic permitted. "Must be an accident," he mumbled.

More silence.

The next day, just before he left high school for good, Delmer told everyone that he and Patch had ripped down the highway at a hundred miles an hour, blaring Deep Purple on the stereo. Yeah, that was a lie, but it was a memorable one. And as there wasn't much he'd *actually* done at school that kids would remember him by…he didn't see the harm.

And really, when you thought about it, it wasn't lying at all. Because he was going to be famous, playing lead guitar for the biggest rock band the universe had ever known. And famous people did outrageous stuff. So if he was famous, then the stuff he did must be outrageous, otherwise he wouldn't be famous, seeing as a famous person wouldn't do stuff that wasn't outrageous. So as a famous person (well, soon-to-be, but that was just a matter of time), any stuff he did *must* be outrageous. And if an accurate recounting of said stuff failed to bear that outrageousness out, he was well within his rights to fluff it up a bit.

See, a lie wasn't a lie if it was told to tell the truth. No sir. It was, uh…

Mythmaking. Yeah. That was it.

He was going to be someone who did stuff that people remembered, forever. He was going to create something that outlived him, that kept on rocking unto eternity, forever surprising cool kids cruising around in one of their moms' cars.

That was something he already knew. And as long as he knew the ending, why not get a jump on shaping how the rest of his righteous story would be told?

Back in the car which was certainly not ripping – barely even *creasing* – down the highway, Delmer thought about what he was going to tell his parents when he got home.

Halfway there, he asked Patch to pull into a rest stop.

A REALLY GOOD IMAGINATION

BUB Bowersox froze, hunched over his little broom, staring at the butler into which he'd been sweeping popcorn off the floor. "Ouch," he realized.

"What's wrong?" Angela Manager (Bub was fairly certain that her last name was not actually Manager, but her name tag made it look like it was which was funny) asked as she kept sweeping. It was very nice of her to ask; some of the other people who worked here probably would not have.

"I hurt my back," Bub told her.

Angela sighed and swept, with her own broom, into her own butler. "Just now? Sweeping?"

"I don't know. I don't think so. Sweeping doesn't hurt my back."

Sweep sigh sweep. "Go help at box office, I'll finish up in here."

Still frozen, Bub lifted his eyes and did his best to look through his eyebrows. "That's okay. I will try to finish in here."

Angela stopped sweeping and smiled at Bub. She smiled at him the way most people smiled at him. From a distance. "Don't worry about it. We're basically done."

"Oh. Ok. Thank you."

Angela Manager just nodded and went back to her sweeping.

BUB Bowersox reached his arm up and over his head, pointing his finger down his back. "What's this muscle called?" he asked.

Harrison rolled his eyes. "That's your spine."

"Hah hah," Bub chuckled, the way he knew people did. "That's funny. I meant the meat part though. The spine is the bone. I was wondering about the m-"

"There are a bunch of muscles back there. I don't know what most of them are called. Customer," he informed Bub as a couple chuckled their way to the counter. They were better at chuckling than Bub was, so Bub stopped.

"Welcome to the Regency Theater," Bub recited. "Would you like to purchase a ticket?"

The girl nuzzled the boy. Bub heard Harrison grumble something.

"Ah," the boy said, "two for *Star Trek.*"

The girl giggled.

18

Bub's face got heavy. "Though it has humor, *Star Trek: The Wrath of Khan* is not a comedy."

The couple stared. Bub stared back.

"In case you wanted to continue laughing," he explained, "I thought I sh-"

"Just sell them the tickets," Angela Manager sing-whispered as she entered the box office.

A practiced smile tore across Bub's face, like a monsoon. He pulled two tickets off the perforated link and presented them to the couple. "I'm sorry. Here you go. Two tickets for *Star Trek: The Wrath of Khan*. I hope you enjoy the show, please. Really," he added.

"Thanks," the boy said, yanking the tickets from Bub's hand.

"Ouch!"

The boy's eyes flexed. "Sorry dude."

"It's fine," Angela answered on Bub's behalf. "Enjoy the show."

The couple walked away. Bub stuck his upper lip into his mouth and turned back to Harrison. "I was asking about the back muscle," he continued, "because mine really hurts."

Harrison spun in his chair and tilted his head towards Angela. "Sounds like Bub can't do his job. Maybe he should g-"

"Do *you* want to go home?" she snapped at Harrison.

He just made a *pffft* sound in response. "Customer," he grunted at Bub.

Bub said "thank you" and then turned. There was no customer.

BUB walked home along Sunset Boulevard, right along the Strip. It was out of his way, but he liked the lights. They showed him interesting things. People laughing, smiling, having a whale of a time. Nobody ever invited Bub to whales of times, but that didn't mean he never saw what they looked like. Or heard what they sounded like. Or smelled what they smelled like. Most nights you could go to Gazzarri's and watch people porking on the yard out back. Some people threw beer at the porkers, which Bub didn't think was all that nice. But the porkers didn't seem to mind, just like they didn't mind that it was usually Ratt whose tunes were spilling out the back door. Bub didn't think he'd like to pork on a yard, listening to Ratt while having beer thrown at him. But he couldn't be sure, because he'd never tried.

You could also slip into Mötley Crüe's house pretty easily without anybody seeing. There were always people having fun there, porking each other all the live long day. Bub could just about stand right over those porkers and watch. They didn't mind. One time he tried throwing beer on them and they *did* mind. That, as far as he could tell, was the biggest difference between Ratt fans and Mötley Crüe fans.

Bub didn't like any of the music. He didn't like music. It all hurt his ears a little bit. It sounded like bugs. Bzzz, bzzz, bzzz. It was kind of scary sometimes, when it was loud. But the lights were cool. Sometimes Bub would go to concerts and clap his hands over his ears and hum so he didn't have to hear the music. He got to watch the lights that way, got to feel the vibrations. The lights at concerts were way cool, even cooler than the lights on Sunset. The lights on Sunset showed him interesting things. The lights at concerts *were* interesting things. So in that way, he liked music. Plus sometimes there was fire. A few years ago he drove nearly six hours each way to see KISS in Dale City. He could have gone to Fresno but in Dale City they were playing at a place called the Cow Palace and he thought that was a really funny name. He imagined a cow king. That wasn't too hard because KISS dressed like cows, all black and white. Anyway they had all kinds of fire and sparkles and stuff. Bub liked it a lot.

Rock 'n roll was like a barnyard. They dressed up like cows and their guitars went cluck cluck cluck, then they went backstage and porked a lady. Probably more than one. That's what Bub had heard. Nobody had told him. People who knew how many ladies were porked by rock 'n roll cows didn't talk to Bub. But that didn't mean he didn't hear about it.

He passed the Whisky and the Rainbow and thought about all the fun activities he'd heard of happening there. He liked imagining them happening to him. Him doing them. It felt weird when he thought about the activities that ended with sad ladies. Like the story he'd heard about everybody urging this one lady to put a banana in her fruit drawer, then a guy bends down and peels it with his teeth. Bub took turns imagining he was everybody there. Even the banana. He had a really good imagination.

Sometimes he would pass back into the nighttime that

was always hanging around the bright of the Strip and feel sad. He didn't know why. He could always just imagine himself more fun activities whenever he wanted. It was better than having real fun activities because real ones ended. Imagination was forever. That only made him feel worse, though. He could never imagine himself back to happy. There were nights he couldn't even imagine himself happy at all.

He tried to imagine his back didn't hurt. The muscle between the shoulderblades. Maybe it was more than one muscle. He had no idea how he'd hurt it. It was easy to imagine ways that he had. Playing tennis, or paddling a boat, or doing a handstand. It couldn't have been those, though, because Bub didn't do any of those. He got dizzy too easily. No way he could do a handstand. But how had he hurt his back, then? Backs could hurt. They didn't have to *be* hurt. Like hearts. There wasn't always a reason. A lot of times hurt just *was*.

This felt like it had a reason though. This ache. It stretched its spider legs across his shoulders, up his neck, down to his hips. Then it squeezed until it hurt to breathe. Bub didn't think it cared. This ache.

The rest of the walk home was dark and quiet. Bub always put his hands in his pockets and his chin on his chest. That way he didn't have to look at other people, and he could count the cracks in the sidewalk. The accidental ones, not the ones between tiles. There were one hundred and thirty-four accidental cracks from the end of the Strip to Bub's house. Once Jan from work had asked him how far he lived from the Theater. He'd said he didn't know, but he was one hundred and thirty-four accidental cracks past the Strip. She didn't know what that meant. He'd told her he didn't need a ride home, thank you. Jan was very nice. Basically the nicest person Bub had ever met.

Except for Dominick.

"Hi there," Bub said as Dominick came hustling down from his seat on the stoop of a duplex.

Dominick smiled and jerked his chin upwards. He used to clap Bub on the shoulder, until Bub asked him not to. Bub didn't really like being touched. There was a word for that. Sometimes he didn't like that he didn't like being touched, but today he liked it. His back hurt already. If Dominick had clapped on it, the ache would've smiled.

"How was the Strip tonight?" Dominick asked. Dominick always had a question for Bub. The first few times Bub had met Dominick, he'd been a lot bossier. He'd said things like "give me all your money!" or "throw me your wallet and fucking run!" But after five nights in a row of taking Bub's money and making him run, Dominick had asked his first question. It was "why the fuck do you keep walking down this street?" Bub had told him it was because it was the way home from work. So Dominick asked another question, which was "are you fucking retarded?" Then they became friends. Life is funny. Ha, ha.

"The Strip was funny," Bub replied. "It's always so funny. Today some people came in and thought *Star Trek: The Wrath of Khan* was funny. If they had seen the

Strip, they'd know better."

"*Star Trek* isn't funny?" Dominick asked.

Bub shrugged. "Sometimes. Ouch. My back hurts today."

"Well shit, what are you up to now? Mike and I wrestled a grill up to the roof, we're gonna get shit-hammered and make burgers. Mike's a funny guy, you'll like him."

"That's ok. The Strip made me sad again. I wouldn't laugh enough. I don't want Mike to think he isn't funny."

"Trust me, ain't no chance of that." Dominick said it in a way that made Bub think maybe Mike wasn't actually that funny.

"Well, that's ok. I'll take a rain check. Even though you can't grill if it's raining. Ha, ha."

"Alright. You take it easy, Bub. Come crash if you change your mind."

"Thank you. Goodnight." Bub smiled. In twenty-seven accidental cracks, he would be home.

HOME for Bub was the fourth floor of a four-story apartment complex. It was a narrow stairwell that got him up. They had to put easily removable windows in when they built each story because that was the only way to get furniture in and out. Seemed like it'd have been easier to just build a bigger stairwell, but Bub wasn't an architect. What did he know about stairwell widths? Very little. That was almost a joke. Bub would work on it and try it out on Dominick. Dominick would definitely laugh.

He shouldered his way up the steps, right elbow scraping along the wall. The sound traveled up his arm and rattled the palm pressed against his right ear. It was like talking on the phone with a landslide. Made his elbow hurt, too. And his back! Bub sprinted up the steps, humming loudly to himself. Not to himself enough, though: he heard a third floor door swing open as he hit the landing, and the person who opened it told him to "SHUT THE FUCK UP." Whoever was on the third floor always seemed to be directly behind the door, waiting to yell at Bub to shut the fuck up. So Bub just imagined it was the door itself yelling at him to shut the fuck up. That way it was funny instead of scary.

Bub always wanted to apologize about needing to shut the fuck up, but if he said he was sorry he would be doing the opposite of shutting the fuck up. So he kept quiet and tiptoed up to the fourth floor, then down the hall to his door. He plunged his hand into his front right pocket and felt two things in there.

Which was wrong.

There was only supposed to be one thing in there. His key.

Humming without quite realizing it, Bub balled a fist around both objects and pulled them up into the light. One of them was a key, which sparkled a little bit.

The other was a human tooth, which did not.

That there was a connection between the ache in his back and the tooth in his palm occurred immediately. Imagination failed to determine what that connection might be.

Squinting, Bub ran the meat of his thumb across his own chompers. All present and accounted for. The tooth wasn't his, then. How strange.

Looking down for a long time hurt his back. So Bub lifted his gaze, plucked the key from the slow clench of his fist and guided it carefully into the lock. The key.

His apartment was just like he remembered it. The mattress over here, the floor lamp over there. Nothing was out of place. He liked that. Sometimes his apartment wasn't just like he remembered it. The furniture would be rearranged, or the pictures would be hanging upside down, or there'd be a new television set in the far corner. Bub didn't like that. He didn't like his apartment making big decisions like that without asking him first.

Maybe that was how the tooth got into his pocket.

Yep, that must have been it.

Bub was satisfied with that.

He couldn't help but wonder what *that* was, though.

DELMER'S PARENTS JUST DON'T GET IT

HIS parents just didn't get it. They weren't listening. They were so wrapped up in what they thought a family "should" be, how kids "should" kowtow to every little thing their poser-ass folks told them, that they weren't even hearing the words he was saying to them.

So Delmer put his fork and knife down on the plate, making sure they landed with a big old *clink* sound, and told them again: "I'm moving to Hollywood. I'm gonna be the biggest rock star the world has ever seen. And you *can't* stop me!"

Delmer's mom looked over at his dad with that same annoying face, her eyebrows slanted up and mouth twisted into a phony little smile, and she said the same thing she'd said last time. "That's great, honey. We totally support you."

"Do you need money to help with the move?" His dad added from across the dinner table.

"NO!" Delmer shouted. "You can't *bribe* me into staying here! I'm an *artist!*"

"We just want to help," his mom told him.

Delmer considered throwing his plate across the room, but then remembered that he was eating off of one of the plates his parents had gotten on their honeymoon about a thousand years ago. So he considered just tilting his cheap-as-hell fish filet onto the floor, except he was still hungry and really wanted to finish it. Utterly trapped, he settled for picking up his utensils again, and once more dropping them onto the plate. *Clink.* "Why do you think I need your help so badly? Don't you *believe in me?"*

"Moving is expensive," Dad replied, a forkful of fish halfway to his face. "Especially that far across the country."

"You can take any furniture you want," Mom piled on. "Except for the loveseat in the TV room, we still sit on that one a lot." She smiled over at Dad. "Don't we, dear?"

"It's the best seat for watching the television," Dad granted, still chewing on a mouthful of his mahi-mahi.

Delmer just shook his head. "I don't want *any* of this goddamned furni-"

"Come on," Dad grunted.

"The swearing isn't necessary," Mom whined.

Delmer sank into his seat slightly. "Fine. I don't want

any of this blankety-blank furniture. I don't want your precious little corporate sheep dollars that you got from your precious little office job, and I don't want your pity, and I don't want your *help*. I'm starting *fresh.*"

Dad dabbed at the corners of his mouth with a paper napkin. "I understand. That's a great sentiment. Great work ethic."

"It's how we know you're going to do so well with your music," Mom joined in.

"But…" Dad returned his napkin to his lap. "It's maybe not the best, uh, thing. Moving is expensive. And we're happy to help."

"Moving's not gonna be that expensive," Delmer fired back. "We're not taking *anything* with us."

His parents exchanged another glance. Another *disbelieving* glance.

This was going to be such a turning point in his story, Delmer knew. He'd write a book about his life, and people would buy it by the millions. And everybody would read this part, and hardly be able to believe how committed to his art he was. This was like a temptation scene. It was like he was a married man being seduced by a sexy temptress, beckoned to a commit a fucking awesome titty sin. Except instead of being married to a human lady, he was married to his music. To the power of rock and roll.

And instead of being seduced by some kind of raven-haired mistress with hips three times as wide as her belly and tattoos all over her chest, it was his parents.

He frowned. Wherever that analogy had been headed,

he was *deeply* dissatisfied with where it wound up.

"You're free to make whatever choices you feel are best," announced Delmer's father. "But I just worry that…you know, I'm just letting you know, moving is harder than you think. We c-"

"You don't know how hard I think moving is," Delmer snapped. "I think it's a lot easier than you think it is, *but*, I also think it's harder than you think I think it is. I think it's exactly the amount of hard that it is."

"We're just trying to tell you how it is," Mom chimed in. "We've done it before."

"I did it before too! Or did you forget I was even *born* then?"

"Well, Delmer, you were eight months old."

"But I was *born!*" Sensing his moment, he rose slightly, pushed his seat back, then snapped the rest of the way to his feet and thumped his chest. "I was *born!* Do you even *know that?* I'm my own person!" He tried to thump the table with his fist, but found it too far to knock without bending down, which he didn't want to do. So he instead swung his right hand onto his hip. Even though his left was hanging limply at his side. It wasn't quite the pose he'd hoped to strike, but it would have to do. "I'm a *rock star!*"

"We believe you will be," Mom said. "But until then, we're more than happy to help y-"

"You'll see!" Delmer shouted. "I'll show you! I'll be the biggest blankety-blanking rock star of all time! Then I'll buy a *hundred* furniture pieces! And I *don't* need your help to do it!"

Dad shrugged. "Okay. I'm sure they have jobs out there that pay enough t-"

"I'm *also* never gonna get a job that isn't *rock 'n roll! ROCK 'N ROLL!*" he added, as he stormed from the kitchen. Which were, fittingly enough, the final words he would ever speak to his parents.

Until the following morning, when he asked his dad if he could borrow an atlas. And when he asked his mom if she could give him a ride to Patch's house.

There were actually a lot of other words he said to his parents after *"ROCK 'N ROLL!"* But Delmer made no effort to commit those to memory; they wouldn't be part of the memoirs.

BA-DA-BA-DA!

"I hear you," the telemarketer interrupted, "but this is, pardon my language here, a hell of a deal. Just a *hell* of a deal."

Silence, save the plastic *squeak* of the phone being strangled. Isley Pultrock heard her knuckle *pop*, and only then deduced that she perhaps ought to loosen her grip on the receiver.

"Hello?" the telemarketer added.

"What do you make?" Isley wondered.

"Uh…phone calls?"

Isley sniffed. "Your *paycheck*, you goofy son of a bitch. What do you make on your *paycheck?*"

"M-"

"If you say *money*, so help me."

"Help you what?" Said with a tinny sneer.

Squeak pop crunch.

"Do you know who the fuck you've called?" Isley demanded.

A theatrical rustling of papers on the other end of the line. "Izz-ley Pultroon, biggest bitch in tinseltown?" She could hear someone laughing in the background. Now the *fore*ground.

Now it was Isley's turn to grin. "Try Detective *Isley,*" she hammered the pronunciation, *eye-lee*, "Pultrock of the LAPD. Now do you wanna tell me how much you make an hour, or do you want me to find out as I'm stapling your last four pay-stubs to your forehead?"

"What," the voice somewhere between man and boy asked, "am I supposed to be scared now? You don't seem like such a hotshot to me."

"Last warning."

"Why do you even care how much I make?"

"That was it!" Isley slammed her fist down on table, leaning forward so the *THUMP* would register over the phone. "The last warning! I'm gonna find you, you bastard! How dare you! How dare you call me, you piece of shit! Get ready to fucking die!" Isley punched the receiver into its cradle, ripped the phone out of the wall, and threw it across the room.

It flew towards the glasstop table upon which she'd been cutting her lines with an expired driver's license, before being *rudely* interrupted by the telemarketer. Isley watched the next bit happen in slow-motion: the phone hit the glass, sending a fissure slashing through a reflection of the water-stained ceiling of her apartment. The pane crystallized and split, shards whirling like glaciers celebrating a calving. What was there to celebrate, though? The ice was knives, and it cut and recut her lines, sprinkling the coke she'd purchased at great personal risk and expense into the high-pile carpet, the acquisition of which had posed only reputational hazards; the cuddly mire now devouring her score had been a cheap get by virtue of being out of style. Coke, alas, was only just hitting its fashionable stride, having reached the west coast quite recently.

The past swallowed the present.

Or maybe that was just the hash talking.

Probably shouldn't have given the kid her name and departmental position just prior to threatening him. Damn. And now she didn't even have the fix for which she'd been so impatient. Double damn.

"Damn," she mumbled to herself, to her high-pile carpet, to her shattered glass table, to the hole in the wall where the phone used to be, to her RCA Colortrak on which Brokaw was flying solo and doing a hell of a job, just a *hell* of a job, to the phone on the floor where the hole never was, to the lump in the wallpaper she'd superglued with what was it, ah, superglue, to the sun through the window that was further down than it ought to have been, to the Diadora Borg Elites on her feet, she'd bought them because they sounded like Star Wars characters but apparently they were fashionable, had been like the carpet maybe were like the coke, but not anymore probably because they were in really rotten shape, to the pants her sneakers were wearing like a tall hat for cats, but they weren't striped red and white they were a dull yellow, the color of a banana in an old photograph, but pleated and high-waisted which wasn't at all like a banana, not one bit, to her dull pastel patterned turtleneck, when had she put *that* on, must have gotten cold, must have gotten cold as *hell*.

"Damn," she repeated.

She would have to change before she went in.

SERGEANT Hollenbeck kept saying things. This was profoundly frustrating, as Isley wanted him to listen to things that *she* was saying.

"Listen sir," she sniffed, "I'm sorry I barged in on you if that's what you're upset about. But listen, listen to me, I'm just trying to tell you, if somebody calls in and says they're a telemarketer and that I threatened to kill them, they're lying. About the second thing. Or the first, for all I fucking know."

More yammering from the Sergeant. Unbelievable! Why did he keep talking?

"Excuse me Sarge, sir, but I still don't think you're listening. Excuse me."

"No," the Sergeant babbled, "*you're* not listening."

Isley threw her hands in the air. "I know, right? That's what I'm saying!"

Next thing Isley knew the Sergeant was across the room, making a respectable effort at looming over her despite his being a head and a half shorter. Either he was a halfsquat or Isley was a giant. She couldn't remember. She sure as hell *felt* tall though. "Are you high?" he asked.

"Either that," she replied helpfully, "or you're low."

"What are you on?"

"I mean, not much. Pot and coke, mostly. Not as much coke as I'd hoped. Only got a bump in before the phone fed the rest to the, uh, um, apartment grass. What's that? Carpet! Shouldn't have said that, huh? Fuck, that sucks!"

Sergeant Hollenbeck shook his head and took a slumping seat on the corner of his desk. "Forget the call. Go home, sober up. Come down enough to at least be *functional.*"

"My table broke though. What call? Exactly. The telemarketer's a liar if he says I tried to kill him, because I haven't yet. Sober *up,* or come *down,* which is it, eh? Oh, alright, maybe two bumps."

She blinked and the Sergeant was back in his chair, on the other side of his desk. "Go home," he said.

SO she did, only she didn't remember doing it. She remembered Sergeant Hollenbeck telling her to go, and then she remembered being at home. There was bottle of red wine on the counter, the kind of wine's got more syllables than it knows what to do with, that she'd never seen before. Must have bought it preowned, because it was half gone. Or half there. Best to stay positive. Too many negatives in the world, who needs more? She did, so she poured herself some more, and then it was gone. She followed it like a clue.

Why not? Wine not, haha, a wine knot to be unraveled, it was a clue and a mystery. She was a dang sleuth and sleuths follow clues, which only rhyme if they're plural. Singular clue came first, when Officer Friend, his name wasn't Friend but he was a Friend and an Officer which wasn't his name either, he was an Officer and his name was Carpet, Officer Carpet, no, what, he had a name, just a *hell* of a name, what was it. Thump thump. No. Knuckles on the door. Let yourself in. Say it loud, say it proud. "Let yourself in, loud and proud. Hee hee."

Carpet let himself in, only his name was Saacks, spelled like that, like he was proud of it. Officer Saacks. He said, "where the fuck were you?"

And so she said, "I'm still not dead yet. I can't believe it."

He asked her, "are you trying?" All serious, like she was. She wasn't. Never would. But she didn't say so.

Instead she said "where wasn't I?"

Saacks, Saaaacks, he had to think about it. He thought about it and he said "at the scene" even though he sounded like he wasn't done thinking about it.

"What scene?"

Saacks made a face that should have been on money. He asked her if she was high, and she said her joke again even though it didn't work because Saacks was about her height, about a hundred feet tall. Finally right away all of an eventual sudden he said "the crime scene, you idiot."

That hit home, where she was. Sarge says go home so where does she go, home, and here's Saacks. Officer. Can't cut that down like Sarge from Sergeant. Where do you go? Off from Officer? Off Saacks, sounds like a baseball thing. Sounds like a game of gridiron and cleats. "Where wasn't I?" she asked again.

"They got a body."

Clarity like a truncheon. Smash, crash, back to Earth. "Holy shit," Isley said, hitting back with her consonants. Holy shi-*tuh*. "The Good Time Butcher?"

"The Good Time Butcher," Saacks nodded.

"Who didn't call me? Why not?"

"The line was busy."

That fucking telemarketer. She didn't even have to ask when the call had come through, not just because it hadn't. It had to have been when she was on with that bastard, that little bastard boy who'd apparently ruined more than one line for Isley. "Oh, I'm gonna kill him," she said.

"We have to find him first," Saacks replied, because he didn't know they weren't talking about the same person. "Let's go."

"Where?"

"…"

Isley nodded. "The scene. Right. Now?"

"They're gonna close it soon."

"Why? It's a scene. Don't tell me. I know. Saacks," she enunciated, savoring both vowels, "I'm high as a kite."

"Yeah, no shit." He reached out his hand to help her up. She needed to go *down*, though.

"If I'd known about the scene, I wouldn't be."

"I'm sure." He wasn't.

"I'm serious," she insisted. "I'm not joking," she elaborated.

"I'm sure you're not." Saacks heaved Isley to her feet. "Come on, up, up!"

"Who's on the scene now? Colby? Don't tell me."

"It's Colby."

"Damn! Fuck shitting, fucking *shit* man. If I'd known about the scene, that's what I'm telling you."

"Uh-huh."

"I am *telling* you. You see about my table? That's something else."

Saacks led Isley out the front door, grunting vague assent without meeting her eye. He must have been scared, she thought, because her eyes were fire and they could shoot lasers. She was a goddamned superhero. Kitewoman. High as could be. She felt incredible. She hated it. Colby was on the scene and Isley was going to miss the case. No clues, no case. She needed the clues. Colby was going to slurp them all up. Goodbye clues.

That was when Detective Isley Pultrock realized that her friend was avoiding her gaze because he was disappointed. Because he'd been at the party where Isley had taken her first bump. Peer pressure. Beat cops, his buddies. Bunch of tough guys. They'd said she couldn't run with them, a lady detective, too delicate. Bull*shit*, pass the nasty. Turned out *nasty* wasn't slang for cocaine, but it had sounded good. And they'd known what she'd meant. They didn't know she'd meant it, though. She had. She'd taken a bump and they'd laughed and slapped her on the back. She never saw any of them again, but she made more than a few visits to the evidence room, then once she'd outpaced the influx of new contraband, directly to the Strip. Saacks told her later they'd been fucking with her. None of them did coke. Now she had a monkey on her back. Not a good look, was all Sergeant Hollenbeck had ever said. Not a good look if you're not a beaner or a glam fag. Whatever though. The monkey could be a pal sometimes, a real chum, even if other nights he ground his thumbs into her eye sockets. Oh yeah, the monkey was a fella. No doubt about that. Before that, though, the other fellas. The ones on Saacks' beat. They still laughed, she bet. But Saacks didn't. He never took that hit. But he never told her not to, either. Bubkes was what he'd had to say on the night. Zilch. Maybe that was why he never looked her in the eyes and said, gosh, what a bummer you are now.

Turned out the back of his head said it better.

"Bummer," she repeated for the first time. "Bummer. Fuckin' bummer."

"What?" Saacks sighed as he led her down the cracked linoleum of the stairway.

"I set out a kite and it flew away."

"Ok."

"No. Not ok. *Ok* is what it isn't. I'm done with it all. You see about my table? That's me. Dusted. Get me through the scene tonight. I just gotta get it from Colby, then it's mine and I'm its. Um, uh, uh, you know. Just help me get it, I need a win. Colby doesn't need another fucking win, *I* do."

"I know."

41

"After this scene I'm clean. This is my clean scene."

"Sure it is."

"You should believe me. I'm telling you. Do you believe me? Don't tell me."

So he didn't, and she didn't ask again.

SAACKS' car was a Crown Vic, maybe one of the first they'd rolled off the assembly line. Who was they? Ford. How Saacks *could* a-Ford one, ha, hee, Isley had no clue. The problem was, was that, that was the problem. She needed clues. Clues were at the scene. Where were they going. Where they were going? To the scene. To find clues.

Isley's mouth said "Money doesn't grow on trees, goddamnit, but cherries do."

Saacks grunted his agreement; even in her state of experiential extremity, Isley caught the condescension.

"Don't patronize to me. Cherries, you dig? You fuck-in' dig?"

"Are you telling me," Saacks asked, "that you'd like to stop for ch-"

She slapped the dashboard. "Hell no! Pedal to the metal! Faster! I'm just saying they grow on trees. I bet you didn't know that." She sighed, melted into her seat and looked out the window. "Sorry." Isley turned on the radio and immediately changed the station. A split second of music became a waterfall. Static. No. Thrashing. White water. "I love this song," she said. A joke. Saacks thought she was being serious. She couldn't blame him.

She found a real radio station, with real music.

"By god," Isley shivered, "I get this case and I'm cold turkey. Brr, gobble. Like that. See?"

Saacks kept his eyes on the road. He didn't always do that. He'd turn if he wanted. Which meant this time, he didn't want. "Isley, don't take this the wr-"

"GODDAMN!" she screamed, cranking the volume as Metallica's "Whiplash" came thundering in through the aether. "BA-DA-BA-DA!" She sounded better than the guitars. She was drums.

"Listen, y-"

"BA-DA-BA-DA!"

"Cut that shi-"

"BA-DA-BA-DA!"

"I swear to fu-"

"BA-DA-BA-DA!"

"ISLEY. ST-"

"Baaaaaaah," she faded out with the rest of the band, except the drums, which were her. She bounced her shoulders with the beat. Or close enough that Saacks could hopefully tell that was what she was trying to do. "You heard this song before? Thrash, man. Adrenaline, like it says in the song, like the man says in the so-BAAAAH! BAAAAH!" the guitars were back.

Her own voice echoed in her heard, *so-BAAAAH!* over and ov-AAAAH until it died a small death and became *sober*.

"Cold turkey," she said to Saacks, and that was the last thing she said the whole way there.

SAACKS hadn't even stopped the car before Isley was

opening the door. "Hang on," he tried to say. Probably. She only heard the "ha-", and then the rest was lost to the dry *smack* of her shoulder hitting the pavement. The tuck and roll was a bust. Too bad.

She pushed herself to her feet, dusted herself off and walked confidently into what may or may not have been the scene. There wasn't nearly as much yellow tape as she'd expected. She'd expected some. There was none. None was less than some. That was a rule. It was one of those rules.

Before entering the apartment complex she slapped herself in the face and did three jumping jacks. On the last one both of her feet hit the ground at the same time. That meant she was sober enough to go in. So she open-ed the door and walked into it. It was locked and she'd walked *into* it. You had to push instead of pull. Third time's the charm.

"Isley!" Saacks hissed from behind her. "No!"

She showed him a rude finger. "We can't wait for backup!"

"That's the wrong building!"

She backed up. "Where's the scene?"

He pointed to a different building. They both follow-ed his finger through the door until they found yellow tape. Then Isley was off and running. She barreled straight through the finish line stretched across the door, to an apartment on the fifth floor. She won the race. "I won," she announced to the room.

It was basically empty. There were only two uniforms putzing around. But Luca Colby was there. Luca goddamned Colby. Nice suit, idiot. Right? Nice suit. Nice fucking haircut. Like, right?

"What did you win?" Colby asked. What a whatsit. Lady bastard. Bastette.

"I won the race, lady bastard," Isley informed Colby with the wide-mawed phrasing unique to those for whom sobriety was an affectation. "Race for the case. They're my clues. Detectette. That's sexist." She spit on the floor. "Fuck." She ground her saliva into the floorboards with the toe of her shoe. Sneaker. She thought she'd changed. Damn.

Colby sighed and lifted her gaze. Looking at Saacks, running up behind Isley. She could hear him.

"Is she high?" Colby asked Saacks.

"Damn right she is," Isley growled. "She's standing here. Fly as a kite." She looked down at her fist. Her middle finger was still up. She'd forgotten to put it down. "That's not for *you*," she teased Colby, like it was cake.

"Listen," Saacks said to Colby, like he always said. It was always listen. Listen.

"No, *you* listen!" Isley snapped. "I might be fucked up, but I won't! I'm giving it the old heave-ho because we got The Good Time Butcher on our paws! The Good Time Butcher is mine!"

Colby made dumb face. Idiot. She couldn't believe what she was hearing. Maybe. Or she could. "You want the case?"

"I won the race!"

"Jesus." Colby threw her hands up. "Thank you. Take it."

For the first time in hours, Isley found stillness. Or vice versa. "What?"

"It's a shitshow," Colby explained. "This is the kind of thing people get trapped by."

"No," Isley fired back, "it's a career-maker. Catching The Good Time Butcher is like, like, *wow!* It's the thing!"

Colby stared at Isley for so long that they all grew old and died. "Ok," came her death-rending declaration, "how's this. I don't feel good about foisting something like this on you if you're not…in your right mind."

"First of all," Isley said.

"…"

"…what were you gonna say?"

"I was *saying,*" Colby resumed, "that I don't want to take advantage of your, uh, state. But I also *really* don't want this case. Given the choice I wouldn't touch it with a pole. S-"

"How long?"

"How long is…the pole?"

"Yeah. How many feet are we talkin' here?"

"The pole is a metaphor."

Isley sniffed.

Colby cocked her thumb towards a room behind her. "You go in, you take a look, you tell me if you see anything that *doesn't* strike you as a total dead-end. If you do, the case is yours for the taking. On the condition you never try to fob it back off on me."

"Cool," was Isley's reply. She charged into the bedroom, snapping at Saacks to "stay."

The room had the color and attitude of dead grass.

Earthy carpet, brown walls. Ug-*ly*. Only thing notable about the room was the grey lump on the bed. It was a human body the same way a chassis was a Crown Vic. The cheeks drooped into the mouth, the teeth visible in relief. The fibula and the tibia on each leg looked like the mast and boom of a fleshy sail. Push a finger into the belly and you'd probably feel the inside of the spine. Isley didn't want to try.

She only knew she was looking at a woman because Saacks had said so.

Isley crouched in front of the bed, studying the body. Looking for the needle mark. Ligature burns on the wrists and ankles. Chafing at the sides of the lips. All restraints since removed. That was The Good Time Butcher's M.O. He, if it was a he (of *course* it was a he), wanted them to look peaceful. Like they'd just deflated in their sleep.

No apparent insertion points at the major arteries. Hard to tell, of course. The skin was so loose Isley had to stretch it out to search for punctures. Still, no signs. The Good Time Butcher to a T once again. The bleedout was meant to be slow. If what Isley had read held true, there should actually have been *two* points of hypodermic contact. One for the needle that sucked their blood, a second for the one that fed the victim TPN. A cocktail to keep them alive, and conscious, for as long as possible. The Good Time Butcher wanted them to feel the life trickling away, drip drip drip. Wanted them to have time to know that their run of good luck was at an end.

Nobody knew why. Maybe the guy'd had a bad run of

it himself, hated seeing happy people having fun. Wanted them to know his pain. Psychobabble bullshit. Isley didn't care why. She just wanted to know *who*. The face behind the stupid fucking name. The Good Time Butcher. Stupid. What, was The Shindig Slaughtermonger taken? What a big dumbass.

She pulled up the girl's top lip. Front right tooth missing. A souvenir. Part of the M.O. Taking away their smile? Conjecture.

Careful. Isley bundled her hand in bedsheet. Lifted up the poor girl's right hip. Count the sores. At least twelve. Isley frowned and let the girl rest. How long did it take for bedsores to form? How long had the girl been held here? How long had she lived?

Isley wanted to know. She wanted to know who had done it to her. She wanted to know because she didn't want to live in a world in which someone could do this to a person and get away with it.

So he wouldn't get away with it. Because Isley wanted to live in this world. It wasn't all that great of a world, to be honest. Room for improvement. Which and so, that was where she came in.

So she came back into the living room from the dying room, the bedroom. Three quick paces into Colby's personal space.

"Um," Colby said.

"Metallica," Isley replied, "ever heard of 'em?"

"…no?"

"There is a feeling deep inside, that something fucking mad. A feeling of a hammerhead, something something bad. Ring any bells?"

"…"

She pointed towards the front door. "Signs of forced entry?"

"…um, nothing except the tape you broke."

"Don't worry. I did that. Don't tell me. I know." Isley shook her head. "Tell me what I don't know. What didn't I see?"

"I…don't know what you saw."

"I'm not asking you what I saw."

"But if y-"

"Who was she?"

Colby cleared her throat, on surer ground here. "Her name was Barbara Dewey. She w-"

"Fax it to me," Isley interrupted.

"…I will, but I can tell y-"

"Fax it to me and I'll look at the fax. After you fax it to me. Her name was Barbara. Right. Okay. I want the case."

Colby's eyes darted to the space behind Isley that was likely full of Saacks.

"Don't look at him," Isley ordered. "He's not taking your case. I'm taking your case. You're giving it to me and I'm taking it. Right? Okay?"

"It's yours," Colby sighed, relieved.

Isley narrowed her eyes. "Why don't I like you?"

"…I didn't realize you didn't like me."

"I don't. For some reason I don't like you. I can't remember why."

"…did I do something to you?"

"That's what I'm trying to figure out. Two cases," Isley shook her head. "Two mysteries. Jesus *CHRIST*, three! Who called me, you know?" She thumped her pointer finger against Colby's breastbone. "Anybody tells you they called me and I threatened to kill 'em, they're liars and I need to know where they live."

"…"

"Don't look at him. He's not taking your case." Isley slapped her cheeks again and did *five* jumping jacks. "Okay. Come here," she called Saacks. "We're going in. Every clue we can find. I want it."

"Uh," Saacks began, "I'm not really a clue-gathering guy."

"Then you wait in the car. After this," she announced to the carpet, low-pile, almost certainly undusted with illicit substances, "I'm going home and getting turkey. Going turkey. Roll down the windows," her wagging finger reminded Saacks, "I don't want you to get heat stroke and die. I need a ride home. Later. Not now."

She returned to the room she now knew had belonged to Barbara. Maybe it still did. Her names were on the paper. Name on the papers. That was how you owned something. Didn't matter if you were alive anymore. What mattered was the name on the paper. Isley imagined The Good Time Butcher's name in the paper. The real one. Next to his face. Then she'd own him. Then he'd belong to the State of California. Even if he wasn't alive anymore. Maybe then Barbara would be free. Wasn't she? Maybe not. Who was?

Isley sniffed.

50

INTERESTING THINGS

IT definitely wasn't sudden, but it felt like it was. Every-body on the Strip was talking about Ace and Slash and Grip, like now rock and roll's not a barn but it's a hard-ware store, then before you know it all they're talking about is the Good Time Butcher. Bub thought he was just another rocker, the Butcher, but only for a little bit. He was a really good listener. Bub was.

"I heard he works at a limo rental company, right? Anybody who rents a limousine, he's driving 'em, he sees, fuck, how much fun're they having? How much? Too much? Then he cuts their fucking throats."

"I heard this little girl won a national science fair, got her name in the paper. Smiled a bit too big in the picture, maybe. Next thing you know she's slashed ear to ear."

"What *I* got told is he don't cut 'em up. He drains 'em, makes 'em know what's happening. Take a tooth out, just to keep."

That last part was interesting to Bub. He'd found that tooth in his pocket. It hadn't been his, and he hadn't had any reason to keep it, but throwing it out had felt wrong. Somebody might be looking for it. So he'd kept it under his pillow like when he was a kid. It didn't turn into a quarter, but he knew it wouldn't. Teeth don't do that without help.

Maybe the Good Time Butcher gave him the tooth? Why would he do that? He didn't seem like a generous kind of guy. That wasn't fair to say, though. Bub didn't know him from Adam.

"Who's Adam?" Dominick asked, because Bub had said that last part out loud.

"Eve's husband," Bub explained.

"Like Adam and Eve?" Dominick considered this. "Pretty sure they weren't married, bro."

"Bro?"

"Like brother."

"Like Cain and Abel."

Dominick laughed. "Hope not."

Given how much Adam and Eve screwed things up for their kids, Bub had just assumed they had been married. Bub never wanted to get married. If he got married, his wife probably wouldn't want him wandering up and down the Strip. He thought the things he saw were interesting, but sometimes he knew they were gross. Other people would find them gross. One time he saw a man porking a lady's face right on Sunset and La Brea. The man was drunk and he yelled his dinner onto the lady's noggin. Then she yelled her dinner onto the fella's frankfurter. Then he grabbed the back of her head and kept porking her face. Neither of them looked like they were enjoying it. Bub didn't enjoy it, but he watched.

That was why Bub never wanted to get married. It didn't seem like something he had to worry about, though. Phew. That was a load off.

What came to worry him more than anything else was the tooth under his pillow. The way people were talking about the Good Time Butcher didn't make him sound like somebody who shared things. Why would he give Bub the tooth? Bub hadn't done anything to deserve it. Maybe the Butcher saw that Bub wasn't having a Good Time, and so wanted to at least give him a Good Tooth? That didn't seem right.

He kept waiting for somebody on the news to say something. Put up a sketch of a tooth and say "if you've seen this tooth, call this number." But there was no sketch, no number. No news. People on the TV were talking about the Good Time Butcher, but not about missing teeth. That was only on the Strip. You only heard about that from people who were having a Good Time. That wasn't a lot of people, as far as Bub could tell.

"Have you heard about the Good Time Butcher?" he asked Dominick.

"You don't know him from Adam, that's all *I* know."

"Of course. I forgot I asked you about him already."

A pair of shoulders with a gumdrop head and toothpick legs came a-thumping up behind Dominick. "Yo Dom!"

Bub felt his face rearrange itself into a different emotion. "You have a nickname?"

Dominick, *Dom*, smiled at Bub and said "what's up?" to the man who looked like a toddler's drawing of a jackhammer.

"Keith got a fucking Ouija board!"

"…why the fuck did he get a Ouija board?"

"Not even a new one from a store. It's an old one. Got it from a yard sale."

Bub shifted his weight from foot to foot. "That sounds like a Good Time," he warned Dominick, whom he struggled to conceive of as anything more concise.

The jackhammer man misunderstood Bub's tone. That was okay, though. Most people did. "Damn right it does!" he shouted. "You wanna come fuck with it?"

Dominick shook his head. "I don't fuck with Ouija."

The jackhammer turned into a paint roller. He smeared a sad color. "It's just Parker Brothers, man."

Uh oh. It sounded like something bad had happened to someone's bro. "Who's Parker?" Bub wondered.

The paint roller looked confused. Dominick also did for a second. Then he laughed. "Parker Brothers," he told Bub. "It's a toy company. They make the Ouija boards."

"Oh." Bub looked to the paint roller. "How old are you?"

The paint roller turned back into a jackhammer. "Nineteen."

"That's too old for toys."

Jackhammer looked from Dominick to Bub, Bub to Dominick. "This the guy you were telling me about?"

Dominick laughed and nodded.

The Jackhammer extended a concrete palm. "Ollie."

Bub studied the hand. It had accidental cracks in it.

"That's my name," Ollie clarified.

"I like that name."

Ollie bounced his eyes between Bub and Dominick some more. His lips were all tangled, like shoelaces he'd just tripped over. "You wanna shake my hand, Bub?"

"He doesn't like touching," Dominick reminded Ollie.

"That's ok," Bub said, surprising himself as much as Dominick. "I'll try to shake Ollie's hand." He tried and succeeded, slipping his hand from Ollie's corset grip as quickly as he could.

Ollie tried to press his luck, inviting Bub to join himself and Dominick. Bub couldn't help but remind Ollie that Dominick seemed unwilling to fuck with the Ouija board, regardless of who manufactured it. Ollie didn't seem bothered, and neither did Dominick anymore, at least not that much.

Naturally, Bub declined the invitation.

When he returned to his apartment, everything was in the wrong place. The mattress was over *there* when it should have been *here*, the floor lamp was *here* when it ought to have been *there*. There was no water in his vase. The plant had died. Bub was sure he'd watered it this morning. His apartment was making decisions without him again.

"Not nice," he upbraided his living quarters. "Not very nice."

He thought about how it had felt to touch Ollie. Not very nice. Manageable, though. He used to not like eating ground meat, but it was really all his mom would give him. So he got used to it. Then he learned to like it. Maybe that was how touching would be.

It was weird that he liked touching the tooth so much. He didn't realize just how much, which was so much, until he thought about how much he liked touching living people, which was not much at all. The tooth was nice to touch because it had no life. Whoever had grown it was a body now. Just a body.

Bub wondered why he knew that, how he could know that. He wondered as he moved his mattress from *there* to *here*, he wondered as he moved the floor lamp from *here* to *there*. Nothing to be done about the plant, but he filled the vase anyway. Then he put his head down on the pillow and the tooth told him secrets from the other side, the cool side. *You took me yourself,* the tooth whispered. *I caught the light. I showed you interesting things. So you took me.*

"You haven't shown me any interesting things," Bub rattled into the warm side. He slipped his hand beneath, to a side that was no longer cool but *cold*. The tooth was ice between his fingers.

It burned. The pain bade him *look*.

DELMER'S MONEYMAKERS

RIDING in the back of the U-Haul wasn't too bad on the highways. Granted, it was high desert they were shooting through, so if you weren't downing about a gallon of water an hour, it was *BANG BANG BANG BANG BANG* on the front until Patch *BOOM BOOM BOOM BOOM BOOM*ed back to say roger dodger, loud and clear. Quite a few times they were pulling over on the shoulder to splash Mick with water until he quit breathing so heavy. How many times did they have to tell him, just drink! Stay hydrated and you'll be fine! Did he listen? No. He didn't. The problem that arose once they got off the highway was less easily avoidable, though. Maybe Patch could have been a bit softer on his turns, but really, how do you stop inertia? They'd lashed their gear to the walls, and thank goodness for that; having to dodge Marshall stacks rattling for the far side with each turn would have been a nightmare. No way to lash themselves, though. It wasn't like there were seats back here. It probably wasn't even legal for them to be riding like this. It certainly wasn't smart. But it was cheap. And that, thus far, had been the Bömerayñ way. *Legal* and *smart* cost money. *Cheap* got them from Pennsylvania to Los Angeles (and without needing to hold their hands out to their goddamned *parents).*

And getting to LA got them more than halfway to a record deal, if half the stuff they'd read in *Guitar Player* was to be believed.

Patch took a right turn a bit too enthusiastically.

"Jesus!" Delmer cried as he stumbled, losing his balance and nearly cracking his head on a hardshell case. "He never keeps his eyes on the fucking road!"

"I'll bet you he missed the turn," Mick chuckled, both arms wrapped tightly around the hitching beam running along the middle of the truck's interior.

"Yeah," Delmer chuckled, doing his best to will the fear away. "You can tell he never took his driver's test."

Rain frowned. "What?"

"First break we get," Mick announced, "we're buying a fucking tour bus."

"He never took his driver's test?"

"Yeah." Delmer glanced to Mick, who wasn't returning his gaze. "A fucking *awesome* bus. Metal as *fuck."*

"I think," Rain offered, living up to his nickname, "a

company owns them, and bands just rent them." Rain's real name was Ryan, but he was a downer, and every rocker needed a nickname. So he became Rain, bane of parades.

Delmer crawled up the wall and mimicked Mick's chokehold on the beam. "With how big we're gonna be, we'll buy the damn thing. And Patch *never* gets to drive it."

"He stays in the back of the bus!" Mick cackled. "He'll be Bömerayñ's honorary nigger, ay?"

"Ah…" That was as vociferous as Delmer's disapproval of Mick's 'jokes' ever got. He hated them, but Mick himself was really cool. He was a year older than the rest of them, having dropped out of school in sixth grade to work in the kitchen at a diner. He was also addicted to cigarettes, which was awesome. So yeah, his jokes offended Delmer, but that was Delmer's problem. It wasn't rock 'n roll to be offended. Besides, there weren't any black people in the band. So it wasn't *hurting* anybody. Delmer was happy to let Mick be Mick. Bömerayñ had never had a Bandfight in the entire year and a half they'd been around, and Delmer wasn't about to kick the first one off over a silly joke that wasn't *hurting* anybody.

It did annoy him, though, that he could tell that *Mick* could tell that Delmer didn't like his jokes. That was why he'd taken to ending each one by saying "ay?" and repeating it until Delmer acknowledged receipt of the comedy joke. It felt…territorial. Like Mick could sense that Delmer used to be the edgy one. Back in school, Delmer was the one who'd messed with all the teachers and said stuff that people just couldn't believe they were hearing. Now, though…he couldn't keep up with Mick. Nor did he entirely want to.

Worth noting: Mick had picked out his own nickname. He'd gone with 'Mad Mick.' He hadn't thought very hard before coming up with it.

Delmer, on the other hand, had cycled through quite a few nicknames. First he'd been Deep Dive, because his real name sounded a bit like "delver." Deep Dive had been his name when he'd been playing rhythm guitar in Bleech; when he got sick of second fiddle, he and the drummer, the very same Patch who was at that moment doing his damndest to flip the U-Haul, broke away and formed Popsickle. Deep Dive took the lead guitar position and became just Dyve. But everybody kept pronouncing it as "D…uh, Dave?", most humiliatingly at the tenth grade talent show. Dyve was jotting new names in the margins of his social studies notes when Popsickle broke up during fourth period. Their singer Reynold wouldn't let Patch copy his test answers, and that had turned into a Bandfight, and right there in front of Mrs. Tripolitis and the whole class, Reynold quit, then Patch kicked him out. That was how most of the kids found out Popsickle was still playing together after their catastrophic gig in the auditorium. The second semester saw Delmer branching off into more adventurous solo material, facilitated by a brand spanking new Tascam Portastudio 244 Delmer's apparently-wealthy Uncle Enoch had bought him for what he'd thought was Delmer's birthday (Uncle Enoch had been off by three months, but Delmer neglected to mention this in his effusive thank you note, the first one he'd ever sent without being goaded by his mother). Delmer's solo act eventually collapsed when he got bored a week later, so he called Patch and they formed Fragile Orphan with the intention of releasing politically charged anthems to speak to the nation's disaffected youth. The one and only song they wrote was called "Boner Patrol," and Fragile Orphan was shelved before any other band members had been hired. After a few months and two calls for talent in the Reading Eagle (the first had accidentally ended up in the personals section, which had gotten quite a few responses of precisely the wrong sort), Delmer, currently between nicknames, and Patch (whose evergreen nickname had long since supplanted his given appellation, "Brandon") met Rain shortly after he moved to Pennsylvania, who subsequently introduced them to Mick, whom Rain had met through semi-mysterious circumstances (though it seemed that a shared affinity for professional wrestling was involved). And so, the boys forged Bömerayñ as a blood oath. Goodbye high school, hello Los Angeles. The rest would be history.

"Did you hear me?" Mick called. "I said like our honora-"

"Hey," Rain interrupted, "Earth to Delmer! What are you thinking about?"

Delmer smiled. "I'm thinking about how I need a new nickname!"

"Delmer!" Mick barked. "Did you hear me?"

Rain and Delmer had a moment of silent communion.

Then the world screeched and all three of them went flying towards the front of the truck. They were hardly on their feet before the back clattered open and daylight caught like a match in a gas leak.

"Rise and shine boys!" A mercilessly backlit Patch giggled. "We're home!"

"Dude," Rain gasped. "You never took your driver's test?"

"What?"

Delmer lifted his eyes. His first glimpse of Los Angeles was a blinding light, clean and pure.

That was a laugh.

DELMER stopped as the hammer touched the head of the first nail. He turned around to Mick, speaking through lips pinched tight around four more nails. "Rwsrdsd-"

"What?"

Frowning, Delmer looked longingly at his pocket for a few seconds before opening his mouth and letting the nails *plinkety dink* onto the floor. He assumed they made a sound like that, anyway. It was hard to hear over the unceasing complaints of heavy industry (e.g. *RUUU-UUUH* and *CRACRACRACRAH)* above their heads. "I was asking if we're sure that th-"

Mick pointed to his ears. "I can't hear you!"

"I *said,"* Delmer shouted, "I was asking if we're sure this doesn't violate the lease?"

"The fuck are you talking about?"

"Nailing the cartons to the wall!"

62

"It's a good point," Rain added. "I don't think we have to worry about being too loud!"

Mick pointed to his ears again.

"TOO LOUD!"

Mick shook his head. "We don't have to worry about that!"

"That's what he said!" Patch screamed.

"I'm talking about the lease!" Mick replied. "We don't have one of those!"

"…" said the band.

Mick saw and raised their incredulity, gesturing wildly around the stinky little four-by-five catacomb that they called a practice space. "Does this shithole look like it has a fucking lease?"

It was a fair point. *This shithole* was in the basement of a basement of a warehouse that, as far as anybody could tell, made basements. That, and a paint-peeling stench. And the noise. An ungodly amount of fucking noise. Which had a silver lining, one uncharacteristically traced by Rain: the practice room itself, located smack in the center of an otherwise doorless concrete hall, was too small to admit both the gear *and* the band. Except for Patch on his kit, the rest of the band could only stuff their amplifiers in the room with him, run cables into the hall, and rock out amidst damp brutalist chic. That left the door to the room open, which flooded what the members of Bömerayñ came to call the Hellhall with sounds of a different, almost certainly less profitable industry. There was no chance of their creating more noise than the roar of jet engines and boom of nuclear warheads above them.

That was the silver lining.

Astonishing that Rain should cling to that, rather than the cloud. It consequently fell to Delmer to broach the essential question: "I thought you said we could sleep here?!"

Mick grinned his 'please punch me' grin. "I did! We can!"

Delmer considered the hammer in his hand. "We're sleeping *here?!*"

"Well, in the hall!"

Patch finished nailing his egg carton into the wall so he could more firmly fix Mick with a glare. "What if somebody comes?"

"Listen, we're all adults, just try to be discreet and do your own laundry!"

"I'm serious!"

"So am I! You think I wanna touch your spunk?"

"Yeah," Delmer fumbled, edgily, "do we wanna, uh, lick our own jizz?" Upon receiving absolutely no reaction, he cleared his throat and said "everybody calm down."

"This isn't a fucking joke," Patch snarled, eyes locked on Mick. "I get neck cramps."

"Oh," Mick simpered, "those come on after your pussy cramps, or what?"

Delmer and Rain locked eyes, instantly confirming each other's intuition. There was a Bandfight incoming. Given how unsettled, how vulnerable Bömerayñ was just then, it could well prove their undoing. Before they'd even done much *doing* to *un!*

Patch looked to be winding up for a particularly punishing verbal swing. It was the set of the jaw. Delmer knew it all too well. He *also* knew that however civil Patch was at baseline, telling an angry Patch to "calm down" was like trying to save a choking person by shouting "spit that out already!"

So Delmer laid aside his rock 'n roll persona for a moment, just a moment…and reconsidered the hammer in his hand.

"Did you *know* this place was such a fucking shithole before we left PA?!" Patch hollered.

Quicker than thought, Delmer scooped up another egg carton off the ground, slapped it against the wall, wound up the hammer, and swung it…at a spot just to the right of his outstretched thumb.

"OUCH!" he shouted, as he yanked his safely un-smashed hand away from the hammer on the wall. A less-than-convincing performance, if he said so himself, but it was enough to cut Patch's fury off at the knees.

"Fuck, dude!" Patch shouted, full of worry. "Your moneymakers!"

Rain caught on quick, thank god. "Was that your fretting hand?"

"Oh," Mick said, "shit."

Delmer drew his left hand against his chest and turned dramaturge. What kind of person *was* he? As in, what kind of person would he want to be, ideally? Would he try to underplay the pain? Would he be freaked out about possibly breaking a finger on his fretting hand? Or maybe overstate the pain as a plea for sympathy? He hated to admit it, but the truth was probably somewhere between those latter two.

But fuck it, he was an artist on the path of reinvention. The truth could be whatever he wanted it to be. *He* could be anybody he wanted to be.

So he took a swing at a chagrined hero's mien, like Clint Eastwood trying to hide a fatal gutshot. "Ah, hell," he growled at Patch, "these old hounds ain't made us no money."

Patch took a page from Mick's playbook and pointed to his ears.

"I said these old hounds ain't made u-"

"WHAT?"

"I'm fine!" Delmer shot another look to Rain, which was returned in kind. This time the thought being communicated was more complex, but no less clear.

The Bandfight averted, Bömerayñ finished cartoning the room (despite having established the illogic of the same), plugged in, and jammed. They only had a few completed songs to their name, all of which were stuck in the "heavy inspiration" stage of development. "Get In My Hair" was basically just "On Fire" by Van Halen. "Dirty Dog" was a glorified cover of Motörhead's "White Line Fever." The main riff of "Boots" had been rather clumsily lifted from Whitesnake's "Take Me With You." Chief songwriters Delmer and Patch recognized the likeness each time, yet allowed it on the pretense of this all being part of Finding Their Voice.

After two or three nights wrapping up practice by

spreading blankets in the hall, plugging their ears with napkins stolen from Mel's Drive-In, and trying to banish rats from their dreams, Bömerayñ got their first opportunity to play their music aboveground: a taqueria in Thousand Oaks called Maria's. Perhaps confused by the tilded 'n' in Bömerayñ, Maria's booked their first and last hair metal band to fill a sleepy Wednesday evening slot.

Prior to arrival, Bömerayñ had hitched a ride to an S&M shop in West Hollywood, pooled their meager funds, and bought Mad Mick a sleeveless leather jacket. The guy behind the counter, recognizing their discomfort, asked them if they were in a rock band (a full half of his current clientele being those with musical aspirations). When they said yes, he pointed out that there were other, less intimate places to buy a jacket. That made them feel foolish, but all the same, there was a transgressive glee the four country boys got from following in the leather-clad footsteps of folks like Rob Halford.

Less delightful was performing at a family restaurant that hadn't understood who they were booking, though Delmer considered this to be on *them*, as the flyers clearly stated "for fans of:", and then they'd drawn a little picture of a rock.

"Ah ah!" the manager tutted as they entered Maria's an hour before showtime. "No ladyboys! Out!"

"You show me a ladyboy," Mick hissed from beneath the bleached topiary of his hair, "and I'll kick his fuckin' faggot ass."

"No! This is a family place! Out!"

Delmer swung out from behind Rain, waving his guitar case. "We're the band," he explained.

The manager took this about as well as if Delmer had said "your son drowned and I watched." He sized each of them up in turn. It didn't take him very long.

"Which of you is Bomerañ?" He pronounced it *Bow-mer-an-ya*, with a drumroll on the 'r'.

"Oof," Rain sighed quietly.

"We're all Bömerayñ," Patch replied, pronouncing the band's name the way it was intended to be pronounced, which was to say, incorrectly: *Boomer-ain*.

"Why…" the manager wrestled with his question, as though struggling to process a great betrayal. "Why do you accent the letters?"

"Because we're a rock band."

"…none of you is called Bomerañ? You don't perhaps play nice music?"

"Nice? *Nice?!*" Mick scoffed. "Our music's not *nice*. It's fucking *rock!*"

The manager moaned. "Family, sir, please."

"It's a bit of a play on words," Rain explained with the muscular condescension of a man who believed he alone had the key to determining whether or not egg yolks are good for you. "It's a portmanteau of *boomerang* and *brain*. Like that's how much we're gonna blow your mind, it'll go flying away and come back around."

"It's like we put them together," Patch clarified. "The words."

"That's what a portmanteau is," Rain sighed.

Patch shrugged. "Well, fuck me, right?"

"Family," the manager whispered without conviction.

Mick stomped his foot on the floor. The three patrons in the restaurant started from their meals, looking up in time to see Mick charging towards the manager, finger jabbing into his chest. "Listen up asshole, we're gonna be big. Bömerayñ, you're gonna see that name in lights, even if they have to make new fucking lights to spell the letters right! So are we playing or what?"

In the end, the manager paid them *not* to play, which suited the members of Bömerayñ right down to the ground. Twenty-five bucks to split four ways. Not bad for their first-ever LA gig! "Which," Delmer happily pointed out, "wasn't even technically our first gig!" They ended up splitting the windfall five ways, each taking five for themselves, with another five constituting the inaugural deposit into the "demo fund." There was a bit of bickering over who would serve as fund manager, until Rain was ultimately decided upon based on his lack of interest in doing so.

The question of what would be done with the other twenty dollars was one without a question mark.

"The Strip won't know what hit it!" Mad Mick shouted into the night as they nursed a handle of Jack they'd picked up for the long walk along Sunset. Delmer couldn't help but imagine there were no fewer than eight other self-styled wildcards hollering precisely the same thing at just that moment. The night, alas, did little to acknowledge Mick's pronouncement, and the Strip did everything it could to affirm the inverse. The Sunset Strip, in all of its preposterous, shameless, scuzzy glory, splattered itself before them like a mirage with poor depth perception; utterly insubstantial, its promised pleasures retreating as they approached. Did the Whisky A Go Go smell of sex? From a distance, but upon closer inspection it was just booze and cigarettes. Could some righteous shredding be heard coming from the Starwood? Only from far enough away to wonder, for up close it turned out to be a load of boxy pentatonic widdly-diddly bullshit. Were those two people in the alley fucking each other? Or was one of them fucking, and the other *being* fucked? It was a fine line. And speaking of lines…

"Wanna see if we can get some coke?" Mick asked. Nobody answered, because they all knew a question like that from Mick was purely rhetorical. To wit: "Hey! Who's got some coke?"

"Keep your fucking voice down," Rain snapped.

Delmer felt his jaw tighten. "We could get some coke, *or,* we could go to, like, a strip club or something, th-"

"Somebody has to help me," Mick insisted, his tone oddly pleading. "This is a lot."

"What's a lot?"

Patch exploded in laughter. "Jesus dude, since when have you been doing close-up magic?"

Delmer cocked his eyebrow at Patch. Patch pointed at Mick's balled fist, which was currently pressing something small, snowy, and potent on Rain.

"Ah!" Delmer squeaked. "How the fuck did you get that already?"

"Take it!" Mick demanded.

"Who…" Rain glanced frantically around him. "Who

70

the hell gave that to you?!"

"These pants are too tight, I don't have any fucking pockets!"

"Did you know the sellers?"

"Did we seriously just buy coke?" Delmer marveled.

"SHHH!" Rain chided.

Patch, still cackling, slapped Mick on the back. "You're down to buy on the street, you just don't wanna carry, huh?"

"Fucking *take* it, Ryan."

"Oh, *hi,*" said a woman none of them had ever seen before, which they knew for a fact because they would definitely have remembered. "You boys look like you're after a good time."

Very slowly, Rain reached out and took the cocaine from Mick, who was all of a sudden loathe to let it go.

"We'd still be at the taqueria," Patch marveled under his breath.

Before Mick had a chance to say anything, Delmer swallowed his terror and stepped up to the friendly lady. "Do you know where we can find one?" He gulped again as two new friends sidled up to the woman's flanks, as buxom as their vanguard. "A good time?"

The woman simply smiled and raised her arms, palms up, like a revivalist on the pulpit.

DRIP DRIP DRIP

SO *this* was why they called it cold turkey, huh? Yeah. Isley curled up in her bed beneath a mound of down, a little baby ball shivering and sweating, bundled up like a turkey at the grocery store, a turkey in the freezer section, yeah, this was *cold* turkey, dip her in the deep fry and have a happy holidays, so many thanks to give. Thanks to Sergeant Hollenbeck for giving her a week's paid leave. Thanks to Saacks for bringing her groceries. Thanks to the Academy. Couldn't have done it without you. You and you and you. Fuck 'em. Fuck 'em all. They didn't think she could do it. Wean, they said. Wean off like she was some fucking piggy on a tit. Wean?! How could she wean when she had a killer to catch? Best way to catch the Good Time Butcher was to have a Bad Time. Never see her coming. She saw all kinds of things. Things he wouldn't believe. Like the guy in the movie says. The blonde guy. The movie. The fucking movie! Call the Academy, they'd know the name. They know all the names. Not the name of the Good Time Butcher though. They ought to. They will. She'd find it. She'd tell them. She'd tell all of them. The world. The city. The difference? The smog. Jesus Christ. Too thick. She'd never find her way through.

She *would* though. They said she wouldn't. They? Said she wouldn't. So she would. Somebody tells her she won't do something, she fucking will. She must. She does. Why? What for? Four weeks. Four weeks and you're through the worst. You or me. Better you than me. Fuck 'em.

Second week she's back at work. Sarge says just the one week off. Then it's unpaid. Who can afford not to pay? To *be* paid? Getting paid is passive. Work for a living. That's Isley's way. Get out there and work. Active. Go *do* it.

Ground it. Build it from the ground up. Up and at 'em. Take the desk to start. It's a desk and she has it. It's hers. It's in the office. Where's the office? On top of the desk. Now we're getting somewhere. We're getting to the office. What else is in the office? She's getting to that. Fuck.

Ease into the seat. Attagirl. Two buns on the chopping block. This chair sucks. What's it made of? Plastic? Metal? It goes *screeeeeee*. When? Round the clock. Nobody's in the office and it's probably going *screeeeeee* in the lonely dark. Spooky thought. *Life* is a lonely dark. Far out, man. Far out. Life is a chair, get used to it. Get over it. Get on it. Sit. *Sit.* She *is.* As hard as she can. Sitting. It's so easy. Gravity's got the hard job. So relax. Oh, hell. Who's she kidding? She's not a detective. She's a god-damned fraud. One time in school she gave a presentation on some shit or whatever and she got a B on it. Now she was a detective? Fuck that. Yeah. No. What's she gonna solve? The dilemma of the chair. Here goes. Here goes nothing. Where? She's already sitting down. Lean on the desk? No. Desks are for writing. What if she's righting herself from tipping? Then don't lean. Oh, save it for someone who cares! But who? Who cares? Who cares about her? Nobody. Life is a lonely dark and it goes *screeeeeee* when nobody's around. Who hears it? Saacks? On the beat. Not in the office. Out of the office. Call back later please. Call back another time. Later. Please.

Everything is made of bugs.

"Pultrock," a life-sized cockroach tells her.

Isley points to herself and nods. Yes. Pultrock. Isley Pultrock. Who wants to know? That's me. Who's asking?

The cockroach is the size of life. Life itself. Nothing to live but life itself. Fear is a chair in the life. A brain is what you make it.

Isley makes hers work for just long enough to seem normal. Normal is relative. Her relatives aren't normal. Who is? Not her relatives.

"Yeah, Sarge?" she yodels. Her tongue is a centipede. It tapdances on her teeth. Teeth! The tapdance master!

No. The Butcher!

"My office."

Music from far away. It's not Metallica. It's neither rock nor roll. It's not metal. It's vapor. "What about it?"

A room full of eyes. Jesus wept. Never got to hear the good news. Good News Butcher! The Spanish Inquisition, more like. Right? Yeah? You hear the good news yet? Snip snip snip, now your face is upside-down. That's history folks. All the News that's Good to Snip.

"Come *into* it." The roach's opinion.

Isley's brain was planets. Planets for bugs. Make yourselves at home. The water's fine. Don't drink it. It's fine. "Into what?"

Do bugs have teeth? *"My office."*

"Oh." Then she was in his office and she asked him "do worms get headaches? Don't tell me. You must know. I don't wanna hear about it."

"You assured me," said a desk with a Sarge behind it, "that you would have your shit together after a week. I didn't expect you to be clean straight off, but I figured you'd be able to work."

"I'm working very hard," Isley replied, which was true, it was a fact, folks, that's history.

"Do you know how long you were sitting there sweating onto your paperwork?"

The bridge of her nose collapsed. There was a lengthy bidding war between construction firms, but one ultimately received a generous federal grant to rebuild it. Most of the money was embezzled. Corners cut. Bound to fall apart once again. One day. It'd be history one day. "Time is a dark house with an HBO subscription but no television."

Then she was where the heart was. Home. Sweethome. Jiggity jig. Alabama. California. Hark, a mattress! Gravity does the hard work. Falling's easy. Gravity never had it so easy. Sleep? Sleep's not something you fall into. It's a heavy thing that falls onto you. Or doesn't. Or it dangles. It just dangles. You can see it. You can't touch it. You can't see it either. It's not there. It's not real. But it dangles. Gravity's slacking. It's fake. Sleep and gravity are made up. They fuck and have babies that are liars. All babies are liars. They say goo when they really mean ga. Fall, sleep. Autumn. The Season of the Turkey. Descend. Deep. Gobble. Crunch.

COULD it make sense to be happy about one's mind-mushing withdrawal? Not in hindsight, as something to be considered chief among one's character-building obstacles, but in the moment? Three weeks into the worst, to get some kind of specific? Could be. Could be.

How?

Well, just as a for instance, to get some other kind of specific: what if one couldn't stop fantasizing, with the unfortunate clarity of experience, about the *where* and *how* of obtaining relief from one's self-inflicted misery? Relief as in relapse. Relapse as in blow, as in dust as in snow as in the big C. The evidence room. Only a few people had keys but guess what, the lock had been picked so many times it didn't even latch. It still went *click* when you turned the key, but nobody ever bothered to find out what the *click* meant. Turned out it was just the lock clearing its throat. No semantic content. The door was open. Drugs were supposed to be locked up in their own evidence cabinet, and all drivers are supposed to come to a complete stop at every stop sign. *Supposed to* is just the law clearing its throat. Laws are like made-up locks. Even easier to pick. You don't need a tool. Just don't stop. Don't stop at the door, go to the far corner, past two shelves. They're useless. Third shelf from the top. Not on the shelves back there. On the one here. Third from the top. In a brown bag, or a plastic bag, whatever they grabbed it in. Whatever kids were carrying it in that week. Bingo. Slip it in a pocket. Bingo. Drive on home. Bingo. No need to hide it, nobody to hide it from. Bingo. Bingo. Bingo. If the powder's easy to get, if it'd make you feel better, make you work, fix you, help you do your fucking job, take the case from poor Luca, poor Colby, poor both who's got the case she doesn't want until you can take it, all that, no if's about it, any of it. No if. The score was simple. Isley could do it. She knew. Which meant every second of every day required an active, conscious decision. I will not score. I will not score. I *will* not score. I will *not* score. It was a manta. A flat fish? Haha, fuck no – a *mantra*. Bingo. Like laws and locks. Bingo. But harder to break. Bingo.

Here's the glad bit. The happy one. Might be enough to justify the whole frozen poultry routine. Here it is. Locks, laws, mantras. Fragile words. Just words. Isley didn't need words. She had all kinds of fucking words. Thousands, millions. Colby sent her a copy of the case.

Everything she had. The *how* and *where*. More than that. The *who*. Half the *who*, anyway. The *where*: Barbara Dewey's apartment. Fifth floor walkup. Two points of entry: the front door, and fire escape through the bedroom window. No signs of force applied to either. She'd let him in. What are you doing out there, please, come in. Like that. Or like Romeo through the window. Only one party got the poison though. One star crossing out the other. Dewey wound up on the bed. Ligature marks on the wrists, but the bed was well made. Tucked in. Signs of struggle all smoothed out. New sheets. No sign of the old ones. The ones on which Dewey's back had split and leaked. Forget them, then. APB on soiled bedsheets? In this city? No. More words: coroner hesitantly confirming that Dewey died in her bed. Didn't appear to have been moved very much postmortem. They can tell these things. Words and charts. Isley was happy to accept the former and ignore the latter.

The *how*, then. Drained of blood. Kept awake and alive all the while. Drip drip drip. No other mutilations before or after death. Drip drip drip. No sexual contact of any sort. Drip drip drip. Just a steady vein drain. Could well have taken two or three days. Conscious all the while. Did it hurt? Probably not. So said the coroner. Like he would know. He would know. But the pain wasn't the point, was it? Isley didn't think so. Not physical, anyway. Not physical pain. The point, the pain, the *purpose*, was the powerlessness. It was in the mind. The knowledge. Drip drip drip, that's how it happens. Whatever you've done, whatever you've accomplished, that's where it goes, your love and your laughter, drip drip drip into a drain. Or a bucket. Somewhere. No blood at the scene. The scene was clean. That was the point. Draining a life of adventure and high drama, ending it in anticlimax. Make it last. Live fast, die slow. And young.

That was the *who*: Barbara Dennis Dewey. How she must have hated that middle name. Had to have been a family name. Or maybe that's what her parents would have named Barbara if she'd been a boy. Maybe both. Barbara had grown up in Quamba. Some backwater in Minnesota. Land of ten thousand backwaters. Quamba was too small to have its own police department, so they used the county sheriff. Colby had put in a request with said sheriff for as much information on Barbara as could be managed. "It'll be a while" said the note scrawled in the margin on the return letter. Nearer to the point of expiration, then: Barbara had come to Los Angeles to be an actress. No shit. She'd gotten a few modeling gigs, nothing to write home about. For a host of reasons. There were some clippings. Isley didn't look at them too carefully. No point.

The important stuff was what Colby had gotten from Barbara's friends. Casual, on-record interviews. As casual as it gets when discussing the murder of a friend, anyway. You could put a timeline together from them. Which Isley did. Her hands were shaking too much to write in a notebook, so she bought some notecards and thumb-tacks and played Hollywood big-shot. Here's the story. Picture this. It's a tale as old as time itself. Dreams, hopes, hustle, lucky break, heartbreak, disillusionment.

And that's the first month. Barbara ground through three years of that before landing a steady gig at the Whisky A Go Go. She was eye candy, seems. Nothing sinister in the job description. Nothing skeevy. But she worked at the Whisky. Skeeve was bound to happen whether she wanted it or not. Her friends said, yeah, it did. All kinds of advances. Most led to withdrawals from her. Some didn't. Boyfriends, she called them, even if it was just a night. Colby had gotten a few names, followed up on them. Suspects, she'd called them, even if the alibis checked out.

After that, a wall. One Isley probably would have hit too. If it hadn't been for the withdrawal. The glad bit of it.

Words were brittle. Isley needed concrete. She needed firmament. Terra firma. Terra fucking firma. Where was that, in Colby's folder? Here and there. Sprinkles. Who ever made a meal of sprinkles, huh? Nobody.

They all assumed the Good Time Butcher had done Dewey. Why not? It was his M.O. down to the tooth. The hole in the gums. The assumption was valid. But it was vapor. It was words. So Isley called up Hollenbeck and said "Sarge, send me everything the department's got on Good Time Butcher cases." And then Sarge says "you can't work on unpaid leave." So Isley says "then fucking pay me." Then she says "sorry." Sarge laughs and says "ok." But it'll take a while. Like the note. Words get it right sometimes. A thousand years later Sarge calls back and says "we've got fifteen." What a number. Fifteen. Nice by fives and threes. Other numbers, not so much.

Ah, one, obviously. Of course. So Isley says "send 'em over." Sarge says "why don't you come in, as long as I'm paying you?" And Isley says "because I'm fucking comfy in my P.J.'s, get a courier and take it out of my paycheck." Courier arrives two thousand years later, on the far side of a sixth ice age.

She looks at the words, the words, the words, for something firm. Terra fucking etc. She can't find it. Then she does. It's insubstance made bone. Jutting out. A spur. It's obvious to a wordless mind. So maybe there's the good part of the turkey. Rise, gizzard king. Ascend. Conquer. Gobble. Drip.

"Sleep?" she demanded.

Sergeant Hollenbeck didn't bother asking a third time why she was in his office. "What you should be doing, you mean?"

"How does he get them to sleep? To tie them down?" Isley raised her arms in a capital Y. "If he had to fight them there'd be signs. Skin under the nails. Bruises. There's neither. So how does he get them down?"

"Hm." Sarge nodded. "You have a theory?"

"We have toxicology?"

"Should have. It's not in the stuff I sent you?"

"No. I need it. Rule shit out." She tried to sit on the middle shelf of a bookcase, found no purchase, and so arose. "Smart money says no anethe…aseneth…a… sleep sauce. But *lots* of booze. He picks em up off the Strip."

"We knew that. It's the only place the victims all have in common."

"That we know of. They might all shop at the same Ralph's, or read in the same park, go watch movies at the same theater. We don't know. But we know the Strip. Everyone's got the Strip nowadays. You're young, you're pretty, you've got the Strip. Not you. But somebody."

"Thanks, Pultrock."

"Don't mention it. Shut up about it."

At that Hollenbeck politely asked her to excuse herself. So she did. And the next day she gets a ding dong at the door; courier. Toxicology reports out the wazoo. Just like she thought. No sleep sauce. Hell of a lot of booze. Which clinched it. Nearly, at least. One last thing to check.

The lock on Dewey's apartment was tougher to pick than the one on the evidence locker. Funny if you think on it. More of value in the latter. Dollar-wise. What did Dewey have? Not much. Not much but it's hers. Was.

Pop. The door swung open. Isley slipped through no *under* the tape. Not making that same mistake twice. She won the race once. Twice would be selfish.

She combed every inch of the place. No. Comb didn't cut it. Not precise enough. Well, maybe if it was fine-tooth. She gnawed her way along the floor, teeth out and more than fine. Terrific. She terrific-toothed her way, thinking on her chompers in someone's collection. Fifteen teeth jingling in his pocket. Oh, wait. Sixteen. Barbara Dewey was sixteen. Neither fives nor threes into that. Twos, fours, and eights. Smush that together and you've got fourteen. Now that's a straight. Fourteen fifteen sixteen, all accounted for. What did that mean?

Nothing, unless you add *those* three together. Then you have forty-five, split that by the center one. Fifteen. Still fine by threes. Three threes. That was six, if you add. Slot that into the sixteen division, it's two four six eight. Who do we appreciate? Isley. Hey hey, Isley.

There it was. More spurs of spaces between. The holes. Yes. That was how she'd find him.

"I have a thing I noticed," she told Colby's front door. Then she rang the doorbell. Wrong order. Oh well. Luca Colby answered the door and Isley said her thing about having noticed a thing again.

"How…what are you doing here?"

"Telling you about the thing I noticed. I have it."

"It's three in the morning."

"Three," Isley chuckled. *"Ha.* Don't get me started on three."

"Everything okay?" called a voice from over Colby's shoulder.

"Fine," Colby called back. She rubbed her left eye and yawned. "You want to work the case, believe me, I'm all for it. But leave me out of it. Soon as you're back full time, it's all yours. I'm not liaising or anything."

"I need to tell somebody. About my thing."

"Call Sarge."

"At three in the morning?!"

Colby looked at her slippers. Seemed like they annoyed her. She shook her head and stepped outside. "Ok. What. Go."

"He finds 'em on the Strip. Gets 'em home by being the nice guy. There's a million guys trying to get in their pants, right? Our guy doesn't. He's the nice guy. Who's teetering around? He picks 'em out and says, hey, I'll make sure you get home safe. I'm a Nice Guy. Wouldn't hurt a fly."

"So how do you account for the male victims?"

"By saying it's the fuckin' eighties, Colby. Everybody fucks everybody now. It's rad. Get with the times."

"*Rad?*"

"Yeah, get with the times. So like I was saying, he gets 'em home. Makes 'em puke in the toilet. Heave, splash. So they don't choke on it, I bet. Then he cleans up."

"We know all of this," Isley mumbled into her fist. "*I* wrote that in the report."

"Cleans up the bathroom with bleach, right? Don't tell me. I'm telling *you.*"

"Bathroom with bleach, cleans the sheets with Dash. It's all in the report. If this is all you have, I'm g-"

"Barbara Dewey's got neither."

"…what? How do…you know what, don't answer that. You're sure?"

"One hundred percent. She's got no detergent – I bet she buys what she needs right at the Laundromat. Got some of that Pine-Trio shit for cleaning, but that ain't bleach. Cabinets are dusty, but there's no rings where stuff got taken out."

"So…the Butcher brings his own cleaning supplies?"

Isley leapt and clapped. "Exactly!"

"…ok? That's something, I guess. But is it helpful?"

"I called Cedars-Sinai. TPN's cadged from there. It's so fucking big, and they're so near the Strip, they're losing all sorts of shit uses needles. Everybody must think it's morphine. Ha! Get a high from TPN, go on, just try! Can't. Won't happen. Anyway. They can keep a closer eye on their cleaning shit. Who's gonna steal that? Somebody. Turns out they're losing, guess, just guess, don't tell me. Bleach and Dash, right? Like fucking buddy cops. Like us. Buddies. You'd be Bleach, no doubt. One hundred percent. So, listen, how much shit is he cadging from Cedars now? IV, let's even say he's got that. Ok, he still needs the TPN bags. Jugs of bleach, Cedars buys 'em by the gallon. So at least a gallon of bleach, and a big box of Dash. That's a two-hand job. Where's he put it? In a bag? Gotta be. Or a box. Does he walk it out or drive it? So here's my thinking. It's simple. We put some plain-clothes in Cedars, stop anybody who's got a box and no uniform. Take a peek inside. If it's TPN and bleach, Hit the fucking floor! See?"

Sarge sighed, because now Isley was talking to Sarge in his office and it was daytime. When had that happened? Who knew. Who cared. "I suppose the idea's not *totally* off the rails," he allowed, "but creeping around Cedars-Sinai and accosting people who could well be there to visit terminally ill loved ones?"

"Or to steal bleach and Dash! The detergent, not run. They might though. Not Luca either. If I'm Dash. It'd be me."

"It's not legal, but," Sarge shrugged, ignoring the words Isley had said in favor of what she'd clearly meant, "that's not what I'm worried about. PR fallout's the problem."

"Plainclothes, chief. Nobody'd know."

"Then why would anyone open up their bags to be searched, if we don't identify ourselves?"

"If they don't, what are they hiding, eh? Huh?"

"You're on to something, but the hospital itself isn't the tack to take. Think of something else and I'll put it through."

Isley would later maintain that Sarge had winked when he'd said that.

THE MAIN DIFFERENCE BETWEEN MEAT AND BONE

IT was just murmurs at first, and they only came through the pillow. Bub would lay himself down to sleep, but he wouldn't pray anybody his soul to keep. He liked his. It was a pretty good one, he thought. His soul.

The tooth didn't agree.

It called him names sometimes. *Dumb* and *retard* and *murderer*. But sometimes it would be nice to him. It would say *it's not your fault*, or *the world does not treat you fairly*. It was nice to hear that after a bad day, even if he didn't know what it was that wasn't his fault. He tried to not do anything wrong in his life. But the world wasn't fair to him all the time. So maybe he did some things wrong sometimes. But they weren't his fault. Even if he was a *goddamned moron* too. Sometimes.

Bub didn't know whether or not he liked the tooth. Could someone be a bully and a friend at the same time? Could a tooth be a someone? He had so many questions but nobody to ask. He tried to tell Dominick about it once but he called it some "Ouija shit" and laughed. He didn't believe Bub had a talking tooth under his pillow. Bub couldn't blame him. It was funny to think about. Not funny that makes you laugh like people do. Funny that makes you go all quiet and look at a wall. Like people do. Bub did.

Nobody at the theater wanted to hear about the tooth either. Angela was too busy being the boss to care. She would just say "Customer" like Harrison said it. Sometimes Bub imagined his coworkers paid the customers to come in so that they wouldn't have to talk to Bub. He couldn't blame them for that. It wasn't their fault. The world wasn't fair to anybody.

Except sometimes it was. Sometimes it was more fair to some people than it sometimes was to some other people. Friends who laughed on the Strip, or porked each other. Life was very fair to them. The world was very fair. The tooth kept telling Bub this, and at first he didn't believe it, but he knew it was true. The world was different amounts of fair. Which wasn't fair.

"You got a fuckin' tooth under your pillow still?" Ollie asked one night when he walked home with Bub and 'Dom.' "If the tooth fairy was coming, you'd have your quarter already. With interest." Ollie laughed at his own joke. Some people did that.

"Maybe you're the Good Time Butcher," said a third

guy whose name was Mike, who had a grill on his roof now. He laughed too. "You sucked any pretty girls dry lately?"

"Chill, dude," Dominick told Mike.

"It's okay," Bub said. He laughed so everybody knew it was okay, and not their fault. "I am not the Good Time Butcher. But he does take teeth. And I have a tooth. So it's possible."

"Uh-uh," Dominick replied, with his mouth still a little bit flatter than usual. "You're one of the good ones, Bub."

"They always are," Mike chortled.

"Ha, ha." Bub replied.

The tooth didn't think it was funny. The tooth said *you need to be more careful* and *you're not hiding it well enough.* Bub didn't know what he wasn't hiding, why he needed to be careful. It wasn't fair that he didn't know. But it wasn't his fault. Then the tooth called him *murderer* again.

"I'm not a murderer," he informed the side of his pillow that was almost always sodden through with sweat now. "I am one of the good ones."

Good. You have to believe it.

"You don't believe me?"

It's not your fault.

"Do you also think I might be the Good Time Butcher?"

Don't be stupid.

"I don't know what you mean."

They laugh at you because you're stupid. When they laugh, they laugh at you.

91

"Who?"

All of them.

"I don't think so. I think they're laughing at their own jokes sometimes. Or someone else's."

You're the biggest joke of all.

Bub shifted uneasily. His mattress groaned. He shivered, but the covers were all on the floor. He was scared that if he reached down to grab them, something would snatch his wrist from under the bed. Maybe a hand that glittered like bone. "I don't hurt people."

They're not people. When they laugh, they're just meat. Meat that doesn't treat you fair.

"Where did you come from?"

Meat.

"I don't like talking to you." Bub reached under his pillow to grab the tooth and throw it away.

The tooth bit him.

"Ah!" he pulled his hand back out. Blood bubbled at the tip of his first finger. The sight of it excited him. The excitement frightened him. The fear was its own thing.

It's not your fault.

IT was funny, ha ha, that when you walked down the Strip you didn't see many people laughing. A lot of them were screaming, yippee screams, look at all the fun screams. But the screams were their own thing. They were born and died. Laughter echoed. So they couldn't be laughing at him. They weren't laughing. Same with the people who porked each other in public. They grunted and puffed but they didn't laugh. They didn't even smile.

Porking didn't seem like such a fun time for them. Maybe somebody had dared them. Or double dog dared them. Cows with clucking guitars dog daring each other to pork. Maybe the tooth was right. Or close to it, anyway. It wasn't just the people who laughed, wherever they were. Life was meat. All things: meat.

Was he meat? Bub considered it. Possible. He could be meat. He didn't laugh, but neither did they.

He imagined what would happen if one of the cars driving down the street accidentally drove off the street and became a car driving down the sidewalk. It was awful. He didn't like imagining it. But he could see it happening. Meat rolling over the windshield, under the wheels. Maybe it would be a convertible and they would fall on the driver. Snap their head back over the headrest of the seat. Their foot would press harder onto the pedal. The car would go faster down the sidewalk. *Thump thump thump*, that'd be the sound of meat being tenderized. It was weird to think about. The meat that screamed, the meat that laughed, the meat that made music. It could be tenderized so quietly. Thump. That was all. Thump.

Or Drip.

The tooth had followed him. How? Inside of him. It was like in that movie. What was the movie? The calls were coming from inside the mouth.

Bub laughed. He laughed at his own joke. He had earned that. He opened his mouth and laughed. When he did, his tooth screamed. The scream was louder than the laugh. It sounded like tires squealing over meat. Rubber tearing flesh from bone. It didn't echo.

He shut his mouth quickly and looked around him. Nobody looked at him funny. Nobody laughed at him. He was just another person screaming on the Strip. In the time it took to realize that, there were two more people screaming. It was a way of letting other people know you were having fun. But Bub wasn't having fun. Was he? Was this what fun felt like? Screaming on the street?

He wanted to ask the tooth, but was afraid to open his mouth. The tooth beneath his pillow had hidden itself away amongst Bub's own. Teeth. He no longer knew which tooth was his and which had belonged to someone else. Someone who was dead. A body. Meat. He wondered where *his* tooth had gotten to. Perhaps it was at home, beneath his pillow. Perhaps he would return and it would be nicer to him than the one in his mouth.

Bub returned and put his head on his pillow. The tooth beneath had a softer voice. It tried to tell him nice things. But the tooth in his mouth just screamed. It screamed and screamed and never stopped, so Bub couldn't hear the nice things. Only the screaming. It was the tooth's way of letting Bub know it was having fun.

94

EYES,
OFF AND ON THE ROAD

THE garage door rose with a rattle and crash, like it was mad about something. Or, come to think of it, had been opened by someone who was.

One of those definitely made more sense than the other.

Delmer started and snorted awake. "Rock 'n roll?" he mumbled. It was the only pleasantry to be found on his tongue.

"The fuck are you?!" shouted a silhouette punched into a grey morning.

"Aaouh. Good question." Delmer looked around. The world twirled and tittered like it had just fallen in love for the first time. *"Aaouh."* He slapped a hand onto his forehead and took stock. A two-car garage with just one car in it. He was lying on the oil-smeared concrete where this disgruntled gentleman perhaps wished to park his vehicle. None of Delmer's buddies, either the Bömer-ayñ boys or the friendly folks whose acquaintances he had undoubtedly made last night (it was hard to live it up on Sunset and not make a few acquaintances, wink nudge ouch) were anywhere to be seen. Safe to assume, then, that Delmer was an unplanned and uninvited guest here.

So, *the fuck are you*. Fair. A fair question.

"Aaooouh," Delmer explained as he pushed himself to his feet. He got a good look at the clothes he was wearing. Spoils from a string of gigs on the perimeter of the greater LA area. Tight leather pants. All manner of chains and studs. A meticulously, stylishly shredded wifebeater. Neon yellow, of course. Topped off with dried blood under his nose. Had he finally tried coke last night? Why yes he had. The verdict? Pretty fucking good. It was a wonder he got to sleep at all. "I guess you probably didn't invite me to crash here, huh?"

"Fuck no I didn't!" the man bellowed. His voice bounced around the garage, slapping Delmer silly from every angle.

Wincing, Delmer raised his hands halfway to his ears. "Alright, dude. Sorry. Just chill out, quit yelling."

"You little hard rock dipshits are what's wrong with this world!" The guy planted his hands on his hips and frowned so hard his chin nearly touched his nose. Boy, he'd be *perfect* for the obligatory Disapproving Authority Figure at the beginning of a music video. He tells Bömerayñ to turn it down, and they're like, "sure thing, *square.*" Close-up on a hand, probably wearing a fingerless leather glove, cranking a volume knob all the way to MAX. Then the stereo explodes and the song starts and it's called "Let's Disrespect Our Elders" or something.

The thought made Delmer chuckle.

Turned out, chuckling was an excellent way to get picked up by his not-so-lapels and hurled out into a day that was much further along than Delmer had expected.

He hit the pavement and rolled a few times, "aaaa-ooouh"ing all the while. The driveway wasn't especially long or steep, but he still managed to tumble about half-way down. He celebrated his eventual stasis by proclaiming (sing it with me now) "aauoh."

"Music used to mean something!" Oh, here came the guy again. Delmer knew he ought to get up and run, but he had an acute case of the birdbones. *Really* good benders, he was discovering, left him brittle. It was wonderful incentive to ensure the bender never ended. Alas, this one was over, a fact to which the churlish fellow's approach dramatically attested. "It was political! It had metaphors!"

"We use metaphors too!" Delmer insisted. "When we say *hard*, it usually means boners and sex!"

The grump wound up and kicked Delmer hard, and *not* metaphorically, in the ribs. *Pow.* "They used nice guitars! They didn't make squealies with them!" Another kick. *Pow.*

"AAOUH!" Delmer rolled his way to the very bottom of the driveway. The guy followed. So Delmer kept on a-rolling right out into the road. "Ha!" he exclaimed from his white-line repose. "This road is public property! You can't batter me anymore! Fuck you!"

Apparently this guy wasn't as up on the law as Delmer was, because he charged right across his own property line. "I have a daughter! She has to grow up with your fucking noise!"

"Ooooh," Delmer sighed. That must be how he'd gotten here. Might also be why the fellow was so mad. But then, how did he wind up in the garage? "Listen dude, if a girl wants to boogie, there's always gonna be somebody to fill that hole. See what I'm saying? Be glad it was me stuffing her, and not some rat boy!"

That stopped the guy. He turned green, then red, then purple. The life cycle of a tomato, in a matter of moments. "My daughter is eight years old!"

Ok, so, scratch that. "…had her pretty late in life, did ya?"

The reply was less than articulate. The only comprehensible thing about it was its velocity.

Delmer tapped a hidden reserve of motor control, launching onto his feet and booking it down the street. Christ, there was the skyline of downtown. He was *way out*. That was where he was. How he'd gotten here, well, he'd piece that together just as soon as that guy back there stopped chasing him.

ONCE he hit the 101 he parked himself at one of those metered onramps and stuck out his thumb. The nice thing about looking disreputable by design was that it

was easy to spot, and be spotted by, one's fellow repro-
bates. Just such a scoundrel pulled over in what appeared
to be a car from the Flintstones. "You heading north?"
he asked, the question nearly inaudible over the jangling
of his chain bracelets and four-inch earrings. Delmer
kicked himself for never having thought of earrings.
Something to tell the fellas.

"Sure am!" Delmer replied.

The cool dude waved him in, and got him back to
Hollywood, leaving him at the corner of Sunset and Cah-
uenga. They said their goodbyes, and Delmer felt that
strange pang of melancholy one gets when bidding adieu
to a ride. What a nice man, who he would never see again.
Such was the life of a hitchhiker. Alas.

Delmer headed *that-a-way* on Sunset. He wasn't entirely sure which way was which, but he resolved to walk for
an hour and see if he got to a part of the Strip he
recognized. If not, he could hitch back. No big deal.
Might do him well to walk this hangover into submissi-
on, at least.

He'd clocked about twenty minutes of shufflefoot
progress when a car coughed up beside him and screeched to a halt, nearly mounting the curb in front of him.

For an instant, Delmer considered that this might be
the man whose garage he had crashed in. But no way
would a suburban square like *that* drive a car like *this;* if
Delmer's ride into town had been Flintstones, this was
the spirit of the Industrial Revolution itself. A thick black
plume of smog rumbled from the exhaust, and the body
of the car was caked in a truly inexplicable amount of

mud and dust. The dust could have been sand, Delmer supposed…but where in Los Angeles was there all that mud, short of a joyride through the tar pits?

The driver's side door of the car swung open, and a kid about Delmer's age popped out like a meercat. From the neck down, he seemed legit enough; what appeared to be a homemade AC/DC T-shirt, one black wristband on his left wrist. Only thing was, he had a close-cropped head of black hair. Sure, it was disheveled…but it was short. Like some office square. *Not* rock 'n roll.

The kid planted his hands on the roof of his car and sneered. "Jesus, found ya!" He *thumped* his open palms on the top of the car. "Get in!" With that, he ducked back down into his car. Which made it difficult for Delmer to do anything but comply, or else keep on walking. Which would have been rude.

Which, therefore, would have been rock 'n roll. Moreso than this kid was. But…his presumption and peremptory tone *were* pretty darn rock 'n roll.

So Delmer nodded, stumbled over to the car, and grabbed the passengerside door handle. It was locked.

The kid rolled his eyes like that was Delmer's fault, then leaned over and unlocked the passenger door from the inside. He had no trouble doing this, Delmer couldn't help but notice, because he wasn't wearing a seatbelt.

"Clutch," the kid said before Delmer had even touched down on the seat. He proffered a hand.

Delmer took it and shook. "Thanks."

The kid narrowed his eyes. "Your name's *Thanks?*"

Delmer, in return, narrowed *his* eyes. "No. What?"

The kid pointed to his own chest. "I'm Clutch."

"Oooooh." Delmer mimicked the motion towards himself. "Delmer."

Clutch scoffed as he cranked his car into reverse, flipping off another car honking behind him. "I saw you playing at Halpin's house party, right? Your band."

Delmer laughed. Ah, yes, Halpin's house party. The one where everybody had stuffed themselves into the basement, a concrete bunker with a big dipshit staircase cutting through the middle. Bömerayñ played on one side of it, while the six people listening danced on the far side, peering under the banister when they wanted a glimpse of the band. That Clutch should have been there, not just listening but interested enough to get a good look at the group, was in its own strange way one of the most touching validations Delmer had yet received for his music. "Yeah, that was us. Bömerayñ."

"Dude, you guys fucking rip," Clutch announced as he stomped the pedal and lurched the car off of the curb.

"Aw," Delmer blushed, "th-"

"I'm stoked I saw you here. I pulled my car over right away." Clutch straightened his car back out on Sunset, flipped off the car behind him once more for good measure, then cranked it into drive. "You probably saw, I pulled it over *right away.*"

"Ah…yeah."

"You can't go around calling yourself *Delmer.*"

Delmer shrugged. Ok, less validating to have one's name spat out like an unexpected crunch in oatmeal, but he knew what Clutch was getting at. "I know, I know. I used to go by Dyve, but everybody ended up calling me Dave. Between Dave and Delmer, I'll g-"

"It's not just between those two. You can call yourself anything."

"Yeah, I *know.* I've been trying to think of so-"

Clutch fixed his gaze on Delmer. "You know Clutch isn't my real name, right?"

An *rrrr* noise emitted from high in Delmer's throat… but of course, Clutch didn't know that that meant *eyes on the fucking road, dude.* So Delmer did his best to say it (without *saying* it) by darting his own peepers towards the windshield. "Uh…I figured."

"Like, my parents didn't say 'ooh, it's a boy, he's baby Clutch now'. You know?" Eyes still on Delmer.

"I know," Delmer nodded, thrusting his forehead towards the bow. "I hear ya."

"I have a band," Clutch grumbled. "Toksick. T-O-K-S-I-C-K. We're pretty good. Could be better. Like, in the guitars department." Once more, he looked straight at Delmer. As opposed to the road. "This feels like *fucking* serendipity, you know? That I'm thinking about, gosh, I have to find a new guitarist, maybe one who can play as good as that guy from Halpin's. Then there you are, dude! Walking around like a jackass! Fucking wild, am I right?"

Delmer faced front in time to see a whole mess of red brake lights. He wanted to shout *STOP*, but his throat closed up. The best he could do was stomp on an imaginary brake pedal on his side of the car. Which he did.

Clutch laughed, then turned to follow Delmer's gaze.

102

He burped quietly, then *slammed* on the brake.

The car lurched to a halt inches from the rear bumper of a sleek number worth more than Toksick could hope to make in a hundred years of touring. "Oh, damn," Clutch mumbled. "Close call." He turned to Delmer and smiled. "Anyway, how does tomorrow sound?"

"Uh…" Delmer (ha) *clutched* his chest. Was he too young to have a heart attack? Probably. Besides, his heart had to be the strongest muscle in his body. He gave it a hell of a workout every damn night. "For what?"

"A jam, dude. A jam sesh."

"Won't that be awkward with your guitarist?"

"He's got work tomorrow. All night at the call center. Maybe he'll give us a ring and try to sell us some drain cleaner or some shit, but otherwise he's out of the picture."

Delmer knew what the right answer was. It was *no*. More than anything, because of Patch. The rest of his band, he could take or leave (except Mick, he could absolutely leave that asshole). But the idea of bailing on his best friend, without whom he'd never have had the courage to move out here…it was impossible to consider.

But just shy of letting Clutch know all of this…he froze. Found himself unable to do anything more than pump a fictive, functionless brake on the conversation. "I…I've got a good thing going with Bömerayñ, I think," he offered limply. "Things are starting to pick up, you know?"

"Oh, sure," Clutch scoffed. "You're playing at *Halpin's*."

Delmer scowled. "Yeah, actually, we *are*. We're gigging in LA. Saving up for a demo. That's a big deal for us."

Clutch shrugged. "Yeah," he grunted apologetically, "I know. That's cool. I'm just…" he glanced from side to side, as though some paparazzo might be listening in. Which was to say, as though he weren't *driving a fucking car* just then. "Alright, listen, don't tell anybody I told you this, but Toksick has a meeting with Elektra coming up."

Delmer shifted in his seat, turning to more fully face Clutch. Speechless once more, but for a different reason than before. "Wh…" he finally managed. "What? How? Are you serious?"

As the traffic ahead began to break, Clutch eased the car back into motion. A faint smile on his face. "We did a demo, just some live gigs we recorded on this gay little Dictaphone thing. Quality's shit, but it got passed around. Somebody at Elektra heard it. They're interested in signing us, doing a regional push on a debut."

"Full-length?"

Clutch shrugged, his smile filling out in the center. "I guess that's what we'll talk about."

The first thing Delmer felt was jealousy. Intense, burning, cheek-clenching jealousy. Who the fuck were Toksick? Delmer had never heard of them, and now they were getting record deals with big, no, *huge* labels? That was bullshit! Fucking posers! They hadn't paid their dues!

The second feeling, hot on the heels of envy, was electric ambition. Because this guy who was just one or two good meetings away from a major label debut…wanted to jam. And then, maybe more.

"Holy shit, dude," Delmer finally managed. "Congrats! That's huge! Let's celebrate!"

Clutch shook his head. "Nothing's signed yet. And besides," he said, drumming his hands on the steering wheel, "I'd want to celebrate with my *bandmates,* you know?"

The drumming put Delmer in mind of Patch. Or, rather, gave Patch a lever by which to force his way back into Delmer's head. With a whole Santa sack full of guilt slung over his shoulder.

Delmer cleared his throat. "What do you play?"

Clutch simply shook his head. "You wanna bring your pal into the band, right? Because you moved out to LA together with big dreams, or whatever bullshit? Right?"

"…right."

"What does *he* play?"

"Drums."

"Drummer we have's better than your pal is. That's a fact."

Delmer's natural impulse to defend his friend was overruled by the acknowledgement that this was, very probably, a fact indeed. Patch was a good drummer…but he was a friend first. Because objectively speaking, if Delmer had to evaluate Patch as nothing but a musician, from a purely technical standpoint…

"Are you gonna let some old friend stop you from hitching your wagon to a quicker ship?" Clutch demanded.

Delmer blinked. "You mean a horse?"

"Horses are all the same speed."

"Uh, well, I actually grew up around 'em, and you'd be surpr-"

"We'll talk on it tonight. What's your number?" Clutch reached his hand back to the well behind his seat and flapped his hand around. The car lurched hard to the right as he did.

Rrrr. Delmer's eyes darted to the steering wheel. He frowned. "You need help?"

"I know I have a pen and paper back there."

"I see a *lot* of paper."

"There's a pen somewhere."

"I can give you my number when you drop me off. After. Also, I don't have a phone number."

"*I* might forget."

"I won't. I also don't have a phone, so I don't have a number."

Clutch vanished further into the backseat of his car. "It's around here somewhere…"

"It's okay, because I don't have a phone."

"Where the hell *is* it?"

"Dude. I don't have a phone. I live in my practice space."

"*There* it is!" Clutch returned his eyes to the road. "So what's your number?"

"Just write down yours," Delmer suggested, like a rookie cop instructing a professional hitman to drop his weapon. "I can call you from a payphone."

Clutch frowned. "*I* don't have a phone. I live in my damn practice space."

"Oh cool," Delmer replied. "Me too."

Clutch pursed his lips and clicked his tongue. "How about this, I'll give you the number for the call center. Don't give this out because nobody's supposed to have it."

"I don't even know who I would give it to."

"Mhm." Clutch put the paper on the wheel and started scrawling numbers into it, horn honking with each penstroke.

A middle finger emerged from the car in front of them. Naturally, this was the one time Clutch had his eyes on the fucking road ahead of him. "Be a pal," Clutch grunted, "and throw him the bird, huh?"

"Uh…I mean, as far as he knows you're just honking at him for no reason."

"Be a pal, huh?"

Delmer sighed, cranked his window down and poked his fist outside.

"Your finger isn't up."

"Eyes on the road, dude."

"Here." Clutch thrust the paper into Delmer's lap. "Talk to your band, have a think, then punch those digits between three and ten today. If somebody who isn't me picks up, either I'm on break or I got fired, so hang up."

"Okay." Delmer folded the paper, a repurposed In-N-Out receipt (for *ten dollars,* Jesus), and tucked it into his pocket.

He smiled and lay his arm across the lip of the window. Things were happening for him. Whether or not he bailed on Bömerayñ, he had people from other bands trying to poach him. He was doing something right. He just hoped he could figure out what that was, so he could keep doing it.

WHICH had seemed like a good way to pitch it at the time. Keep it light, keep it positive. So as Bömerayñ wrapped up their next practice session, Delmer clapped his hands like he'd just remembered something wonderful. Instead of having been thinking about it during the entirety of practice.

"Oh!" he added, which along with the clap sounded quite authentic to Delmer's ears, as far as just remembering something went. "So I met this guy named Clutch the other day, and he asked me to join his band."

Patch paused in a half-crouch over the stool of his kit. The look of deep hurt on his face wasn't something Delmer had counted on. Should have, in hindsight, but hadn't.

"You tell him to fuck his dumbass self?" Mick asked, not so much wrapping a cable as pre-tying a series of knots into it.

"Clutch?" Rain clarified. "Who does he play with? Maybe we could open for them!"

"They would open for *us,*" Mick insisted.

"Not if they're bigger than us."

"Nobody's bigger than Bömerayñ!"

"I know you know that's not true, Mick."

"FUCK!" Mick smashed one of Patch's symbols with a closed fist.

Delmer flinched.

Patch didn't, despite his head being right next to the

108

damn thing. He just kept staring at Delmer, with those soggy shelter-dog eyes of his. "What did you tell him?" he asked.

As everyone else caught up to Patch – the person in the room who knew Delmer best, after all – they slowly turned to look, and then frown, at Delmer.

"I told him I would talk to you all," Delmer replied limply.

"Why would you tell him that?" Patch demanded as he rose to standing, his tone making clear he already knew the answer.

Delmer sighed. So it was gonna be a Bandfight. He should have known.

"Are you…considering it?" Rain wondered, his approach far more delicate than Patch's.

"They have a deal," Delmer grunted. Which wasn't quite true; Toksick only had a *meeting*. But saying that would have made Delmer sound like a lot more of an asshole.

"Ah," Patch scoffed, shaking his head. "Chasing fame, is that it?"

"Isn't that what we're doing too?" Mick asked.

"Yeah, but we're doing it *together*. As a *band*."

"Oh." Mick nodded. "Yeah!" He took a step towards Delmer and jabbed a finger at him. "Fuck you!"

"Come on," Delmer whined, throwing his hands out to either side, "it's not like I said *yes!*"

"You should have said *no!*" Patch shouted, stomping out from behind his drums.

"You should have *kicked his ass!*" Mick suggested.

"Yeah, well, I *didn't,*" Delmer replied, cocking his head as he spoke. "Because I'm not a bunch of *assholes!*"

"Alright," Rain cooed, pumping his palms out in front of himself. "Let's all take a breath."

Mick shook his head and pointed at Delmer. "I'm not taking a breath if he doesn't take a fucking breath."

"Yeah," Patch sneered, "why don't you go take a breath with your new band, Delmer?"

"I…they…" Delmer sputtered for nearly two full seconds. "They're not my new band yet! All I w-"

"Yet!"

"All I…thi…I didn't *do* anything!"

"You betrayed this band," Patch growled.

"Oh, fuckin'…*betrayed*, gimme a break."

"Yeah, *betrayed,*" Patch doubled down. He flailed his hands wildly at the rest of the band. "We're all one hundred percent for Bömerayñ. We're dedicated, yeah. We wouldn't even *consider* it if somebody else asked us to j-"

"Easy for you to say," Delmer snapped, "nobody's *asking* you to join their band." He jabbed himself hard with his thumb. His nail caught flesh through his shirt, but he managed to suppress his wince. "They're asking *me.*"

Patch said nothing. Just stared at Delmer.

Delmer felt the needle in his head skip.

Patch put on a mean mask, but Delmer knew how to see through that. And right now, beneath that mask… there was Brandon. Delmer's best friend, from further back than either could remember. Looking like he was about to cry.

Suddenly, Delmer felt the way Brandon looked. "Oh," Delmer whispered. "That w-"

He never finished the thought; Mick's fist interrupted him, by rocketing into his jaw.

GOOD OLD-FASHIONED POLICE WORK

STAKING out Cedars-Sinai didn't work. The place was too fucking big. Besides, close proximity to easily-filched narcotics was fucking with Isley's head. She was nearly out of the four week tricky bit. The trickiest bit, that was about four weeks. Almost there. Boy, it was hell though. Sweating, twitching, trembling. There she'd been, prowling around the hospital looking for suspicious characters with large bags. Turned out *she* was a suspicious character. Couple of times she was asked to relocate herself. One time the guard said it like that. "Relocate yourself," as in "I'm going to have to ask you to," as in "ma'am." Funny shit.

Hospital was a dead end, then. So Isley spent the last

week of her tricky bit combing through those fifteen cold cases. She used the full week, too, after realizing on the second day that none of these cases made any fucking sense. In terms of being done by the same guy. The big picture, that was always the same. Drip drip drip. Meticulous for a fella folks were calling a Butcher. A Butcher that meticulous, he'd have an eye for detail. Right? He doesn't just drain them, after all. He does their sheets, makes their bed. Except when he doesn't. Because sometimes the bed wasn't made. Sometimes there was nothing on the mattress except a plastic tarp. Sometimes a light was left on in the bedroom, sometimes they were all off. About half the time there was bleach rubbed onto the doorknobs. One of the murders yielded a usable print not belonging to the homeowner on the baseboard beneath an electrical outlet. It didn't match anything the LAPD had on file. Sometimes the killer took the "wrong" tooth, not a front tooth but one of the canines, or in one case a molar.

Which made Isley wonder if these fifteen cases might not be the work of more than one person. A conspiracy of killers, then? Or a coterie of copycats? It was a *cuh* sound either way.

Cuh-rap. This was all just a bunch of crap. *Shit.* Stuff. She had to turn the stuff into things. Useful things. So Isley set about organizing the stuff according to a simpler metric: which of these murders appeared to have been done by the person who'd killed Barbara Dewey, regardless of whether or not he was *the* Butcher? Hard to say. There were a lot of *maybes.* Easier to say which hadn't. So she tried sorting out the *yeses* from the *noses*. No's. Sniff.

After three days, Isley had it down to five cases. Three and five. Fifteen. Was that from something? Isley couldn't remember. The cases, though. Five. Five crimes she felt halfway confident had been committed by Dewey's killer. They started early last year, the first in March, then another in April, then nothing until October. The other two, not including Dewey's obviously, had been committed this year. The oldest of the cases from the discard pile went all the way back to two years ago. 1981. One nine eight one. Adds up to nineteen. Like the number from the book about the guy who was looking for the thing in the place? What…what the fuck was Isley supposed to do with nineteen? Something about it wasn't right. Something really basic. Something super obvious. She couldn't see it because it was so obvious. It was poking her in the eardrum. Doink. *Hey*. Doink. *Hey*. Bddd-doom-pa-DOM-pa-doom-pa-DOM-pa-*doink*.

"There are people that will, uh, uh, doom-pa…*ah!* They'll *investigate* you!" Isley shouted. Holy shit! "doom-pa-DOM-pa-doom-pa-DOM-pa!" Do Anything You Want To, by Thin Lizzy. The first track off Black Rose. An album that came out in 1979. It was just after that came out that Isley had first heard about the Good Time Butcher. She wasn't sure how she knew that, but she *did*. What was more, she knew she was right. Her memory might not have been much for shit that didn't matter, but when it came to album drops it was a steel fucking trap. '79. Hell Bent For Leather, Highway to Hell. Hell of a year, ha, ha. 1979, and she's at a bar looking for a dope to buy her a drink. Doesn't take long to hook one. She waits to tell him she's a detective until he's paid for a brew. Tends to put most guys off. Well, either that or they'll say something about handcuffs while their eyebrows do calisthenics. This one was a rare middleground. He got real interested. Full of questions. What's the worst thing you ever saw. Who's the baddest guy you ever caught. That sort of shit. Then he asked if she'd spent any time going after the Good Time Butcher.

"The what?" she asked. So he told her again. The Good Time Butcher. She said she'd never heard of such a fucker. The dope gave her the skinny, the only skinny he'd be giving her that night, heyo. Drip drip drip. The Butcher doesn't cut 'em up, he drains 'em. Like a real butcher. Wow, Isley only just made that connection. Real butchers drain their hogs. Huh.

Anyway. No hog-draining that night, heyo again. She got another round out of the dope then went home and cranked "If You Want Blood You've Got It", which had come out the year before. 1978. This was 1979. 1979 and she's got a dope telling her about a serial killer she's never heard of.

Here in 1983, she rifled back through the fifteen cases. '81 was the earliest. 1981.

So she picked up the phone. Ring, ring.

"Yeah?" Sarge says.

"You sure you gave me every Butcher case we've got?"

"Fuck, Pultrock. I've got a goddamned bone to pick with you."

116

"Specifically cases from earlier? I'm trying to find the earliest one might even be a maybe."

"I…you have them all."

"Are you sure?"

"Isley, d-"

"*Isley*, he says. Uh oh."

"Yeah, fucking uh oh is right. Do you happen to remember threatening to kill a telemarketer?"

Ugh. "Jesus, I forgot all about that. Until you just said it. I guess that's how memory works though, huh?"

"If you need a refresher, I can play you the tape of the call."

"I don't need a refresher, I just said, I remember. *I* told *you* about it, remember *that?* Way back? A while ago?"

"I think you're missing the thrust of what I'm saying here."

"I'm not missing a goddamned thing, you said there's…a, uh…uh oh."

"Yeah. Uh oh. You know they record most of the calls at those call centers, right?"

"…I did not know that. But he, I mean, do we know it was me? Did you hear the recording?"

"I did."

"Well didn't you hear him call me a big bitch? Giggling with his fucking friends and calling me a big bitch?"

"…that didn't happen."

"Yes it did! They must have edited the tape! If it's even *me* that's on the tape, how do we know?"

"Even *if* they did, he's a kid! You're a goddamned

adult detective! Why are you cussing out teenagers on the phone?"

"Maybe I didn't. Maybe they edited that part too, somehow! We don't know how deep this conspiracy goes."

"We try for that defense, first thing that's gonna happen is you have to take the stand and testify that you were sober enough to have accurate recall of the incident. You prepared to do that?"

"First of all, coke gives me flashbulb memory, *allegedly*. Second, that depends on what the sentence for perjury is."

"It's a prison sentence. Put you shoulder-to-shoulder with people you probably helped put away."

"Alright listen Sarge, it was me. I did it. Tell me whose boot I've gotta lick and then I don't wanna hear another fucking word about this goddamned telemarketer."

"You and me both. Not likely, though. They're suing the department."

"Who is?"

"The plaintiff." Papers shuffling. "Kitchens. Gareth Kitchens."

"I got a kitchen company suing me?"

"Kitchens is his name."

"Are."

Sergeant Hollenbeck breathed like sandpaper. "So anytime you want to make a sterling case for why I shouldn't drop your dumb ass and let you play defendant on your own, I'm all ears."

"That's not why I called you. I'm asking about the

Butcher files. It's actually important. Don't tell me about a Kitchen boy is upset, I've got a killer to catch."

"I'm not even sure you caught what I just said. I said I've got more than half a mind to fire y-"

"Yeah yeah yeah. I heard you the first time. Do I have to ask *my* question a *third* time?"

"I already answered your goddamned question."

"See? That wasn't so hard!" Isley hung up the phone and nodded at the files scattered before her. Ok. Yes. This was fucked up.

She grabbed a coat that was far too heavy for the weather and hauled ass to the offices of the LA Times. "Excuse me," she said to the very first person she encountered upon entering. "I need to talk to someone who can help me."

"Uh," the hale fellow replied, "my mommy?"

Upon closer inspection, the fellow was a toddler. "Useless," Isley muttered as she found someone who was sitting behind a desk and old enough to vote. "I'm a fucking detective. Who's in charge around here?"

The secretary puckered her face. "Check the masthead, Sherlock."

"Ha, ha. Funny. No. I need to see some records. Don't tell me to go to Amoeba. I'll tear off your jaw and wear it like a necklace." Isley leaned forward and peered down at the desk. "You don't have a tape recorder down there, do you?"

Isley tried to explain to the security guard how it was all just a big misunderstanding. He didn't get it. Poor listening skills. Hell of a lot of upper body strength though. Got her on the street right quick. So she walked once around the block, found a bank, asked to use their phone, pointed out that she was a detective with the LAPD and so would be using their phone, and called the LA Times. "Hello," she said to whoever the hell it was that picked up, "my name is Sergeant Hollenbeck of the LAPD. I'd love to talk to somebody who knows their way around the back issues. Oh, really? That sounds like it was probably Detective…Colby. That was probably Luca Colby who was just in there. She's a real firecracker, huh? Yes, I'll hold." Thus began, much to the chagrin of the bank manager, an hour and a half long marathon of holds and transfers before Isley finally got connected with the resident archivist, Spiro.

"Alright pal, here's the problem: I wanna know when's the earliest the Good Time Butcher ever got mentioned in the paper."

"Is this information time sensitive?" Spiro asked.

"Well I'm pretty fucking impatient. How's that?"

"…ok. Well, give me a few days. Maybe a week."

"A *week?!*"

"Job like that takes time."

"What the hell am I supposed to do for a week?"

"…"

"Well?!"

"Um…fight crime? Other police things?"

Isley gave him her address to send the clippings to, and hung up. A week! This was heading into week five of sobriety. It was supposed to get easier. Only now she didn't have shit to keep her mind occupied. Just other cases. Boring. *Bo-ring.*

She shushed the bank manager as she punched in Saacks' phone number. "Yo boy," she told his answering machine. "On the beat, I guess? Just wondering if having a beer counts as relapse. Let's hang out! I'll just have some coffee if it does. Doesn't kick like the white stuff, but hey, you know? Hey. Later." She hung up the phone and turned to the bank manager. "Thanks for your phone, pal." She searched his chest for a nametag. "You're not wearing what you're called. *Christ* it's hot. Why did I bring a jacket?" She laughed at herself and left the bank. Every footstep ridiculed her. *A week. A week. A week.*

The hardest part was not thinking about that evidence cabinet.

OR AND/OR AND

TOOTH or dare. Ha, ha.

Dare. Bub dared himself to wonder. Out loud. He went to Dominick and he asked him "what if I'm a bad person and I don't know it?"

Dominick shook his head and mumbled *something something "Mike"* under his breath. *"I'd* know it. And you're not." Then he didn't want to talk to Bub about that anymore.

Tooth. It wanted to talk about it. It had so much to say. Bub didn't always want to listen, but he didn't have any choice. Cupping his hands over his ears did nothing; it spoke from the skull. It was a wider smile that dug into the cheek. Sometimes he tasted blood. Other times he just imagined it.

Dare. There was a KB Toys in the Beverly Grove. You had to pay to park there but Bub didn't have a car. It was free if you just walked in. So Bub walked in and went to the toy store. It was very colorful and smelled like diapers. They sold Ouija boards though. Bub took one to the front counter and the girl behind it said "hope you're not planning to use this on your own, ha ha."

"Ha, ha," Bub replied. "I am."

The girl stopped smiling. She told him "don't." She told him "it's too dangerous."

He asked her "then why are you selling it to children?"

She seemed like she was offended by his question. He hadn't meant to offend her. He'd just wanted to know. Why sell something dangerous to children?

"I'm sorry if I offended you," he said. "I've never used one of these."

"If you use it by yourself," the girl said, as though the past seven seconds had never happened, "you open yourself up to evil spirits. Demons and devils. Maybe even Satan himself."

Bub nodded. "There are some bands on the Strip that sing about this. They don't say Ouija though. They just talk about Satan."

The girl's eyes boggled. "You shouldn't even be listening to them. That's evil music."

"It's okay. Mostly they just sing about how war is bad. Nowadays they sing about girls, and porking girls."

"You want anything else?" the girl asked like she was mad at the idea that he might. But he didn't. She seemed mad about that too.

Bub took the board back to his apartment. The furniture was all rearranged again. It usually was now. He'd taken his artwork off the wall because it was always upside down when he came back and that was creepy to him. Sometimes it would be back on the wall even though he'd left it in the closet. Today it was still in the closet. Probably. All he could say for certain was it wasn't on the wall.

Tooth *and* dare. He put the dangerous game board on the floor right in front of his door and read the instructions. It kept talking about making connections to the spirit world. Fingers on the planchette. That was the little wooden thing with the hole in the middle. The ghost or whoever moved the planchette around, and positioned it over letters so you could see the letter through the hole, and then it spelled a sentence. That was how the ghosts talked. Bub didn't understand why they didn't have telephones yet. The guy who had invented it for living people was dead. Why hadn't he done one for dead people? Oh well. Kneeling before the board, Bub put his fingers on the planchette and said "I want to talk to anybody who got killed by the Good Time Butcher."

Nothing moved anywhere. There were no moaning and groaning noises, or crashes of thunder. Cabinets did not open and close, windowpanes did not rattle. The planchette stayed right where it was.

"Excuse me. Sorry to bother you. I have a very important question."

Stillness. Quiet.

"Can you see my face? Does my face look like a face

you've seen before?"

All at once: nothing.

"Do you see through this?" Bub bent down and held his face three inches from the hole in the planchette. "I don't know if the camera is on but this is what my face looks like."

This is stupid.

"Yeah," Bub told the tooth, levering himself down to a seat. "It's pretty silly."

It's a children's toy.

"It's not scary like everybody said."

Or maybe nobody wants to talk to you. Maybe even the dead have no use for you.

Bub shrugged. "I guess."

Maybe not, though. Right? Couldn't it be possible that the victims of the Butcher have no interest in speaking to their murderer?

"Maybe. I don't know."

Try again. Try again and speak to someone else. Your mother?

"She won't want to talk to me either."

Father Brockman?

"I don't want to talk to him."

Well who, then? Isn't there anybody? Just a single dead person you could talk to? Think, Bub. Think. It's important.

"I can't think of anybody."

Hm. Well, is there anybody living, *then?*

"I would just meet him in the world. I wouldn't talk to him through the children's toy."

Then I guess we'll never know. We'll never know if you're a bad person or not.

Bub stared at the board. He had a powerful feeling

about it. What was the feeling? It wasn't one he recognized. It stung, but in a good way. Like when you sit on your leg funny and it starts to tingle. Except this was for his heart.

He placed his hands on the planchette and said "is Abraham Lincoln busy? I could talk to him."

Hmmm. Looks like Honest Abe doesn't want to talk to you either.

"Oh. That's t-"

Do you...do you mind if I try?

"How?"

I can take your hands from the inside. You just have to let me.

"How?"

You close your eyes. Then I'll open mine.

"You don't have eyes. You're a tooth."

Not just that anymore. I've grown myself a Bub.

"Oh."

Close your eyes.

Bub did as he was told.

Now open them.

He opened his eyes and it was daytime and he was sitting on a fire hydrant outside the Rainbow and he was wearing different clothes than he'd just had on a second ago and his back hurt and his hand was bleeding and his left ear was ringing and his tooth was screaming and he shot to his feet and fell over because one of his shoes had a wet sock in it and he pulled the sock up and it looked like blood and he had bruises running all up and down his right leg.

"What…" he panted. He flopped on the sidewalk like

a fish. It was the kind of fish that whimpered and reached out for people to help him as they passed. Everybody else was the kind of fish that ran away. "What…I don't know what happened. I don't know where I am. Somebody help me."

You know where you are. You're on your favorite street in the whole wide world.

"Woaaah," some glam kid fresh from a night of partying said as he passed. Then he stopped passing. He crouched down next to Bub's head. It was a crotchfirst crouch. Bub smelled a bad smell. Like somebody had told mothball smell to cheer up so now it was being nice in a sarcastic way. "Hell of a night, huh?"

"I don't know what happened," Bub gasped.

"Fuck yeah dude! You with a band?"

"I was at home."

"Sounds like art pop or some shit. You guys play art pop or some shit?"

"I was playing Ouija."

"Like Ravi Shankar? Get with the times, man. It's all about the guitar now!" He pantomimed playing guitar. Then he moved his right hand halfway up the imaginary neck and started wiggling his finger around. "Eruption! *Be-diddle-ee-be-diddle-ee-be-diddle-ee-be-diddle-ee-be-di-*"

"My hand is bleeding."

"*ddle-ee* so's Eddie's, when he starts fucking tapping! Rock and roll!"

Someone further down the street shouted "rock and roll!" The glam kid perked up like a dog to a whistle. He said "rock and roll!" again, and then he walked away.

128

Was this what rock and roll was? You closed your eyes and then the tooth took over? Then you woke up on the street and you were broken and didn't know why?

You know why.

"No I don't."

Yes you do.

And he did.

BACK at his apartment after a long walk home, hands on the planchette. The blood on the right hand was still wet. It stained the little gizmo with a red fingerprint.

You're gonna want to keep an eye on that. It was teasing him.

"I don't know what I'm doing."

That's a lie. You promised to tell the tooth, remember?

"I didn't tell you any promises."

You did. You may not remember them, but you did. Now connect. Concentrate. There's somebody who wants to talk to you.

Bub felt his eyes getting sad. That was what it felt like. His eyes were crying but his heart wasn't. His heart was tingly. That was all.

"I don't think you're a very nice tooth." But that was a silly thing to say. Teeth were never particularly kind to the things they were chewing up.

Say his name. Let him speak.

"Dominick."

The planchette slid, slowly, surely, to the word YES. Bub hadn't moved it. But that didn't mean much. His hands were no longer his own.

TWO TABOOS

WEEK seven. The worst was indeed behind her. By this point, she really only felt like shit one hundred percent of the time, as opposed to six thousand. The craving was omnipresent, but the flashes of clarity that made them conquerable were becoming more and more frequent. The ultimate high, it turned out, was a moral one.

"I said I was gonna go cold turkey," she boasted to Saacks. "I fucking said it, and I fucking did."

Saacks raised two palms. "You did. We're all impressed. We all said that."

"Didn't think I could, eh?" she leered at Sergeant Hollenbeck.

"Like I said," Sarge did indeed say, "no. But you did.

Cool. Now get the fuck out of my office."

"It was never easy! But I knew it had to be done!" This she declared to her Hitchcock-looking lawyer, Fletcher Spruance.

Fletcher just shook his head and reminded her that he billed by the hour.

Isley darkened. "Well what's the fucking hold up?"

"The hold up," he harrumphed, "is that 'I was just joshing' is not a credible defense in a felony case."

"So what, I'm supposed to say I *wasn't* joshing?"

"Whether or not you were joshing is irrelevant. You made a criminal threat, in your capacity as a detective. You were clear about that. It's on tape. The question is do we fight this down to a misdemeanor, or settle out?"

"Have the judge overrule it."

Whenever Fletcher got really upset, the wrinkles and folds on his face deepened. It made him look like a wet thumb with a comb over. The sight never failed to lift Isley's spirits. "I am utterly perplexed as to how you can be a…"

"Detective?"

"I was going to say functioning adult human being."

"Easy does it, Houseman. From *The Paper Chase*. You see that one?"

"The film?"

"No, the book. Of course the fucking film."

Fletcher shuffled some papers and cleared his throat. "Your defense will run as follows: y-"

"I thought they were suing the department, anyway? What gives?"

132

"They are. Nobody's suing you. This is a *criminal* charge."

Isley slammed her palm on the table. "Double jeopardy! Case closed. The fuck do I need you for?" She ended up not discovering what she needed Fletcher for until the day of the trial, which was also when she discovered how her defense ran. It was: she had been battling a drug problem at the time. She had since conquered it. The likelihood of her conducting herself as she had on the phone with one Mr. Gareth Kitchens, i.e. making threats, joshily tendered or otherwise, was inversely correlated to her sobriety. Despite appearances, Ms. Pultrock was quite contrite. Fletcher even managed to cajole an apology from her while on the stand. This was, alas, not quite enough to counterbalance the damage done by her more forthcoming admission that, had she known the poor son of a bitch's name was Gareth Kitchens, she'd have offered to kill him as a kindness.

"Has the jury reached a unanimous verdict?" the Judge asked after the lawyers had taken turns pretending to cry at the jury.

"Yes, your honor. We find the defendant guil-"

Isley launched from her seat. Fletcher flung a hand up to stop her. What he got for his trouble was a fistful of sweaty shirtback and a nearly dislocated shoulder. "Objection!"

The Judge looked at Fletcher like he was disappointed in him.

Fletcher just shrugged at the Judge and shook his head.

"Ms. Pultrock," the Judge said, "you'll retake your seat this instant, or we'll set a date for your contempt hearing."

"Can I just ask one question?"

"Can it wait, perhaps, until after the verdict is read?"

Isley plopped down in her seat, slumped her head into her right hand, and waved her left at the jury. "Knock yourselves out."

The Judge made a hungry lion noise, but he didn't bang his little Donkey Kong hammer, so fuck him.

Turned out the jurors unanimously found Isley guilty of making a criminal threat. But Fletcher, demonstrating precisely why Isley needed him, managed to finagle it down to a misdemeanor charge, just as he'd said he would. A non-striked offense. On the strength of character testimony offered by Sergeant Hollenbeck and Officer Saacks (both of whom perjured themselves mightily in the process), Isley would be dodging prison time. Two hundred hours of community service was to be her penance.

"Easy. A fucking cinch," she haughtily informed Sergeant Hollenbeck in the courthouse lobby. "My *job* is a community service."

"It's also not your job anymore," he replied flatly.

"…the fuck you say?"

"You just admitted to using an illicit substance, under oath. You can't wear a badge with that on your record."

"Don't talk to me about records, I've got a bunch coming to me any day now! Records as in old clippings. From the LA Times." She straightened out her posture.

"The Butcher! I've almost got him!"

"You've been saying that for weeks!"

"He told me it would be a week! The guy did! It's not my fault!"

Sarge just shook his head. "Send the shit to Colby."

"No! It's my case!"

"That's an order!"

"I don't work for you anymore, motherfucker! Remember?"

"Send them to Colby or I'll have you back here for obstructing justice!"

"For the record, Ms. Pultrock," Fletcher announced as though there were a stenographer close at hand, "I will not be representing you ever again. For any reason."

Isley waved Fletcher away. She took a deep breath. "Ok," she said to Sarge, "listen. Sorry I called you a motherfucker. I'd like to keep my job, though, because I'm right on the fucking cusp of so-"

Sarge leaned in and spoke in a low, soft voice. "There's no job for you to keep. This isn't my choice. It's the law."

"There's no law about cops can't do drugs. You wouldn't have a force anymore. It's absolutely your fucking choice."

"Believe what you want. Comes to the same thing. The Butcher case goes back to Colby, and you're out on your ass."

Shoving her face in so close to Sarge's that she could feel the scratch of his chin stubble, Isley whispered, "so you're telling me I can run the case by proxy?"

"...how could you possibly have inferred that from what I just said?"

Isley grinned. "You clever bastard. It's not illegal for me to talk to Colby. Just as friends. She and I, the old pals we are."

"Since when?"

Isley thumped Hollenbeck hard in the solar plexus. "Good boy," she giggled. She turned to find herself face to face with Mr. Gareth Kitchens, who'd once upon a time called her up to offer a hell of a deal, just a *hell* of a deal, and subsequently cost her her job.

Isley stuck out her hand. "No hard feelings, pal."

It was a testament to Kitchens' astoundingly poor judgment that he took her hand with alacrity.

Under the audible groans and gasps of those assembled, Isley shook his hand once, twice, three times.

"They're all scared I'm gonna do something rash," she explained, shaking the hand four, five, six, seven times. "I don't know why. I think things through a lot more than people realize." Eight, nine, ten. She winked and wondered if *that* counted as perjury.

SHE returned home to an answering machine full of Sergeant Hollenbeck. He was really leaning hard into the wink nudge wink thing here. "Leave the case alone" and "just give Colby the documents and go away" and "if you want any chance at a decent recommendation, just drop this." Sounded like he didn't get the *say no more* memo, eh? At any rate, the messages weren't all that was waiting for her. A courier-delivered package, courtesy of the LA

Times. Addressed to Sergeant Hollenbeck. Ha! She'd forgotten she'd done that! Which, now that she was no longer working for the LAPD, was probably some kind of big legal no-no. Just one more reason to not actually turn this shit over to Colby, whose voice was now running out the tape in Isley's answering machine.

The package, then, was a series of photocopied newspaper pages, along with a handwritten scrawl making the rather bold ontological assertion that "this is everything." It took approximately ten seconds for Isley to confirm her suspicions. There were pieces in the paper dating as far back as 1979 that mentioned the Good Time Butcher by name (well, not *name* name, but…uh, stage name), and described his preferred method of execution in gruesome detail. The problem with that, of course, was that the LAPD had absolutely no record of any such killer having existed until 1981. It wasn't as though they hadn't heard of him – one of the articles, from August 3rd, 1980, pointed out that the LAPD "refused to acknowledge the fact of the Good Time Butcher's existence" in their response to the LA Times' request for comment. The *fact* of his existence, said the paper. Said…Clea Greenstone. Journalist. Holder of the byline on every Good Time Butcher article prior to this year. Hm.

Isley called up her good friends at the LA Times and asked for Clea Greenstone. Police business. Urgent. None of these statements were technically lies; they were very *simply* lies. What came they? Of them? Of…fuck. To naught, came they. Clea Greenstone had bailed on one Times and joined another, moving to New York and taking up a more lucrative gig running Broadway gossip for the Big Apple's Times.

Hm.

Isley wrapped the pig-squiggle phone cord around her left wrist. "She did a lot of gossip for you all, did…which Times am I talking to?"

"…what?"

"Am I talking to New York or Los Angeles?"

"…this is Los Angeles."

"Great. Why did I think I was talking to New York?"

"…I just mentioned that she moved to N-"

"Right, right," Isley nodded. "So she did gossip for you?"

"…yeah," said the secretary whose name Isley had no interest in retaining because memory was finite and life was for the living. "You said you were a detective?"

"She wasn't a crime reporter?"

The secretary sighed. "Not unless there was a celebrity involved."

"So she's a wannabe Winchell, that's all?"

"Who?"

Isley tutted. "Walter Winchell, ever heard of him?! You call yourself a fucking journalist?!"

"No. I'm a secr-"

"You got a number I can get Greenstreet through or what?"

"…Greenstone?"

"Like getting blood from a stone, that's talking to you. Fucking Christ. Thanks for something and then nothing! One of those I *mean!*" She hung up and rang an operator.

"How many Clea Greenstones you got in New York City?" The answer, after a predictably contentious back and forth, turned out to be *four*. Pretty crazy. Clea Greenstone didn't sound like such a common name. New York was a *big* apple, though. All sorts of people there, all sorts of names. Four of which were Clea Greenstone. The third of which, in the order Isley rang them up, turned out to be just the one she'd been seeking.

"Hello?" the third Clea asked.

"You the Clea Greenstone used to write for the LA Times?"

"…yes. Who i-"

"Phew! Found ya! Hi! How are ya?"

"I'm fine. Who is this?"

"My name's I…Luca Colby, of the LAPD." She explained something that was *almost* the whole truth, about the latest Good Time Butcher case, the police records only dating back to 1981, the articles under Clea's byline stretching back two years prior to that. "So," Isley concluded, "what I'm trying to figure out is, who's giving you a line on this killer two years before he kills anybody?"

"Well, all due respect ma'am, and no offense intended, but I think what we have here is a story about bureaucratic incompetence in the LAPD."

"Uh-uh. I know what our bureaucratic incompetence looks like. This is something else."

"I don't know what to tell you."

"How about who some of your sources were? Names, if they've got 'em."

139

"I think you know I can't do that."

Isley's first thought was to revert to old habits. Namely, select a part of Ms. Greenstone's anatomy, threaten to remove it in a nonsurgical fashion, and use it to bludgeon another vulnerable part of her corpus until both of the aforementioned sections were just bones with mushy meatloaf dripping off. Then she remembered what had happened the last time she'd conducted herself thusly on the telephone. Just in time, too.

"Listen, I'm gonna rip…" She sighed.

"What?" Clea asked in a tone of voice that leaned forward.

"…up the rule book. Ask *you* to, anyway. I'm trying to catch a really nasty piece of work here. Anything you can tell me would be more than I've got now, which is a timeline that doesn't make any goddamned sense." And then she said the word she made a point of avoiding in all but the most dire of circumstances: "Please."

Clea made thinking noises. Clicks and clacks and crackles. Or maybe that was just a poor connection.

"Ok," Greenstone finally said. "I'll be honest, I don't remember a lot of my exact sources. It was mostly hearsay. I just floated around the Strip and asked people what was up. Just fishing for a juicy story. I didn't really take the Good Time Butcher seriously until I'd heard about him about five or six times, all from different peop-"

"What was the context?"

"Kids on the Strip were sort of laughing nervously about it. Worried about having *too* good a time, or this maniac was gonna sneak into their house and drain them dry. It was almost like the way *real* kids, like, under ten, laugh about a ghost story around a campfire. Deep down they were all scared, they just didn't want anybody else to see it."

"Ok. So after you hear about him five or six times, then what?"

"Then I started actively asking people about it, instead of waiting for them to bring it up. Everybody knew who he was. Which was crazy to me, because I'd never heard of him outside the Strip. But he was their boogeyman. My theory is he was picking off the wannabe rockers because he knew they wouldn't be missed. They're just kids from the country bumming in on train cars to chase fame."

Isley scoffed. "Train cars? They coming right from the dust bowl?"

"Is it cool with you if I keep compromising my journalistic principals for your benefit, or do you wanna do snappy comments all night?"

"Sorry." Another taboo word. And so soon after the last!

"Thank you. My point, the whole point of my articles if you'd bothered to read them past the publication date, was that the police were allowing these kids to get picked off because their disappearance was just solving a problem for the cops. I assume the Strip's not any less of a Wild West now than it was in '79. So if you're looking at '81 and wondering why the Good Time Butcher doesn't show up in your records before then, you're looking at the problem the wrong way around. Records don't tell you what happened, right? They tell you what people cared enough to write down. So the question you should be asking is: why did the LAPD suddenly start caring?"

"…sounds like you shoulda pitched this to your editorial, instead of becoming a wannabe Winchell."

"Who?"

"How the fuck…" Isley pinched the bridge of her nose. "You know what, nevermind. You got a theory about *that?* Why you think nobody gave a shit til '81?"

"No to the theory, sorry. It's not like the victims who started showing up past '81 were upstanding citizens. They were, I don't know what the nice way to say this is, but scum. Just faceless wastoids from the Strip. So what changed? No clue."

"Who died before that? You got names of his prehistoric victims?"

"Maybe somewhere in my notes. Those are in a box in storage, if they haven't been shredded already. Old employer doesn't want any of their property getting carried over to the competition. You know how it is."

"Oh, fuck yeah I do. Don't tell me, I know all about it."

"I'd suggest seeing if Wesley still works at the Billymark."

"Come again?"

"It's a dive just off the Strip. Head west and keep going till the lights start to die down. He *seems* like the kind of guy who keeps to himself, but he knew more about what was going on on the Strip, and who was doing it, than anybody I've ever met."

"Wesley?"

"Yeah."

"What's his last name?"

Clea chuckled. "The Billymark's not a *last name* kind of place."

"Gotcha." Isley paused. "How have I never heard of this place?"

"Who's gonna tell a cop about it?"

"I was thinking more as a drinker than a detective. But hey, we have CIs."

"Who presumably want to hang out *somewhere* without worrying you'll show up."

"That's…plausible." Isley looked up to the ceiling. "Well, lemme go see what Wesley's up to. You've been a fucking doll though."

"Always happy to help."

"Oh, I bet." Isley hung up. The moment her phone hit the cradle, it rang. So she answered it. Why not? That last conversation had gone so well. "Who's this?"

"Ah…hi there. It's Luca."

"Luca! I was just thinking about you!"

"Oh, um, ok. Well, Sarge told me in no uncertain terms, I've gotta get th-"

"Sure, sure. I'll bring 'em right on by." Isley's eyes darted to the papers spread across her desk. "I don't need 'em anymore."

"What does that mean?"

"Wink wink, just ask Sarge. Wink and a nudge. Just make sure he knows about say no more, I don't like flipping that tape more than twice a month." Isley slammed the phone down and hummed "Hell Bent For Leather" as she stuffed the clippings back into the package and headed out the door. This would work perfectly. Headquarters was right on the way to the Billymark.

BRAINFACE

SOME crummy old dive on the far end of the fun stuff didn't seem like a great place to celebrate the last night of recording, but it wasn't Delmer's decision to make. The producer, a label-appointed fella called John Van Eiden, who turned out to have a deft touch with some of the larger egos in Toksick – which was to say, Clutch, though bassist Dr. Nosebleed wasn't exactly given to fits of agreeability – had told them "fuck the Rainbow, fuck Gazzarri's, you want a g-"

"Fuck the Whisky?" asked drummer Spots, who was, in fact, a stronger musician than Patch, though that fact did nothing to ameliorate Delmer's guilt at having not spoken to the latter for weeks.

"Fuck the Whisky! You wanna do something might

be worth celebrating, you go to those places. You wanna celebrate a worthy thing you've *already* done, you go to the Billymark.

"Also," Van Eiden would add en route, in a lull between adrenaline spikes, "they don't card."

And so they went, because they had indeed done a worthy thing. Their debut album, coming December 8th via Elektra, was something special. Was it vain to say it was unlike anything else the world had ever heard? No, Delmer didn't think so. The band was tight, playing rhythmic, riff-heavy grooves, but with an expansive, almost prog-esque emphasis on constructing sonic journeys. And Clutch, good god! The man could *sing*. Delmer could scarcely believe the sounds that came out of his mouth. He had the intensity of your typical rock vocalist, but with a range that was downright operatic. *Soaring*, that was what the critics would all say. And what would they write of Delmer's guitar playing? Probably *blistering*. *Virtuosic*. Was that a word? Whatever the adjective for *virtuoso* was. What they'd recorded was the best playing Delmer had ever done, in his entire goddamned life. And as if that weren't enough to be proud of, he'd also been the one to come up with the title of the album: Brainface. He'd meant it as a subtle tribute to his old band, but Van Eiden was mostly taken by the cover art opportunities. He imagined Toksick taking a sort of "elevated shock rock" route, one he described as "like if Alice Cooper had ever read a fucking book in his life." *Brainface*, as he saw it, would be fronted by an illustration straddling Da Vinci and Bosch. Clutch's frustration that he wouldn't appear anywhere on the cover was quickly quashed with the promise that it would feature a face modeled after his. This led Delmer to wonder if anybody else could visualize what Van Eiden had in mind, because he sure as hell couldn't.

But who gave a shit? They had a powerhouse fucking debut on their hands, and the full support of a major label behind its forthcoming release. So Toksick went roaring into the Billymark feeling four drinks deep before Van Eiden had ordered the first round. Granted, the cocaine might have had something to do with that. It almost certainly accounted for Delmer's ferocious, *ferocious*, as the critics would call it, playing lately. But it wasn't the whole story. The boys in Toksick were high on *life*, high on *triumph*, high on *rock and roll*.

They ended up far more than four drinks deep. Probably. The night became little more than a blur in Delmer's memory, a smeary riptide from which there were precious few gasps for air. Among these, though, was; climbing onto a detached garage with Dr. Nosebleed, from which Delmer descended by lowering himself down onto a trash can, while Dr. Nosebleed opted to leap, rolling his ankle as he landed; getting the cops called on them at Mel's for starting a sing-a-long to "It's A Long Way To The Top (If You Wanna Rock 'N Roll)" which was what AC/DC was *for*, goddamnit!; Clutch throwing some girl Delmer couldn't remember ever seeing before off a pier, it wasn't the Santa Monica pier, the water was dark and the girl couldn't get back up on the dock, but Clutch was laughing a lot, so Delmer waited to help her up until Clutch lost interest; laying flat on his back in a place he didn't recognize, it looked like the inside of a helicopter or some shit, getting a blowjob from some chick he'd never met, wondering if she was hot or not, whatever though, nice tits, he reached down to give 'em a squeeze but then it was back to the blur; seeing some guy getting mugged and stopping to help, only the guy getting mugged turned out to be just some homeless loony so Dr. Nosebleed and Van Eiden joined in kicking the shit out of him, which Delmer thought was way off base, so he just stood by and watched and waited for them to be done; and, finally, waking up naked on the floor next to a bare mattress with a big brown stain in the center.

Eyes tracking around the room independently of each other, Delmer pushed himself to a kneeling position and sat on his heels. He really wanted to throw up, but that also sounded like a lot of work at this hour. Which, by the way, was what? He turned his eyes to the window. They burned up in their sockets and rolled out onto the floor. Raising his hand, Delmer heaved himself onto the bed and plopped down next to a woman whose eyes were wide open and staring right at him. Like a spider studying the moth who'd come a-fluttering into her web.

"Ah!" he shouted as she spun up on top of him. She wasted no time grinding his instrument of mere adequacy beneath the weight of her hips.

"Come on baby," she cooed between pursed lips. She bounced and whirled and gyrated, like a NASA scientist testing the effects of high G forces on male genitalia.

"Come on, come on. Fuck me. Fuck me like you did last night."

"How was that?"

"Hard."

"…like my dick was hard, or the fucking was difficult?"

"Oh, baby. Fuck me."

Delmer looked around the floor for a wrapper. A slip of colored plastic. Maybe a mushy water balloon. Anything. Please god. Anything. "Did I use a condom?"

The girl sighed and stilled herself. "You said you wanted the no condom rate. Don't you fucking try to walk that back."

"You're a, uh…um?"

"Prostitute?"

"Yeah."

"Obviously."

"Well Jesus, don't say it like that."

"I mean…" she gestured to her body, and then Delmer's. She had a point. Delmer didn't. He had round edges.

More glancing around the room, which appeared to be a modestly chic studio apartment. "My wallet's in my pants. Where are my clothes?"

She smiled at him. "Honey, that's a very good question. You were naked when I found you."

"Where was that?"

"Heading south on North Highland."

Fuck. Drivers license, what little cash he'd had, the condom his drunk ass had apparently paid extra to not

149

use even though he hadn't had it on him…all gone. "Well," Delmer sighed, "can I run a tab?"

CLAD in the few articles of clothing from the woman-whose-name-was-probably-not-actually-Joy's closet that fit him (a pair of wide-legged jeans that threatened an implosive brand of castration, a swoopy kimono-looking deal that had only one cinch at the midriff), Delmer trudged his way back to the practice space, head ringing and stomach churning all the while. Four times he stopped to throw up, only going through with it the first two times. No cargo left to jettison, it seemed; that second purge in the bushes outside the Consumer Value Store had been downright biblical. And speaking of burning bushes, he really hoped Joy hadn't given him more than he'd paid for. Mad Mick had the jack, and holy hell did it sound unpleasant. The word "discharge" was involved. No thanks. Of course, it was worth worrying about a different sort of bustle in Joy's hedgerow: what if he'd knocked her up? The world wasn't ready for another little Lippincott; it hadn't even met *this* one yet! He consoled himself with the knowledge that Joy didn't know his real name. He didn't think so, anyway. Granted, he'd told her his name was "Delmer," but when she'd asked for his last name "in case you forget to come back and pay" (which, like, how could she even entertain the prospect that she would *ever* see him again?), he'd had the presence of mind to say "Llllippitysplit." Not his best work, but he wasn't a damn lyricist. He was a guitarist.

Which was terrifying in its own right. When Toksick

hit it big in just a few months' time, his face was going to be everywhere. Billboards, television sets, maybe even movie screens. Joy would recognize him, point at his face, and say "that's your daddy" to some little halfsquat with a Delmer-esque splash of freckles. Lawyers would *leap* at the chance. Who wouldn't want to sue the biggest rock star on the planet? A prostitute suing him for child support. God, the headlines. It might give him some cred – what was more rock and roll than sex before marriage, after all – but he didn't want to pay fucking child support.

He wanted to create something that outlived him, yeah. But not a fucking *kid*.

The first thing he said, then, after swooshing into the practice space (still a basement, but this one was a sound-proofed, air conditioned, and carpeted wonderland beneath Clutch's mom's house) was "I need a stage name and I want to wear face paint."

Van Eiden lifted the towel from over his eyes and glanced at Delmer from his prostration. "I don't want to hear anything about music ever again."

"He peed himself," Spots giggled. "Last night he peed his pants."

"Oh." Delmer gestured down at his clothes. "Well, I lost mine. I don't know if that's better or worse."

"Depends on did you pee in them before you lost them or not."

Delmer sighed. "I have no clue. I don't remember all that much."

"Join the club," Dr. Nosebleed's voice harrumphed from under a pile of pillows.

Delmer slugged his way to a chair and turned his bones off. "Where's Clutch?"

"We were hoping he was with you," Van Eiden said, this time not deigning to lift the towel.

"I don't even know where *I* was."

"Join the club," Dr. Nosebleed harrumphed.

Spots giggled. Nobody asked him what about.

Delmer took a deep breath. One of his ribs popped. "Ah," he hissed. "Fuck," he said a bit louder, when nobody asked him what was wrong. "Hm. Does anybody know where we split up?"

"We were definitely together at the Billymark," Spots asserted.

"No shit," Van Eiden grumbled.

Spots drummed his hands on his knees. "They're all in such a bad mood. Hungover big time. I just drank a lot of water before bed. You drink a lot of water and you don't get hungover."

"You threw up."

"Yeah, but *you* peed your pants."

Van Eiden waved a lazy middle finger towards Spots.

"Um," Delmer wondered, "when should we worry about Clutch?"

Dr. Nosebleed's face breached the sea of throw pillows. "He's a big boy," said the blowhole. "He doesn't show up for a gig, we'll fret."

"Maybe I'm just being a bit of a…uh, country kid, but I feel like in a big city, uh, maybe we shouldn't wait that long?"

"This ain't my first rodeo," Van Eiden mumbled.

152

"Frontmen are always the same. They disappear for a while, pop back up at the show. One time we lost Iggy for three days, but when the next Stooges show rolled around, he just jumped right on up out of the audience and joined the band."

Spots stopped drumming his legs. "Woah. You produced The Stooges?"

"Elektra did. That's who I meant by 'we.' I was barely in college when the band broke up." Van Eiden levered himself up onto his elbows, squinting and wincing at the effort. "How old do you think I am?"

Spots shrugged and resumed drumming.

"So…" Delmer began without having any productive follow-ups planned. "We just wait for Clutch to show up?"

"Fuck no!" Van Eiden shouted from back under the towel.

"Dude!" Dr. Nosebleed cried from his cocoon.

Spots giggled.

Delmer felt like there was a black hole between his eyeballs. He pinched the bridge of his nose and sank deeper into his chair.

Van Eiden grumped himself all the way to a seated position. "You guys are practicing every goddamned day before this record comes out. You wanna party, fine by me. But you're gonna be tight for the *Brainface* tour, or… a bad thing. I don't fucking know." He lay back down and sighed. "I don't want to talk about music."

With a start, Delmer realized that they weren't.

153

GOOD, IN A WAY

MIKE invited Bub to Dominick's funeral. It took a long time to happen because the police wanted to look at the body for a long time. Bub was scared about that because he was afraid they would find a fingerprint on it. Maybe one that belonged to him. Or the tooth. He knew teeth didn't have fingerprints, but teeth also didn't have hands. Yet the tooth had had Bub's hands. So maybe it had his prints too.

Dominick had used the children's toy to tell Bub that he was sad that he was dead. He was also mad at Bub because it had been Bub who killed him. But in a way it was also good because now they could talk whenever they wanted. That didn't seem right to Bub but that was what Dominick had said. Through the children's toy.

The police said something different though. They said that it was probably a drug dealer that killed Dominck. They said that Dominick was a drug dealer, and maybe he made another drug dealer mad, and so the mad drug dealer killed Dominick. Bub didn't think Dominick was a drug dealer. Ollie said he *knew* 'Dom' hadn't been a drug dealer, that was just some bullshit excuse the cops were using to drop the case. But the police said he had been. A drug dealer. They also said that another drug dealer killed him. If they were wrong about the first thing, they were probably wrong about the other thing too.

Bub learned a lot of interesting things about Dominick at his funeral. He learned that his full name was Dominick Stacey Hendricks. He didn't have an x like the rock and roll guitarist. He had a cks, like the last two letters of his first name and first letter of his middle. Dominick was a Good Christian Boy. He said prayers and had lots of friends. One lady was crying. That was probably Dominick's mom. Bub was sad that she was crying. He wanted to tell her that her son was kind of mad that Bub killed him, but thought that in a way it was also good. He wanted to tell her she could come over and use his Ouija board whenever she wanted. He didn't think that would make her feel any better though. So he didn't. Tell her.

A lot of Dominick's friends looked grouchy. They were sitting in the pews near the back of the church, like they were late and there was nowhere else to sit. But those were both not true things. They stayed in the back, still. Bub had never seen them before. The only friends of Dominick's he'd known were Ollie and Mike. They both sat in the front. That was where Bub sat. He liked looking at the picture they had of Dominick. He was smiling in it. And young. It looked like it was from school maybe. There was nothing in the background. Just grey with him smiling in front of it. It was kind of creepy to see Dominick in the middle of nothing like that. That was where he was now. Just grey nothing. But it was a nice picture anyway, and it was the only way to look at him because the casket was closed up tight.

The more he heard about Dominick, the less it made sense to Bub that he would have killed him. Because Bub was afraid that he was the Good Time Butcher, but Dominick hadn't had a good time. His mom had died when he was young because his dad knocked her block off with a baseball bat. The lady crying over there was a Foster Mother. Which was a bit like a Parker Brother in that it wasn't a real Mom. She was crying like one though, because she'd raised Dominick right and the guy standing up front in the religious bathrobe said so, and he also said that Dominick had conquered so many challenges that would have stopped a less impressive man in his tracks. Some of the challenges were that he was dyslexic, which is when you can't figure out letters. But he knew how to read and that was good. Dominick also had something that made his head hurt really bad but you'd never know because he was such a tough customer. He worked two jobs, one delivering pizzas and the other digging holes for people to plant flowers in, so he could help his Foster Mother pay for her house and other things, because she'd had An Accident and couldn't do it all by herself. He also still went to school. Bub had thought Dominick was too old for school but maybe it wasn't the kind of school Bub was thinking of. Maybe that was why Dominick and his friends played with children's toys.

Anyway, Dominick didn't have a Good Time. So it didn't make any sense that Bub would Butcher him. Even though he didn't, because the tooth did it. So maybe the tooth wasn't the Good Time Butcher. Maybe the tooth was a Bad Time Butcher. Bub wondered if that meant maybe *he* wasn't the Good Time Butcher. Because he didn't remember ever Butchering anybody. But then where had the tooth come from? It was all really confusing and made him start humming in the church. An old man next to him put his hand on Bub's back, and then picked it up and put it down again.

Bub flinched.

The old man took his hand away.

"I'm not crying," Bub informed him.

"Let it out," the old man replied.

So Bub hummed louder. And it felt okay. He couldn't hear the tooth when he hummed. He liked that. He could tell it was trying to talk to him but he couldn't tell what it was saying. Then it screamed but he just hummed louder and that was fine.

He couldn't hum forever though, and when he was walking home the tooth said *you don't believe me*.

"About what?"

You know what.

"About the Butcher."

About you.

"I don't know."

So you're calling me a liar.

"I don't know."

Red filled Bub's head. It was all he could see. He felt the pavement *smack* him in the face. It was all red though so he couldn't see it. After a while the red went away and he pushed himself back up. His face was bloody again. His mouth hurt.

"Why did you do that?"

You should trust me.

"I don't think you're my friend."

I don't have to be.

Bub took a deep breath. "I don't think I'm the Good Time Butcher. I think you're just confusing me because you're a Bad Time Butcher."

Then where did I come from? How did I wind up in your pocket, hm?

"Maybe you're my tooth. Maybe I lost a tooth then I found it."

Well then who's out there sucking all those fun-loving people dry, hm?

"I don't know. Maybe it's you."

Aren't I your tooth? Isn't that what you're telling yourself now?

"I don't know. Maybe you aren't."

Then where did I come from?

Bub wanted to say "I don't know" but then he closed his eyes to blink and when he opened them he was in a room he'd never seen before and it was somebody's bedroom and there was a bed in front of him and there was a guy on the bed and he was all stretched out with ropes and he had a sock in his mouth and two wires in his arms and one was connected to a clear bag and the other one was attached to a red bag and the red bag was getting bigger and the clear bag was getting smaller and the guy on the bed was trying to wave his arms and legs but the ropes were tight and he had one around the sock so it didn't come out and Bub wanted to take out the sock and say who are you and what's going on and how did I get here but if he took the sock out the guy would just scream and scream and then Bub would get in trouble and the police would yell at him. He didn't want anybody to yell at him so he just stared at the guy and watched the red bag get bigger.

Look, the tooth told him. *You did this*.

"*You* did."

Check your watch.

"I don't have a watch."

Yes you do. Because he *had a watch, and now it's yours.*

Bub looked down at his wrist and there was a watch. "Oh." He looked at the guy on the bed. "I'm sorry I took your watch." The guy didn't look like he accepted Bub's apology.

What time is it?

"Um…two…seventeen?"

What time did you leave the funeral service?

"I don't remember."

Think. You stayed and mingled, and left around ten.

160

"I don't remember mingling. That doesn't sound like something I would do."

You left around ten and now it's two. Look at how much blood is in that bag. Is that four hours of blood?

"I don't know. I don't know how much blood is an hour."

Not that much.

"…what day is it?"

It's today, you useless piece of shit.

"If it's two o'clock AM, and yesterday was Tuesday, then today should be Wednesday."

No shit.

Bub walked to the door and stepped out of the bedroom. The guy on the bed was screaming but you couldn't really hear him if you shut the bedroom door. You *definitely* couldn't hear him if you walked out of the apartment and stood in the hallway and hummed. So Bub did that and then he went down the stairs and outside. He was in a part of the city he'd never seen before. It looked like he was on the wrong side of the Hills.

"How did I get here?" he asked the tooth.

It didn't say anything.

Bub went around to everyone he saw and asked them what day it was. They all said "Thursday," except for a few who said "Get the fuck away from me."

"That's a whole extra day," Bub told the tooth. "You did lie to me."

Did I?

"I don't think I'm the Good Time Butcher. I think you want me to think I am."

Really? Oh good, the man bleeding out on the bed will be so relieved to hear, it was all just a mix-up.

"Oh!" The man! Bub needed to help that man.

He retraced his steps at a run, thumping through the night for what felt like hours. But from out here all of the apartments looked the same. Even if the buildings were all different, the insides he wanted to see through the windows were all dark. A thousand and one dark rectangle shapes. In one of those dark rectangle shapes there was someone screaming through a sock while he leaked into a bag. Bub just couldn't remember which one. There were so many. Then some of the rectangles lit up. The guy definitely wasn't in any of those because he couldn't reach the lightswitch. Then the sun came up and the rectangles all looked the same again. The guy was probably still screaming but you couldn't hear him because of the doors and the walls. And the noise. The rest of the world had gotten noisier. Hummier. More hummy. Part of that was Bub. "Where is it?" he shouted. "Which one was he in? I can't find it! Help me!"

Who?

"You!"

Which one?

An unfamiliar voice. Bub froze and reached into his pocket.

He felt a lot of wet with something hard in the middle. It bit him.

THUD

TWO practice sessions in a row, and still no sign of Clutch. He'd made no effort to contact any of his band-mates, nor even those members of his family that Van Eiden knew how to reach. Delmer kept calling his number at the call center, the one he'd given Delmer on that fateful, surprisingly-not-fatal car ride. Nothing.

"Relax," everybody kept telling Delmer. "He'll turn up." But increasingly, it was only their producer who could assert this with any kind of confidence.

"So what," Dr. Nosebleed exclaimed, apropos of nothing, in the middle of a full-band beer run, "are we worried like he died or something? We'd know if he died. It'd be in the paper."

"Have any of us been *checking* the paper?" Delmer asked.

"I bet Van Eiden has."

Spots made an *eeeeh* noise. "He doesn't seem like a big reader to me."

"The fuck are you talking about? He reads contracts all day! That's his job!"

"I mean like for leisure though."

"Bah."

Delmer became acutely aware of the sound his shoes made as they smacked against the sidewalk. It was a dull *thud* with two gasps on either end. The soles of his shoes were loose. As with most things that had transpired over the past few days, he couldn't begin to account for how or why.

He hated himself for thinking it, but Delmer couldn't help wondering: what would happen to *Brainface* if Clutch…weren't able to go on tour for it? He was undeniably charismatic, and while it would be a disservice to the rest of the band to say that Clutch carried them on his scrawny little shoulders, it wouldn't be *entirely* inaccurate. The Elektra deal had, it was openly acknowledged, been tendered and inked only because Clutch had busted his ass to get it.

So why wasn't he here, with them, getting ready to enjoy the fun part of all that hard work? Delmer frowned and stared at his shoes. From above, they looked perfectly fine.

WHERE EVERYBODY KNOWS YOUR (FIRST) NAME

MOST bartenders, in Isley's considerable experience, made a point of looking busy. Polishing glasses, that was the go-to bit of business, but they also like pressing a little button on the fountain that made a *pssh* sound. As far as Isley could tell, that didn't do anything except go *pssh*, and make the bartender look busy.

The guy who turned out to be Wesley, he wasn't that sort of bartender. He just stood around until he was engaged, at which point he interacted with customers as though nothing would have pissed him off more than someone leaving a tip. Isley watched him, as she had the past few nights, from the dark end of the bar, nursing a drink or four. Nursing it the way you nurse a war hero whose skin fell off. *Lots* of attention.

Anyway, yeah, attention: Isley fixed quite a bit on Wesley as he glared at his latest cash-bearing nuisance. The guy was wearing a pastel blue turtleneck sweater. His gal had a tasseled jacket of a matching hue. Not like a leather jacket though. A cowboy number. Isley instantly felt a pang of sympathy for them, as one does upon seeing a blind person tapping their way towards wet cement.

The guy laughed as he approached the bar. He placed his hand on it delicately, as though worried about smudging it. "Hi sir!" he chirruped at Wesley. "How goes it this evening?"

Wesley said, for the benefit of the entire establishment, "god*damn*it." He hip-bumped himself out of his lean against the back of the bar, followed his knuckles over to the new arrivals, and slapped the bar hard enough to make Isley's glass jump.

The guy jumped too, then chuckled nervously. "Uh, that good, huh?"

"You order this second," Wesley snarled, eyes fixed on the spot where their reflection would've shown up on the bar if it were anything approaching clean, "or you're out on your ass."

It was always some variation of that. Order or go screw. Isley was relieved she'd heard him deliver that ultimatum to someone prior to her approaching him. Wesley was a prickly one, what Saacks would call a "hostile witness." Typically there was some sort of jurisprudential muscle the department could flex to compel testimony from such fuckers, but Isley had lost her access to it. What she had – *all* she had – was her scintillating personality.

So she'd realized pretty quickly she'd need to plot her approach carefully. Because if she *didn't*, she'd be like these two dumb yuppies asking Wesley to run through what he had on tap. The barkeep narrowed his eyes, then closed them, then squeezed the lids together. He sucked air through his nose and blew smoke out his ears. If he'd had any hair, it'd almost certainly have fluttered like the curtain of a haunted house. Then he opened his eyes and drilled them into the guy – not his face, but his Adam's apple.

That was Wesley's answer.

The Adam's apple bobbed up and down. "Ah…do you have Budweiser?"

"Did I say we got Budweiser?" Wesley rumbled.

"Come on," the gal whispered to her husband. "Let's go."

"Oh, too good for my joint?"

"Hey, pal," the fella said as he pointed his finger towards Wesley, which was when a few of the other patrons started to take an uncommon interest in the strange invaders. "I just wanted to get a drink with my lady. I'm trying to pay for alcohol. It's not rocket science."

"Let's *go,*" the gal hissed.

"Ok, great," Wesley said in a tone of voice that contradicted both of those words. "That was the problem. I didn't see why you came in for, until you mentioned it. Ok." Wesley reached behind him, grabbed two shot glasses, slammed them on the counter, and slopped them full of Jägermeister. "There you go. Two alcohols." He thumped his knuckles on the bar, palm up. "Now pay me."

The guy recoiled slightly from the glasses. "We don't want Jäger."

Wesley shook his head. "All you said was that you wanted to pay me for alcohol. There's alcohol. Now pay me."

"We're not drinking that."

"Pour it in your ear for all I care. It's yours. Now pay me."

Inspiration struck. Isley raised her hand and said "I want 'em."

Wesley turned his head juuuust enough to catch her in his peripheral.

She pulled out her wallet and flitted through the two bills she had in there. "Two each, do I have that right?" A five dollar bill materialized. Isley stretched it out towards Wesley.

He shrugged and lumbered over to take it.

"Oh," the guy scoffed at Wesley, "so now they're *your* shots again, is that it? You better be getting that money to give to me!"

Wesley laughed. It was the sound of an approaching tornado.

"Hey, hang on!" the guy pulled four singles out of his pocket and slammed them down on the bar. In one fluid motion, he threw back one of the shots. "Drink up, honey," he ordered his gal.

She sighed but complied.

"This place stinks!" was the guy's parting shot, one he

likely imagined had been free.

The joke, of course, was on him. Those shots were only a buck a pop. Which the guy would have known, if he'd bothered to read the chalkboard behind the bar.

Isley returned to her drink and waited. Guys like Wesley, they always had a soft spot. She imagined his was fucking with yuppies.

She'd imagined correctly.

"What do you want?" Wesley asked her, not unkindly. Isley looked up to find him approaching with an empty shot glass in hand.

She smiled. "We splitting the take?"

"Call it a finder's fee."

"Knock of Jack, then."

Wesley poured amber into the glass, and a heavy hand at that. Isley took it up, presented it to him in the universal *cheers* gesture, and threw back her reward.

When she brought her head back down, Wesley was leaning full on the bar, forearms planted, fists threaded into one big meat mallet. His entire six and some vertical feet tilted at her, tonsure gleaming like the business end of a warhead. "You're a cop." He said it with a declarative flatness that told Isley he wasn't just guessing.

"Was. Not as of earlier this week. I bet you know that."

"Cokehead."

Isley twirled her hand in a mock bow.

"Why are you in my bar all of a sudden? I don't sell coke."

"Oh, I'm sure." She tapped her shot glass. Wesley

smiled and refilled it, with a less generous pour. "I hear you're the guy to talk to."

She didn't specify about what, and Wesley didn't ask. What he did was wonder "this something I should close early for?"

Isley *really* wanted to ask what the hell that meant, but the savvy side of her took that sort of statement to be bait. "Not unless you're the Good Time Butcher."

"Oh, this'll be a short talk then."

"You got something concise to tell me?"

"I got *nothin'* to tell you."

Isley gave a little more love to the bourbon she'd been sipping prior to the unwelcome arrivals. "You answer a few questions, I'll quit darkening your doorstep."

"Maybe I think you're good company."

"Glad to see you're a shit liar. When's the first time you remember hearing about the Good Time Butcher?"

"Skip to the end."

"What?"

"You cops," Wesley began, pouring Jäger into Isley's glass and tossing it back himself, *"ah,* you always got one question you wanna ask. But you don't wanna just start there. You got a bunch of warm-ups before the main event. So just gimme the question at the end."

Isley smiled. "People on the Strip were talking about the Good Time Butcher two years before the LAPD got wind of him. I want to figure out why. How you all knew about him so long before we did."

"Sounds like cops not knowing how to do their fucking job."

"Plenty of people think so. That's my next stop. But I wanna chase *this* end before I go up to the other."

"You mean the beginning. You're chasin' the beginning."

Isley thought about that. "I guess so."

"Mhm. No clue the first time I heard it in here. I can tell you in '80, maybe mid '80, some band did a song called The Good Time Butcher. It was about the guy, obviously. A lot of people got pretty pissed. Up until then, everybody talked about the Butcher but nobody *talked* about him. That kind of thing. This band was *talking* about him." Isley had heard of people 'chuckling to themselves,' but had never really appreciated what a *truly* private chuckle sounded like until she saw Wesley gobbling down his own mirth. "Pissed a lot of folks off," he finally continued. "I think somebody threw a used johnny at the singer or something. Mad about the song sort of thing. So they changed the name to something like Don't Have A Good Time. Not that, but something like it. Maybe *Don't Have A* was in swoops."

"Parentheses?"

"Yeah."

"What was the band called?"

"I just told you everything I got. Don't recall the band name, or who was in it. Just that it happened in '80. It was a thing people talked about."

"Who should I talk t-"

"I told you everything I got, I said. Go sniffin' around for whoever got a full rubber hurled at em."

"On the Strip? That's not gonna narrow it down

much."

Wesley chuckled again…but maybe a little more openly, this time? Maybe.

Isley slammed her bourbon and pushed the glass towards Wesley. "You're not as much of an asshole as you seem."

"I gotta work on that," Wesley grunted. Isley pulled her wallet back out. Wesley waved it away. "You catch the guy's been killin' my customers. We're square." He pointed a finger at her. "But you come back here, you better not be bringin' any questions."

"Then how am I gonna know what you have on tap?"

Wesley's mouth betrayed him: a smile. "Get the fuck outta here."

THE PROBLEM OF MOTHERFUCKERS

"IT'S not a problem yet," that was what Van Eiden kept saying. "It'll be problem if the show starts and he doesn't show up."

Well, it was just about problem time. Toksick was en route to their first show since Clutch had gone AWOL, a shitty gig opening for some act whose gimmick was that their singer strapped the microphone to his face like Dylan with a harmonica and did circus activities with his hands, like juggling and making balloon animals. Toksick was opening for *them*, and not just opening but *opening*. Doors at seven, they go on at six. Like that. Indignities of the sort Delmer had joined Toksick to avoid. This, too, was not a problem to Van Eiden. When *Brainface* dropped, it'd be like an elevator straight to the top. "Weight goes down," he said, "car goes up."

"So what's a problem to you?" Delmer asked in the cab to the club. "Anything?"

The producer shook his head. "A problem is something that doesn't have a solution."

Spots slapped his thighs. "Uh, I thought solutions were *for* problems?"

"Right. You have a problem, then you throw a solution at it, then it's not a problem anymore."

"But it *was* a problem."

"And," Delmer dogpiled, "doesn't that mean that everything that needs a solution is a problem, until you have a solution for it?"

Dr. Nosebleed groaned. "Shit like this is why I ditched school."

"No," Van Eiden fired back, ignoring Dr. Nosebleed, whose doctorate must certainly have been honorary. "You might come up with a solution for something that isn't a problem."

"But then it wouldn't be a solution," Delmer replied.

"You'd think it was. But it wasn't." Van Eiden raised a professorial finger. "Attempting to solve a problem that isn't a problem creates a new problem. So if you think about it, sometimes solutions *are* problems."

"If you all don't shut the fuck up," Dr. Nosebleed hypothesized, "I'll quit the fucking band. There's your problem."

Van Eiden rolled his eyes. "Oh yeah, how would we *ever* carry on without a *bassist?"*

"The fuck does that mean?"

"We're here," the cab driver said with evident relief. "Goodbye."

They disembarked, Delmer being careful, as always, to leave his door open until all of the gear was liberated from the hatchback. Granted, if the driver really gunned it, he could probably close that passengerside rear door with the force of his getaway, off to sell Toksick's shit at whatever gargoyle market cabbies sold their stolen goods. But it made Delmer feel better to leave it open, and sources of relief had been in short supply lately.

As they hustled their hardshell cases off the street and around to the back door, which was glamorously located next to two dumpsters whose emphatic signage announced that the club (fittingly called "Good Grief") shared the alley with a neighboring check cashing operation, Delmer kept a close eye on Van Eiden. He watched him as he pounded on the door, grumbled disapproval at his watch, pounded again. Was he genuinely unconcerned about Clutch? Or was he putting on a brave face for the band and chewing up his fingernails in private? Delmer hoped the latter, but all the same it would have enraged him to discover that was the case. He'd given Van Eiden countless opportunities to reverse his "just chill out" position without losing face. Each time, he refused. He would rather launch a philosophical investigation into the very concept of *problems* than grant that Toksick might be experiencing one.

Even now, pounding on the door, ducking beneath the arm of the meathead who opened it and greeted the band by saying "this isn't my fucking job," threading their poorly-protected gear through narrow hallways, grabbing drinks that weren't comped but were given at the low, low price of 15% off (the discount based on the non-happy hour prices of course, which ended up being still more expensive than the happy hour prices, which deals the band were barred from enjoying after identifying themselves as performers), taking their drinks up on stage as they began soundcheck, being told to start playing after three minutes of attempted hook-up, watching morosely as confused patrons filed in with faces that said *the door is open but I don't know if I'm supposed to be here…* through all of this, until *now*, eight bars into their first number ("Never Wrong"), Delmer watched Van Eiden every chance he could. Not once did the man betray the least hint of concern. Indeed, there was a look of distant pleasure spreading across his face.

"If there's one thing I know, it's everything!"

The first line of the song, right on cue! Delmer started, glancing about for who it was doing a credible impression of Clutch…only to discover Clutch himself, up on stage, dressed, made-up, and hard at work trying to impregnate the mic stand.

So stunned was Delmer that he missed a one-measure fill he was meant to do. He looked at the rest of the band, who appeared just as stunned as he was. Then he looked back at Van Eiden, who was tapping his foot, bobbing his head, and grinning with his eyes shut, like he'd just sniffed a bicycle seat.

Motherfucker.

Another sort of problem occurred to Delmer. It was the kind that one person deliberately makes for others, a problem designed in such a way that only the trouble-maker could provide the solution. It was, perhaps, the worst of all the problems.

But not, Delmer reminded himself, for the person making it.

THE mood amongst the members of Toksick could best be understated as *tense*. Forgiveness for Clutch was a question of degree; that forgiveness was required was un-disputed, even by Van Eiden.

The frontman insisted that his life was his to lead, to which Delmer, easily the least magnanimous of the bunch, agreed. *But* with the considerable caveat that Clutch had a responsibility to the band, and that his pro-longed, unexplained absence was a dereliction of that duty.

"Responsibility?!" Clutch yodeled. "That's gotta be the least fucking rock 'n roll word ever!"

Van Eiden, who came and went according to the dic-tates of Elektra contracts, wiggled his hand in the air. "Rock 'n roll doesn't happen without *some* discipline. But," he added to Delmer, "he hasn't missed any shows yet."

"Don't say *yet,*" Clutch grumbled

Delmer crossed his arms in front of his chest. "He also hasn't come to any fucking practices."

"I don't *need* to!" Clutch huffed.

Spots spoke: "If you never come to practice, though,

177

how are we gonna write new stuff?"

"We don't *need* to write new stuff yet. Our first new stuff isn't even out!"

Leaving the *yet* off that last sentence proved prescient.

The blow that came one eerily still morning in early October was one from which a more tightly knit band might have recovered. It was delivered by proxy via Van Eiden, in the tape deck of his crusty-ass Corvette, with a cassette that glimmered like a gemstone freshly carved from the Earth. "Listen to this," he bade them. Into his car they piled, into the deck went the tape, and into their ears went the music. It was a pisspoor quality recording of a tremendously powerful band playing rhythmic, riff-heavy grooves, but with an expansive, almost prog-esque emphasis on constructing sonic journeys. Alright, maybe *prog-esque* wasn't quite right…but all the same, over top of the music, there soared a goddamned operatic voice, executing daring aerial maneuvers.

It was, in short, a band that sounded a hell of a lot like Toksick.

"That's our fucking sound!" Clutch marveled. "These fuckers stole our sound!"

From the backseat, Dr. Nosebleed grabbed the head-rest (along with a few strands of Van Eiden's hair) and yanked himself forward.

"Ow," Van Eiden mumbled.

Dr. Nosebleed ignored the outburst, offering his own instead: "How the fuck did they get our sound? They heard *Brainface* or what? How'd that happen, John?"

"I hope they're not trying to get theirs out first," Spots

offered from next to Dr. Nosebleed. "They really do sound like us."

Van Eiden sighed. "I have very bad news, fellas. They don't sound like you. *You* sound like *them*. Because *they* are Black Sabbath."

Dr. Nosebleed laughed. "You gotta introduce me to Ozzy's vocal coach, then."

"No way that's Sabbath," Delmer declared, with a conviction that would conquer any and all facts Van Eiden might throw at him. Because it was simply impossible that this was Black Sabbath, the godfathers of all heavy metal, that they were listening to. Black Sabbath was raw, loose, bluesy. This was stadium-ready rock of the highest caliber. Yes, the superlative fit: it was the *highest* caliber. Toksick's *Brainface* was, Delmer wasn't afraid to admit, *very good*. This, whoever it was that Van Eiden was trying to convince them was Black Sabbath… they were *great*.

"They kicked Ozzy out," Van Eiden explained. "This guy's name is Ronnie. And I feel it valuable to mention here, Sabbath kicked Ozzy out for out-of-control substance abuse." Van Eiden mugged at Clutch, then dragged his gaze across all the other members of Toksick.

If Delmer wasn't mistaken, he heard quite a bit of dry *gulp*ing. Impossible to say whether or not any of it had originated in his own throat.

Dr. Nosebleed broke the silence with a laugh. "No way is Black Sabbath fronted by a guy called Ronnie!"

Van Eiden sighed. "Ronnie James Dio."

"Oh shit!" Delmer marveled. "The Rainbow guy?"

179

"The club?" Spots asked.

"No. The band. He did, uh…"

"*Rising,*" Clutch cut in.

Delmer folded his arms. "I was just about to say that. He was on *Rising*. 'Tarot Woman,' I know."

"You guys wanna focus?" Van Eiden snapped.

Spots folded his arms too. "We *are* focused."

Van Eiden sighed at the transmission, then turned down the music. "Here's the deal," he said without lifting his gaze. "These are some demos nobody's supposed to have. So everybody has 'em, obviously. Which means it doesn't matter when Sabbath starts touring or recording with Ronnie Dio, they've already beaten you to market. *You* sound like *them.*" Van Eiden took another deep breath, this one more ragged than the last. "They're on Warner right now. Sometime in the next year or so, maybe as soon as Q2 next year, the new album comes out. With Dio." Finally, he met the gaze of the condemned. It was to Delmer that he looked first. *Read my mind*, those eyes said.

"They're gonna crush us," Delmer deduced.

Van Eiden nodded. "Metal legends on a major label, with the natural publicity coup of a new frontman. And the new sound they've got is almost exactly the same as yours."

"But better," Spots admitted.

Dr. Nosebleed recoiled from Spots. "Fuck you, dude!"

"Man, come on. We're not better than Sabbath."

"Be honest," Delmer added. "Listen to it. A real

recording would be three times as awesome."

Through all of this, Clutch remained largely silent in the front passenger seat. He pursed his lips at the tape deck and wrinkled his brow. "So," he finally offered, "then Elektra has to drop our album right now. Get as far out in front as we can."

Van Eiden shook his head. "That ship has sailed. These demos are out. That they're bootleg is only stirring up more buzz."

"So what, then? We just…what?"

As soon as the producer lowered his gaze, Delmer knew what he was struggling to say. So once again, Delmer helped him out: "Elektra's dropping *Brainface.*"

Clutch cranked himself forward in his seat. "That's what I just said they should do!"

"No, I mean…they're *not* dropping it. They're *dropping* it."

"Like," Spots wondered, "into a garbage?"

Slowly, but *very* surely, all eyes turned to Van Eiden.

Beneath the molten scrutiny of Toksick, Van Eiden nodded with uncharacteristic timidity.

Silence, save a ripping, two-fingered solo from Iommi.

"They're gonna give you another two days in the studio," Van Eiden finally explained. "They're not trying to kill the band. They know you've got talent. But you need to change your sound. S-"

"We can't just *change* our fucking *sound!"* Clutch screamed. "We worked hard on it! It's *ours!"*

"Not anymore," Spots offered.

Dr. Nosebleed slammed his fist onto the paneling beneath the window.

"Easy," Van Eiden snapped.

"Fuck you, easy!" Dr. Nosebleed pounded the door a second time.

"Hey!"

"Fuck you, hey! *Brainface* is gonna go fucking platinum, if you motherfuckers put it out! So put it out!" *Thump* for a third time.

Van Eiden unbuckled his seatbelt and spun nearly one hundred and eighty degrees. "Listen you little shit, Elektra called me up and told me I have to fuck you over. Nobody's heard of you. They haven't put any real money behind you yet. The way they see it, it makes more sense to eat the cost of the recording session than try to debut you against Sabbath. It's not my fucking call. But I went to the *mat*, fucking *combat,* and I got you two days' studio time. That's my reputation on the line, shithead. *And* I'm not getting paid for it, that was the compromise. I'm giving up two days' wages for you to have a second shot, because I believe in you stupid motherfuckers. So quit hitting my fucking car and show some goddamned *gratitude!*"

Dr. Nosebleed seethed, his fist still balled over his lap. "Well…I didn't know that."

"Thank you," Delmer offered on behalf of the band.

"You're *welcome,"* Van Eiden grumbled.

Clutch sniffed. "So what happens to *Brainface?!"*

Van Eiden appeared to be chewing on a rather large portion of his tongue. "It sits on a shelf, then maybe one day when you're big we c-"

"Fuck that! Give it back to us!"

"There's no *back* to give it. It belongs to Elektra. Always has. I explained this shit to you."

"Give us the fucking masters!" Clutch lunged for Van Eiden, grabbing a handful of his shirt.

"Don't stretch my shirt!"

"I'll rip your shirt, you bitch!"

Delmer raised his arms, a *break it up* gesture rather undercut by his inability to extend his arms much further than a foot from his face. "Chill out guys! A lot of this is stuff there's no point arguing about. We can play around until we find a new sound, and g-"

Clutch torqued himself around to face Delmer, his spine *pop pop popping* in more than a few places. The whole car rocked from the force of the crank. "And when are we gonna make that happen, huh?"

"Well," Delmer heard himself say, "maybe at the next practice you decide to fucking show for." He immediately said "sorry" and tried to lift his hands again.

Not quick enough: Clutch availed himself of the spacious front seat, drew his elbow back, and punched Delmer hard in the nose.

Delmer's head snapped backwards. It bounced off the useless headrest, whipped forward, and tapped Clutch's still-extended fist.

The car, still a-rocking from the knocking, settled into stasis just as Dio was suggesting they all "die young," over and over.

Blood trickled from Delmer's left nostril. He didn't

have to run his hand under it to check; he could feel it, smell it, taste it.

"Ew," Dr. Nosebleed said.

Delmer felt a scream stirring in his throat. Oddly enough, all that made it out into the car were a few rogue "tee hee"s.

Clutch swung open the door, practically leapt from the car, and slammed the door behind him.

Die young, die young, die young.

MEET YOU
ALL THE WAY

WHAT was that quote? The definition of insanity is doing the same thing and thinking something different will happen? Who had said that? It was Einstein, Galileo, Moses, a guy with white hair. Probably not Moses. You don't really have a lot of credibility saying who is or isn't insane when you're going around talking to shrubbery. So one of the brainboxes then. That's insanity. It was insanity, for example, that Isley told the guys at Tower Records "that doesn't fucking matter" for the *eighth fucking time*, and expected it to suddenly take.

There were two of them, one a tubby bugger whose tit said he was called Rupert. The other was a pair of stilts with oversized glasses called Ray. They were like some cut-rate vaudeville act, except instead of zippy wordplay they just corrected people about music.

"Sorry lady," Ray said, "but it *does* matter. I know too much about jazz to let him get away with this."

The *him*, being Rupert, harrumphed and returned fire. "I don't care how many obscure jazz names or whatever you can say, the idea that *Toto IV* marks a 'jazzy departure for the band' is insane. It's actually insane."

Isley considered demonstrating her own insanity by making a moot point for the ninth time, but held her tongue. Perhaps the thing to do was let them tire themselves out before returning to her original question, tendered in a different geological era, which had been: *hey, do you know any bands in the Valley that had a song called 'The Good Time Butcher' that they changed to something like 'Don't Have A Good Time,' or something? Singer got whapped with a condom on stage for it?*

Alas, that question was ancient history.

"Look at 'Rosanna'," Ray insisted. "The st-"

"'Rosanna' isn't jazzy!"

"The *structure* is what I'm saying! Look at the structure of it, the time signature changes, it's not just your usual, like, Beatles verse verse chorus kind of thing."

"Jazz isn't just about structure!"

"Then what is it about?" Ray planted his hands on his hips. "Since you know so much about jazz?"

Isley T-boned one outstretched palm with the other. "Alright. Hold up. Stop."

"No! I want to hear his answer! If h-"

"*Shut the fuck up.* I asked you a simple goddamned

question, I would like a simple goddamned answer."

Rupert and Ray looked at each other, then back to Isley. "What was the q-"

"Oh!" Rupert shouted. "About The Good Time Butcher song!"

"Riiiight," Ray said. "I should have retraced. Pretty obvious. We were talking about Toto because Bobby Kimball w-"

Isley reminded him just how much that mattered.

"Right. Sorry. Anyway. I think that Good Time Butcher song, it was by Spitwish."

"There," Isley sighed. "See how fuckin' easy that was? Now, who wants to get me a copy of their album so we can see who wrote the damn thing?"

Rupert chuckled condescendingly, because he didn't realize how near he was to having his face cratered by Isley's fist. "Spitwish didn't record any *albums.*"

"They split up before they had a chance," Ray chimed in.

"…fuck," Isley mumbled. "Ok. Goddamnit. In *the fewest words possible*…where would I find the members of Spitwish now?"

"Aaah…hm," Ray pressed his thumb into his chin.

Rupert chuckled. "Not so smart now, eh?"

"I never pretended to be an expert on, like, hair metal glam bullshit, or whatever Spitwish is."

"*Was.*"

"What*ever.*"

"So," Rupert preened, "the only guy I know from Spitwish is Brandon. He's g-"

"You're on first name terms with him, huh?"

"I've been to his house like six times, yeah I am."

"Ooooh," Ray waved his palms in front of him, *"woooow."*

"Anyway, shut up dude, I'm trying to tell the story." Rupert scratched his fuzzy upper lip with his thumb. "So, Brandon sang and did keyboards for Spitwish. They didn't always have keys but they added them after Queen did. *The Game*, summer of '80. Th-"

"You mean *synths,"* Ray sighed with a truly heroic eye roll. "Queen *always* had *keys."* He knocked on Rupert's forehead. "Uh, hello? Anybody in there? Who knows about music?"

Rupert swiped Ray's hand away. *"Obviously* I mean synths. If I meant piano I'd say so. Everybody knows keys means synths."

Ray thrust a hand at Isley. "I bet *she* didn't."

Neither of them so much as looked at Isley. If they had, they'd probably have stopped talking.

Rupert, quite obviously agreeing with Ray, opted to ignore the point. "Synths, yes, Brandon did synths. For Spitwish. Before that he was a drummer. Talented dude."

"Oh shit, I forgot all about that."

"Yeah man. Hold No Bar, Bömerayñ, he was a beast."

"Too bad he switched to keys."

"Oh, don't you mean *synths?"*

Ray laughed. "Fuck you, dude."

It was only the wound steel of Isley's frown that kept her from saying anything rude.

"Yeah, so, uh. Yeah. Brandon, I think he actually did

a tour with Toto." Rupert snapped his fingers. "That's how we got to that!"

"He didn't play *with* Toto. He played a gig with Floyd Sneed – that's why he swapped off drums, because if you got Sneed you're not gonna say, like, shove over dude, I'm on drums – and Sneed had done S.S. Fools with Bobby Kimball."

"Very excited to see how this all comes back to Brandon," Isley growled.

Rupert shrugged. "He's playing in Eager Bleeder now. Back on drums, doing the hard rock thing."

Isley perked up. "Okay! Now we're talking! Why've I never heard of these guys, they're such hot shit?"

"I didn't say they were."

"They're in the area?"

Ray shook his head. "Bay Area, right?"

Rupert nodded. "Like all the other hard rockers. They got chased out of LA. It's a glam town here now."

Isley sighed and hung her head. "Fuck. San Fran. Okay. Either of you got a phone number for this fucker?"

"No."

Ray mock-gasped at Rupert. "I thought you were on first-name terms with him!"

Rupert sighed. "I've only been to his house like six times! That was when he was here, anyway."

Another mock-gasp. "Just go to San Fran," Ray suggested to Isley, "and look for Eager Bleeder posters. Otherwise go to some metal bar and ask for Brandon Lamonica."

"If you can't find him, you could also ask for Patch.

That was what he called himself here."

"See fellas?" Isley asked as she scrawled *Brandon "Patch" Lamonica* onto a rumpled notepad fished from her pocket. "See how fucking easy it is, when you stop making things so fucking hard?"

A TREE OF TEETH
(A TREETH!)

NONE of it had been real. Bub told himself that for as long as he could but then the newspaper told him it was real. He didn't read the newspaper but this one read itself to him. Body found, it said. Clearly the Good Time Butcher. That was what it said. Then it gave the address. Bub went to the address and it was the building he hadn't been able to find before. The one that the body had been found in. When he'd seen it though, it hadn't been a body. It had been a guy.

The newspaper didn't say what the body had been named when it was still a guy. It said he liked to have A Good Time though. A Good Time on the Sunset Strip. That's how they knew it was the Good Time Butcher that killed him. Also because of the way he was killed.

Drip drip drip. The thing that this newspaper article was confused about was why the blood was still there. Usually the Good Time Butcher always took the blood away. This time the bag was still there. How come, they wondered.

Bub wanted to call somebody and say that it was because he couldn't find the house again. He had forgotten what the address was. If he could have found it he would have let the guy go. He wasn't the Butcher, even though he'd killed the guy like he was. It was the tooth. Now the teeth. He had his old one, and one from the guy who was a body. Since he got the second tooth, the old one didn't talk to him so much. The teeth talked to each other now. Bub didn't like that. He didn't know why.

Until one day he was crying and so he knew that he was sad. He didn't know why and nothing ever happened that told him.

He never called anybody and said what he wanted to say though. Like the police. They wouldn't believe him about the teeth taking his hands. They wouldn't believe him that *he* wasn't the Good Time Butcher. They would say he was a crazy boy and lock him away. Or maybe they would kill him. Drip drip drip but instead of out it'd be in. They had drips that were the reverse of what he… what the Butcher gave to people to make them live until they had no blood left. They were drips that went into your blood and then you died. That was how some places killed you. Others they just zapped you. Bzzz. There were special circles you could put in your hand and then when you shook somebody's hand it gave them a little zap. It was like that except instead of getting a little zap you got fried and your brains melted out your ears.

He didn't want that. But he also didn't want things to be the way they were anymore. So he thought about burying the teeth. They couldn't talk to each other if they were under the dirt. The teeth. Or maybe they could, but Bub wouldn't have to hear their whispers. Sometimes he asked them what they were talking about. They would just get very quiet for a few seconds. Then they would start talking again. Bub didn't like that. But he was afraid that if he buried them, they would grow a tree. If they grew into a tree, and the tree grew a thousand teeth, and they all talked to each other…Bub wouldn't like that even more. He would be deaf. The whole world would sound like whispers.

He still went to the Strip most nights, but he watched movies in the afternoon before work. Not as many people in the theater. Bub liked being alone in the movie theaters. Just him and the movie. No whispers. From anything.

A movie came out called *The Thing*. Bub thought that was not a very good name for a movie because it could be about Any Thing. He told his joke to Angela Manager but she just said "Ha" which meant she didn't think it was funny. Anyway he got to see the movie for free because Angela was nice and let him watch all the movies he wanted for free. *The Thing* was a scary movie about a snow monster that looks like people that you know. It was so good at looking like other people that it could even look like dogs. That was pretty cool. There was also a movie that came out on the same day called *Blade Runner*, but Bub didn't see that one until two days after he saw *The Thing. Blade Runner* was also a bad title but for different reasons. This one didn't have anything to do with running blades but there were robots that could look like people, and you didn't know who was a robot and who was a person. At the end the bad robot says "I've seen things you wouldn't believe." Bub pretended that he was talking about *The Thing* instead of just things. It was funny to think that a character in one movie had seen another movie that Bub had seen. Especially because the one movie was in the future. Even though in real life they came out on the same day. It was funny that two movies like that came out on the same day. Movies about people who might not be people even though they looked like people.

Then there was one called *Tron*. It was about a guy who got eaten by a computer and then he had to fight cartoons. Bub liked that idea. Of getting eaten by a computer. Or maybe a movie. He imagined which movie he'd like to be eaten by the most. He couldn't think of which. All movies were scary at least once or twice. There weren't any movies that were just nice the whole way through. That made sense though. The real world wasn't like that.

Bub imagined what kind of movie he might already have been eaten by. It would be one where everything had a shadow and there was always smoke coming out of the street. Instead of being scary once or twice, that was how many times it would be nice.

A lot of the bands on the Strip now were scary. The drums were going *duddladuddladuddla*. In the music Bub usually listened to they went *bop BAH bop BAH*. There was more room for sun to get in. The new stuff was the shadows. That wasn't always a bad thing. Sometimes it was nice to have scary music, because the world was scary. Ozzy Osbourne sang about scary stuff, but the music wasn't always so scary. He told Bub to bark at the moon, but the guitar sounded more like sunlight. Iron Maiden came through Los Angeles and talked about the Beast, but they had funny accents and anyway they had to go back to where the flag they were always waving was from. One of the bands was called Metallica, but after the first time Bub ever saw them they left to go to San Francisco which made him sad. They didn't even have any real albums for him to listen to yet. Spitwish was the name of another scary band Bub liked, and they even had a song about The Good Time Butcher. One time Bub found one of them after a show and told him "Thank you for writing a song about me, but I only did it once or maybe twice," and the Spitwish guy walked away from Bub very quickly. Then the band went to San Francisco too, but probably not all because of Bub, maybe also because there was A Scene there, and maybe at the Scene people didn't throw wet porksocks at you.

After all the scary ones left, the old stuff didn't sound the same to Bub. It didn't sound right. It sounded wrong.

Sometimes people having Good Times still died. Bub was watching people pork on the yard at Gazzarri's one night when somebody next to him said "those two better watch out, the Good Time Butcher'll get them. Just got another person last week."

"Oh good," Bub said. "I didn't do that one." This guy also walked away from him very quickly. Bub didn't mind. He was used to people walking away from him very quickly. He was mostly relieved that people were still getting Good Time Butchered even though he wasn't doing it. He knew he wasn't because his back wasn't hurting and the teeth weren't talking to him. They were talking to other people, maybe.

It was bad that people were being Good Time Butchered. Bub didn't like that. He just liked that it wasn't him doing it this time.

Still, he was afraid to get rid of the teeth. Because what if he threw them in the garbage, and somebody pulled them out, and then *they* started Good Time Butchering? Then there would be a bunch of Good Time Butchers. More than there already were.

So Bub kept the teeth in a drawer, and he put a lot of underpants on them. Then he kept going to movies and his job and the Strip to watch people have Good Times. They acted like there wasn't somebody who wanted to Butcher them. It was weird. The Good Times must have been really Good. Bub didn't know – he'd never really had one. A couple times he'd tried but nobody wanted to pork him on the yard at Gazzarri's, or share their scream powder with him. One time somebody gave him a silly cigarette and it made him sleepy. He didn't like being sleepy. He didn't like his dreams. The scream powder didn't look like it made people sleepy though. It looked like it made them awake. But nobody wanted to give Bub any, at least not unless he paid them a lot of money. He didn't have a lot of money, but he told them they could see a movie for free if they wanted. Most people laughed at that, except for the guy who'd slapped Bub in the face. That guy really did not like movies.

If nobody wanted to share the powder, then Bub would just act like he'd had some. He watched people who'd put it up their nose. The way they moved, the way they talked, the way they looked. A lot of them danced. It was bad dancing, but they would just throw their arms around when there was music playing. It was because of the music that Bub knew they were dancing. There was always music on the Strip. You didn't even have to go into the clubs. You could just hear it. So Bub would hide in one of the alleys and run in place until he got really sweaty like the people who had powder in their noses. Then he would walk down the street like he was on a broken VHS tape, and whenever he heard music he threw his arms all around. Everybody gave him a lot of space to dance in, but nobody wanted to dance with him, except for some people who seemed like they were making fun of him. It was okay. As long as they didn't touch him, it was okay. He was having a Good Time. A Good Time on the Strip. Maybe he would get Butchered. It was a scary thought, but scary like barking at the moon was scary. The feeling wasn't as shadowy as the words were. Just to make sure everyone knew he was having a Good Time, Bub tried to laugh as loud as he could. "HA HA," he said. "HA HA."

A WHOLE NEW SCENE

ISLEY hated packing toiletries. Not that she enjoyed packing clothes, but, well, that wasn't so bad. It was kind of fun. She wasn't the type to lay out ensembles on her bed and coo over them, but she still enjoyed forecasting her sartorial needs. The toiletries, though, were mandatory. They were an obligation. Plus they leaked sometimes, so Isley had to put them all in little plastic baggies. Then when she got to wherever she was going, she just had these little plastic baggies in her suitcase. It was stupid. She hated it.

Part of her wanted to make a whole weekend of her trip to San Francisco, but that would require packing her toiletries. So, she decided, she would drive up early one morning, sleep in her car, and drive back the next day.

Cheaper than getting a motel, no doubt about that. Little plastic baggies need not apply.

She was just about to hit the road, a literal one-foot-out-the-door situation, when her phone rang. Oh, how tempting it was to just keep going, close the door behind her, let the machine eat whatever bullshit somebody was calling her with and forget she'd ever heard the ring. For some reason, maybe this was just what getting sober did to a person, she decided to do the mature thing and answer the phone.

"Pultrock," the phone told her. "It's Hollenbeck."

"Shit, man, I'm heading out the door. What do you want?"

"To ask you why Luca Colby is following leads and discovering she's actually following you."

"She's tailing me? You tell that silly bitch that I respect the hell out of her, but I'll file a restraining order if I have to, don't think I won't, tell her that."

"…"

"I'm kidding."

"I wasn't sure. That might be something to think about, that I wasn't s-"

"What do you want, bucko?"

"…bucko?"

"What do you want?"

The Sergeant sighed. "Why were you, a private citizen, talking to Clea Greenstone about an active police investigation?"

"Listen," Isley said to the ceiling, "I'm heading out the door, remember I told you that? I don't have time to t-"

"To do your community service? Because you haven't logged a single hour."

"Well Jesus, *Mom*, I've been a little busy lately."

"Interfering with an active police investigation."

"Who's interfering? How am I interfering?"

Hollenbeck sighed. "Just stop. I can't begin to imagine why you haven't already, but, ah, just cut it out. Turn whatever you have over to Detective Colby and I'll consider this a settled issue."

"I don't have anything to turn."

"Not for one goddamned second do I buy that. Where are you going?"

"Out the door. That's the third fucking time I told you that, you might wanna yank some of that hair out of your fucking ears." She slammed the phone back into its cradle and, at long last, headed out the door, walking towards her car a bit more rapidly than her typical gait.

LA to San Fran was pretty much a straight shot up the I-5, although it wasn't much of a shot. More of a slog. A straight slog up the I-5. That sounded almost like a physics equation to Isley, mostly because she hadn't touched the subject since high school. Slog slog slog she went for about six hours, and then she took the 580 through Hayward and San Leandro and Oakland and then over to the 80 which became the Oakland Bay Bridge, which was kind of like the Golden Gate by way of Ingmar Bergman (i.e. grey, boring, and way too long). That was ok though, because it gave her a serviceable view of San Francisco rising up out of the Bay like it was checking to make sure the coast was clear. It wasn't, of course; it was locked in the thick fog of cold Pacific air trying to cover for the ever-rising heat of a California summer.

Near the end of the bridge, she remembered where she was and turned on the radio, prowling the airwaves for some authentic thrash from the Bay's nascent scene. Surely *somebody* must be playing it here. Right?

Right. It was some college station, apparently, and they were spinning a demo track from a new band called Death Angel. Not bad. Isley got to headbang her way into San Fran. The energy flagged a bit as she had to focus more on navigation, then shot back up with a less enjoyable valence when she learned via a flyer on a street-lamp post that the venue Eager Bleeder was playing at tonight, Ruthie's Inn, was back in Berkeley, back the way she'd come from. Over that boring-ass bridge. Alright then, see ya later San Fran. How ya been, Oakland Bay?

Isley got to the squat stucco hut that was Ruthie's Inn around six. She found a parking spot after twenty minutes of cruising, then popped in to some no-name dive that made the Billymark look positively space-age. Within fifteen minutes, she'd sucked down a burger and two beers. She was at the door when Ruthie's opened at seven – her first stop was the merch table for Eager Bleeder, not much larger than the sort of pull-out upon which Isley had consumed many a microwave dinner (though Eager Bleeder's had a black tablecloth on it, which, damn, who knew they made tablecloths that small?). Made sense that the table was so tiny, with just two shirt designs – er, wait, no, that was the same shirt, there were just two set out to showcase the front *and* back – some patches for denim jackets, and a few demos on cassette. Why would they have more? Eager Bleeder was only opening. The headliner was Exodus. Isley only knew them because that one curly-cue fuck from Metallica used to play for Exodus. Their merch looked pretty shit. Eager Bleeder's was better.

"Shirt's ten," the guy jockeying the table told her. "Patches are a buck a pop, or five for four. Tape's fi-"

"I'll be sure to spread the word," Isley replied. "You with the band?"

"Hell yeah."

"Are you Brandon? Or Patches? Whatever the fuck."

"Patches?!" The merch kid threw his head back and laughed, like he had James Bond right where he wanted him. "No, I'm not 'Patches.' He's probably unloading. Or getting loaded," he winked.

"Which one are you then?"

"Do you mean what instrument do I play?"

"No, I mean your star sign. Of course I mean what instrument."

"*Reeeer,*" the guy hissed, jutting a clawed hand at Isley. "Take a breather, lady. It's gonna be alright."

"You wave your left paw at me like that again, so will you."

"…what?"

"You'll be all right. Like I'm gonna ri-"

"Oh. Gotcha."

"No left hand."

"I get it."

Isley waved her right hand limply in the air for a moment, then let it fall and asked "which one are you?"

"I play guit-"

"No one cares." Isley spun on her heel and charged towards the stage. This being a club for longhairs and skinheads, there wasn't much in the way of security to keep her from slipping through to the backstage area. Just a curtain, by which she was more stymied than she'd have cared to admit, but it was a thick fucking tarpaulin with aspirations to sensuality, just a shit load of folds with only one that opened to the other side. After a harrowing twelve seconds she made it, and discovered a drab, stained room with a high ceiling cluttered by rigging. Way more rigging than a rinkydink operation like Ruthie's Inn had any right tucking anywhere in its bowels. Scuttling beneath the ropes and wires were a bunch of fellas trying to look busy, pushing boxes on castors hither and yon, picking up amp cabs by bending from the waist which, Jesus, Isley knew rock and roll was about taking risks but that was just unnecessary.

"Bend from the knees!" she shouted at them.

Everybody stopped what they were doing and looked at her, apparently relieved to have an excuse to quit pretending to work.

Isley pointed to the kid picking up the amphead, then bent her knees and mimicked grabbing a heavy load. "Bend from the knees. Back straight, knees bent. Then you go up," she demonstrated, "like that. With your legs."

"It's not that heavy," the kid said of his equipment.

"Nobody's as heavy as Metallica," Isley replied in a

schoolmarmish sigh, "but we try, don't we? We try. And anyway, let's clarify, who the fuck is *we* here?"

No answers were volunteered.

Isley gestured to the men before her. "Eager Bleeder, yes?"

The kid who had spoken to Isley looked to his friends, then to his shoes, accepting his *de facto* role as the chief negotiator. "Yeah," he said.

"Are you Brandon?"

"Who the fuck wants to know?" asked a guy who'd taken a seat on the corner of his box, and was pretty obviously Brandon.

"Hi Brandon," Isley said to him. "I wanna buy you a beer after the show. Ask you a question about Spitwish. Are you seriously gonna say no to that?"

"I think she wants to suck your dick," another one of the fuckers chuckled.

"If I wanted to suck dick," Isley said to that churlish young man, "I'd join the band."

"Man, who is this bitch?"

"Somebody who wants to buy Patches here a beer and ask him a question. So?" she asked Brandon. "I haven't got all fucking day, and you don't either."

Brandon studied her, hand to his chin. "How long will it take?"

"If how long you're taking to answer *this* question is any indication, six years."

Brandon chuckled. "Alright," he said, gesturing for Isley to follow him, "let's get this over with now. *After* the show is for girls who put out."

They decamped to what passed for a private space here, an alley out back where Eager Bleeder's van was busy leaking itself a puddle to fester in. Isley, only too happy to be done with this guy as soon as possible, launched straight in: "You wrote a song called 'The Good Time Butcher'?"

"We changed the name."

"But you wrote it?"

"With Jeff. He played bass."

"This…you're killin' me here. Just say *yes* or *no.*"

"Yes," Patch sighed. "We wrote it."

"You know you were performing that song before The Good Time Butcher ever had a recorded kill to his name?"

"No. I didn't know that."

"Well, you were."

Brandon shrugged. "Ok. So?"

"So where did you hear about the Butcher?"

"Word on the Strip. Everybody knew about him."

"There's no evidence that he ever existed before '81. Yet you're singing about him in '80. So I'm trying to figure out, how'd you swing it that you know enough about this guy to write a song for him?"

"The song wasn't *for* him, first of all. And I didn't 'know stuff about him'," he huffed, scratching quotes into the air as he did, "I knew he existed, and th-"

"How did you know that?"

"People said so."

"That's it? People said so?"

"*Everyone* was talking about him."

206

"Who saw him? Who knew somebody who'd been killed by him? Who knew somebody who *knew* somebody?"

"Are you a cop or something?"

"I'm 'or something.' You're doing me a solid. I'm just trying to catch a nasty guy."

"It seems like you don't think he's real."

"There's still a nasty guy somewhere in here, that's clear enough."

"Well…" Brandon took a deep breath, wincing slightly at the end of his exhale. "I mean, I actually haven't thought about this in a while, but I think *I* might have seen the Butcher once."

Isley was pretty damn sure she'd never blinked so much in such a short period of time. "…you *what?*"

"Yeah." Brandon eyed her nervously, then leaned against the van. "This was *after* I wrote the song, I thi-"

"You *and* Jeff."

Brandon sighed. "Right. I think that was why…whoever he was came. It was just this weird little guy who came up to me after a show once. He h-"

"When was this?"

"Probably about a year ago. He comes up to me, and he's got, like, these glassy eyes. Like a doll's eyes."

"You quoting *Jaws* at me right now?"

"…yeah. It's a great flick."

"Oh, I know. Great flick. Don't quote it."

"Why not?"

"Don't quote any movies at me right now."

"Oh. Well, it still fits. Doll's eyes. It's a good line. Any-

207

way, he's got this weird little smile on his face," a smile Brandon did his best to imitate by taking his forefingers to either corner of his mouth and lifting, ever so slightly, "and he says to me something like, 'oh, thanks for writing that song about me, but I only killed one or two people actually.'"

"…are you serious?"

"Yeah."

"Why didn't you…have you told anybody about this before?"

Brandon shrugged. "Friends. Some girls, I guess."

"No cops?"

"No."

"So…this guy tells you he's the Butcher, and what did you do?"

"I just sorta ran. It freaked me the fuck out. Then I, uh, I forgot."

"You forgot about the ffff*fucking* Butcher," Isley seethed.

"There was a lot to get distracted by back then," Brandon said with a wistful smile.

"You didn't have a little pang of *hey, maybe I'm an asshole* every time there was another Butcher victim in the papers?"

"Like I said, I was distracted."

Isley took a deep breath, and flopped her arms at her sides. "Okay, well…think you could do a sketch of him?" She blinked, but just the once this time. "You'd talk to the artist and *they'd* do the sketch."

"I don't know. It's been a while."

"You wanna have to think about that answer next time you read THE GOOD TIME BUTCHER STRIKES AGAIN in the funny pages? When I come up here and throw the relevant funny page through your window? Wrapped around a fucking brick?"

Brandon glared at Isley for an instant, then drifted off into a land of distraction. "I guess not," he finally sighed.

"Great," Isley snapped before Brandon was halfway through the word *not*. "Anything else slipped your mind you think might be kind of fucking helpful for the cops to know?"

"…" Brandon bit his lip and squinted, as though scrutinizing one of those insoluble mathematical formulas and letting himself wonder if *he* might not be the one to solve it. "No. But you're not a cop, right? You're *a something?*"

"Sure am."

"Ok. Well. Please don't make a big thing of it, or go to the, uh, the *proper* cops with this, because I don't want to make it a circus for him. But…I played in a band once with a guy whose sister got killed by the Butcher."

"…are you…fucking…" Isley struggled for words, then gave up.

"He only told me about it once, and it was pretty obvious he didn't want to. But, I mean…I guess I get that. Not wanting to talk about it. So I don't want him to have to get grilled about it by a bunch of cops, you know?"

"Yeah. Yeah. I get it. No cops, just me. How do I find this son of a bitch?"

"He's not a son of a bitch," Brandon replied, defensive enough that Isley braced for a glove-slap. "He's just kind of an asshole. But after he told me that, about his sister, I guess I get that too."

"What's his name?"

"Last I heard, he was calling himself Grip or Stitch, or some stupid shit. I don't know. I don't even know if he plays anymore. His real name's Delmer Lippincott."

Isley fished a pen out of her pocket and started writing DELMER on her arm. "How do you spell that last name?"

THERE'S A MONSTER AND A DOCTOR

"IT wasn't my fault," Delmer tried to explain.

Dr. Nosebleed was having none of it. "You were goading him."

"I wasn't *goading* him!" He looked to Spots for moral support. The drummer offered what consolation he could with the top of his head. Oh, if only Van Eiden hadn't been whisked off to oversee recording on another band, Delmer might have had an ally in all of this. But as long as Clutch remained incommunicado, there was no Toksick to take advantage of two more days in the studio. Of course, there was no sense returning to the studio in the first place unless they could create a *new* sound, one that hopefully wouldn't get scooped by some English fuckers playing fast and loose with their lineup.

And try as the instrumental three-piece had, they found themselves floundering without the creative whirlwind that was Clutch. Even Delmer, whose nose ached so much it nearly put him off coke for a whole evening, had to concede that Toksick without Clutch was all rocket and no fuel, bound to catch a case of the Not Going To Make Its, a terminal condition that claimed dozens of well-intentioned LA bands every month.

"We could start a new band," Delmer suggested, in the same plaintive whine with which he'd made his other, equally ill-fated bids to dodge his duty, "we could call it Talk Sick, to ca-"

"No, dude. You have to apologize to him."

"For what?! For calling him out on his bullsh-"

"Yes," Dr. Nosebleed replied. "You can't hit guys like him head-on with that stuff. Frontmen are fragile. You should've known better."

"So it's *my* fault for not…fucking…using kid gloves? We're supposed to just tolerate his bullsh-"

"Yes," Dr. Nosebleed repeated.

Back against the wall, Delmer played his very last card, one he himself knew how to trump: "Even if I wanted to apologize, I don't even know where he is."

Spots, the unassuming bastard, was the one who called Delmer's bluff: "Didn't you call him at work way back when?"

"Yeah," Delmer replied a bit too quickly, "and I kept trying him there the first time he disappeared. He never pi-"

"He didn't disappear this time," Dr. Nosebleed pointed out. "He's just avoiding us."

"He was avoiding us when he disappeared, too."

"You should try him," Spots prodded, gently. "Call him."

Delmer set his jaw. "I called him last time. A bunch of times. No answer."

"But he'd disappeared then."

"Yeah," Dr. Nosebleed agreed. "This time he's avoidi-"

Delmer threw his hands up. "If you avoid somebody, you're disappearing! They're not different!"

Spots considered this with an intensity that was, quite frankly, adorable. "But not everybody who disappears is avoiding somebody."

Dr. Nosebleed nodded. "They could be fucking dead."

"I'm not *saying,*" Delmer clarified, "that everyone who disappears is avoiding someone. I'm saying that everyone who is avoiding someone disappears."

"Their family still knows where they are."

"Not if it's the family that the person is avoiding."

"I think you're trying to distract us," Spots suddenly declared with an incisiveness that silenced both of his bandmates. "Call him, dude. You need to apologize. We need him back."

Delmer sighed. The guy wasn't wrong. But Spots' gambit left Delmer with two choices, which he deliberated for a full day: swallow his pride, bury the hatchet with Clutch, and become immensely successful with a guy he couldn't stand...*or* refuse to call for patently petty reasons, run the risk of Dr. Nosebleed and Spots dumping him, reuniting with Clutch, finding a new guitarist, and becoming immensely successful while Delmer pursued more artistically rewarding, though less lucrative, proje-

Clutch answered on the first ring. "Who's this?"

"Please don't hang up," Delmer spat out in one long word. "Please."

"…I'm working."

"I'm really sorry I gave you shit for not coming to practices and stuff. I'm really just, like, I get really anxious about what we've got. It feels like we're so close to breaking through, and, like, it just makes me a little shitty I guess." Delmer tried desperately to keep his teeth from audibly grinding as he tendered his *mea culpa*. This was such bullshit. It was *hea culpa*, goddamnit! Clutch had fucked up, Delmer'd called him on it, then Clutch had fucked up *again*, and now it was the whistleblower being thrown to the wolves? Fucking bullshit. "So," he concluded, "I'm really sorry."

A long pause greeted this apology. Delmer could hear the low mumble of the call center in the background.

"Hello?"

"4 Winthrop Street. Way down in West Hollywood. Let's talk." Then Clutch hung up.

Delmer frowned at his phone. "We *were* talking," he informed it.

Getting to West Hollywood required four hitched rides over the course of an hour and a half; as Clutch hadn't provided any sort of time frame for the meetup,

214

Delmer had no idea if this would make him early, late, or right on time. He wanted to assume that Clutch wouldn't have any temporal expectations at all, given Delmer's lack of reliable transportation, but to assume that would be to imagine Clutch a reasonable, rational human. That was a leap Delmer wasn't quite ready to make. And as long as he was thinking along those lines: Clutch really hadn't been kidding when he'd said this was *way* down in West Hollywood. The Strip threw off quite a bit of light, but the good Samaritans who insisted they knew where they were going invariably carted Delmer further and further from its reassuring sparkle and stench. If Clutch was bonkers enough to throw a punch merely for Delmer's pointing out his attendance record…was Delmer severely misjudging what this guy was capable of? Was Clutch drawing Delmer into some seedy off-the-grid tenement, to be jumped by junkies or worse? Should he have informed his bandmates exactly where he was going? Or anybody? Probably. He probably should have done that.

"Here we are," his last hitch told him. "Door to door service."

"Ah," Delmer replied. He'd definitely started this journey at a door, and presumably that concrete pancake with the big 4 on it had a door somewhere…but it was pretty hard to spot without any goddamned lights. "Thanks?"

Not wanting to dignify his definitely hysterical, totally not at all plausible, absolutely not something to actually be worried about fears, he forced himself to climb out of the car and wave at the vanishing hellfire of its brake-lights.

Then it was a matter of waiting for his eyes to adjust to the perfect dark.

As he did, he kept his ears sharply peeled for any particularly sinister sounds. Quickly approaching footsteps, heavy breathing, cracking knuckles, knives making a little *shing* sound like in the movies even though as far as Delmer knew knives didn't actually go *shing*. Nothing, though. Nothing to worry about. Just the sound of a timid breeze, rattling the leaves of trees lost to shadow.

Delmer shivered.

Ok. He could see the outline of the low warehouse. Good enough. He put his arms out in front of his face like Frankenstein and began a slow approach, his shoes crunching over what sounded like an assortment of broken glass, peanut shells, parking tickets, and mouse skulls. Stop thinking about skulls. "You know," he mumbled to himself, "most people think Frankenstein isn't called Frankenstein. They call him Frankenstein the monster. Actually though, Frankenstein *is* the monster. You're supposed to call the other one Frankenstein's Doctor."

"You've got that the wr-"

"AAAAAAAAAH!" Delmer replied.

A *click* blinded Delmer with white light.

He staggered back, hands in front of his face. "Don't shoot!"

The other guy lowered the flashlight. He was wearing ratty sneakers with a big swoop on them. "Hey, haven't

I seen you play before?" The guy swung the flashlight up to his chin, like he was about to tell Delmer a spooky story. "I'm in Mold Soul. Matt."

"Oh. Ah. Delmer." He squinted and pointed at Matt's face, split in twain by the shadows his prominent chin and nose were casting. "We split a bill with you guys once, right? With Bömerayñ?"

"Yeah man. Good night."

"Oh. Uh, goodnight!"

"No, I'm saying that was a good night."

"Aha."

"You doing alright dude? You're bugging like fucking crazy."

"I, um…what are *you* doing out here?"

"…if you want a job, you should come back sober. You can pull off a high shift now and then once you've been here for a while, but Fluck's always got his eye extra hard on the new guy."

"I'm not high," Delmer half-fibbed. "I just don't know where I am or what's going on."

"You were just talking to yourself about Franken-stein."

"Well that was because I was walking like him." Delmer demonstrated by stretching his arms out in front of him. "Point the light at me so you can see."

"You were walking like the monst-"

"Point the light. Look."

"Uh huh. That's how the *monster* walks."

"I know."

"Frankenstein i-"

A door slammed.

Delmer and Matt both jumped.

Clutch swung out into the night, backlit by the dull, milky light of building number four. "Jesus dude, there you are!" He waved Delmer in. "Come on, let Matt have his fucking cigarette!"

"Frankenstein is the doctor," Matt offered as a parting shot.

All Delmer could think to say in response was "enjoy cancer." It would be but the first of the evening's regrets.

"AH," Delmer said as he entered the call center. Cubical after cubical, six across and twenty deep it seemed like, bristling with the nerviness of ambitious people doing mind-numbing desk work. He glanced to one of the cubicals near him and spotted someone he was positive he'd seen onstage at the Whisky.

Clutch followed Delmer's slowly extending pointer finger and nodded. "Almost every band on the Strip's got at least one guy who works here. No clue why it's so popular for the rock guys. Easy to do hungover, I bet that's why." He led Delmer through the labyrinth, to a cubical indistinguishable from the others.

"This one's yours?" Delmer asked.

"Mhm. It can be yours, if you want."

Delmer chuckled.

Clutch didn't.

"What does…what?"

Clutch thumped a hand onto Delmer's shoulder and squeezed. "All these rock guys in one place, obviously

218

we shoot the shit. 'Oh, let's play together, let's jam,' shit like that. Well, when *Brainface* fell through…I was commiserating with the fellas. One thing led to another."

"…"

"Me and a few of the guys here, we're starting a new b-"

"Fuck you."

Clutch's grip tightened as a smile broke out on his stupid fucking face. "Keep your voice down. I brought you here as an olive branch. You're gonna need a job, since Toksick is fucking done. This one pays a little better than McDonald's. No free food, though."

Delmer felt something warm and heavy bubbling up inside of him. Something…well, whatever it was, it wasn't vomit; that he'd have recognized straight off. "Look, if you wanna quit the band, quit, but don't drag me out here just to… humiliate me!"

"There's nothing humiliating about gainful employment!"

"What did I do to you? I just wanted you to bring your best, for the b-"

"By talking to the other guys about changing the name and playing without me? 'Talk Sick'? At least I have the balls to do this shit to your face."

Tattlers. Either Spots or Dr. Nosebleed, or both. Tattlers.

That warm heavy bubble plunged down into Delmer's feet. Once again, he could only rule out something that it *wasn't*. "…ok, wait, that was just due di-"

"Oh, and guess what our band is gonna be called?"

"What, is it Delmer Sucks or something?"

"No." The furrow of his brow sloped to match his grin. "Brainface."

"…WHAT?! That's my fucking word! You can't use my wo-"

A slightly older fella approached from over Clutch's shoulder. "This the guy?" he asked with a thumb cocked towards Delmer.

"Yep," Clutch nodded.

Delmer shook his head in disbelief. "So you're one of the assholes starting a new band with him?! You wanna rub my fucking face in it? What did I ever do to *you?!*"

"No," the fella replied in a serviceable impression of patience. He pointed to his nametag, which said *Frank Fluck,* and then screamed *MANAGER.*

"Oh."

"You want a job, it's yours. I don't get to be picky." He sized Delmer up with a darting of the eyes, up and down. "But I'll take an apology right now for the out-burst, if that's the case."

Delmer's jaw tightened so hard that his vision blurred.

Things he wanted to do just then: plunge his thumbs into Clutch's eye sockets, rip his head from atop his fat fucking neck and punt it across the room, ideally into any industrial-sized shredders that might be lying around; find Frank Fluck's office, drop trough over his desk and squeeze out his discontent all over any and every cherish-ed family photographs he could find; burn this fucking place to the ground, not just the call center but the city of Los Angeles, move back home to Pennsylvania and get a real job, working at a steel mill or bailing hay or whatever. Maybe he'd go hang out with the Pennsylvania Dutch, take a trip three hundred years into the past, marry his first cousin, then have eighteen deformed children and die from toothrot at the age of thirty-two.

Fuck everything, that was really what Delmer wanted to do. Not fuck everything like "holy shit, I've had so much coke I feel like I could fuck *everything.*" More along the lines of "holy shit, I'm out of coke, fuck *everything.*"

Including, maybe especially, himself.

He considered one other thing he wanted to do: track down his old bandmates in Bömerayñ, ask them for his slot back. Look into Patch's eyes…into *Brandon's* eyes, and tell him he was sorry, ask for his forgiveness.

But that was harder to imagine than shitting on Frank Fluck's desk. There was no going back. Be it back to Bömerayñ, or back to Pennsylvania. Because if he went back…it would mean he'd done something wrong. That *he* was wrong. That he'd made a mistake.

Which wasn't very fucking rock 'n roll, was it?

So Delmer looked ahead. To the call center full of rockers trying to pay the rent until their next gig came together. By Clutch's own account, fertile ground to form a new band. A *better* band. The best fucking band the world had ever seen, maybe.

And if not the *best* band…then a new one, at least.

Delmer took a long, deep breath, and used it to apologize to Fluck. The manager of the call center nodded, while Clutch made a noise just shy of cackling.

PUMPKIN TIME

THE teeth stopped talking. They weren't even talking to each other anymore. Now Bub's drawer just sounded like a drawer full of underpants.

At first he liked that all he could hear was underpants. It made him happy for about a day or two, and then it scared him a little bit. Because why did they stop talking? Had they agreed on something? Were they waiting? Did one of the teeth die, or did both of them die? Bub didn't think teeth could die, but he also didn't think they could talk, so what did he know. These weren't normal teeth.

After four days of the teeth not talking he pulled the underpants out of the drawer to look at the teeth. When he saw them he stopped moving and thought as hard as he could.

One of the teeth had turned into something else. There was a regular tooth, and then there was a little white rock. Bub recognized the regular tooth: it was the one that had come from the guy on the bed that one time. That one had a lot sharper edges on the bottom, and then the top of it was kind of wrinkly. The tooth that wasn't a tooth anymore was the one Bub had found in his pocket a while ago. Now it wasn't a tooth at all. Now it was a rock.

Bub's fingers were shaking a bunch so it was hard to pick the rock up. When he did though, he saw that it wasn't a rock. It was a candy, or a sweet treat, or something. He stuck out his tongue and poked the rock with it. It had a sweet taste. Bub didn't want to eat it though. He knew that if he did it would make him sick. Maybe he would get so sick he died. This wasn't a normal sweet treat. It was one that had been a tooth. He wondered if it had started out as a tooth and become a sweet treat, or if it had been a sweet treat first, then turned into a tooth, then back into a sweet treat. Like the pumpkin that turned into a carriage. Then back into a pumpkin. It wasn't midnight, though. It was three in the morning. Which was weird because Bub thought it had been today still. Just after dinner. Instead it was tomorrow, way before breakfast.

Bub took the sweet treat and the tooth and walked them down to the Strip. By the time he got there it was kind of light out, but some of the party boys were still out having a Good Time. He wanted to talk to them, and ask them a question, but if he tried to walk up to them they all just walked away and laughed. One person threw beer at him. The beer came from a can, which the person had crumpled up before throwing at Bub's head. He wondered if the person had wanted to throw that at two people porking, but hadn't seen any. It didn't seem believable you could go to the Strip and not see people porking. Stranger things had happened though. A lot of them involved teeth.

"Excuse me," he said, after finally finding people who would stop. It was a group of three women. They were dressed like music videos. Bub held out his palm, in which the tooth and the ex-tooth sat silently. "Are both of these teeth?" he asked.

"Fuck outta here, creep!" the tallest of the three women shouted.

The smallest one shoved Bub, hard.

Bub stumbled backwards and then fell down. "Oh!" he gasped as he hit the pavement. As he felt the tooth and the sweet treat fly out of his hand.

He rolled over as fast as he could, which was so fast he could still hear the tooth and the sweet treat clicking along the street as they bounced away. But he couldn't see them. It was so dark, and they were so small, and his eyes were also not working very well after his head hit the ground so hard.

The three women just kept on walking. They laughed. Probably at Bub. That was what the tooth would have told him. They were laughing at him.

But he couldn't know for sure, because he couldn't find the tooth. He crawled into the street on his hands and knees, slapping and dragging his palms across the asphalt.

The tooth was still calling to him. He knew this but he couldn't hear it, couldn't follow it. Why did he want the tooth? He didn't want it. He just wanted it to stop calling his name in the dark. *Bub, Bub, Bub.* Like the sound of somebody drowning. *Bub, Bub, Bub.*

Eventually someone grabbed him under the shoulders and dragged him out of the street. Just a nice person. They asked Bub if he was okay, and then they asked him if he had been crying.

Bub asked them, "when?"

YOU BLIGHT UP MY LIFE

"**YOU** assholes, you're a fucking…a blight! That's it! You're a blight!"

That was a new one. Delmer had been called all sorts of things in the course of his first day at the call center, things like *asshole* and *cocksucker* and *motherfucker* and *punk-ass bitch* and *douche* and *fag* and *whore*, but *blight*, that was a new one. In a way, it cut Delmer nearer to the quick than the others did. Those earlier insults were boilerplate, ire offered reflexively. This guy here, he'd sought for a word, deliberated, and come back with *blight*.

At least he had made clear he was referring to telemarketers, as a *category*, when he said blight. Rather than Delmer specifically.

"I'm sorry you feel that way, sir," Delmer replied.

Maybe his tone of abject humiliation rang all the way through the line, because the guy on the other end shifted into a lower gear. "I bet you're better than this. I've never met you, but I bet this is beneath you."

You're right, Delmer wanted to say, but here came Fluck puttering into his personal space. He could well say *you're right* and not immediately arouse the boss' suspicions, but if Fluck were true to his reputation amongst the phone jockeys, it was eminently possible to imagine him playing back the tape after close (because of course he recorded the calls) and discovering Delmer's small rebellion.

So he sighed and said "sir, if I might return your attention to the offer prese-"

"Oh, fuck off." *Click*.

Delmer hung up and glanced at Fluck as a dog bracing for a kick.

The supervisor shook his head. "You have to be more engaging," Fluck told him. "You *have* to. Longest I ever let somebody go without closing a deal is three days. Three days, that's how long I give people between sales."

"Yeah, I'm trying. But it's harder than you'd thi-"

"Go longer than that without closing and you're back on the dole."

Oh, how Delmer wished he could suggest anatomically improbable activities for Fluck to go do, starting with that threat, continuing on through this job, and all of the phones in the warehouse, maybe the warehouse itself for good measure. But he couldn't. Because he had no money, no band, no prospects, no skills. He'd very

228

quickly put his ambition to find new bandmates here on hold; his primary concern was getting a fucking roof over his head. He *had* been staying with Clutch, which was obviously no longer an option, which meant he had nowhere to live. Last night he'd pulled a book out of a dumpster, hunkered down in the darkest corner of the Billymark, propped the reading material (which turned out to be a Gideon Bible, damn!) up in his lap, and tried to sleep in such a way that he might just appear to be *very* interested in scripture. The barkeep Wesley had shaken him awake around three and told him he could crash on the floor behind the bar for the night, as long as he didn't come back until he was flush enough for a round or three. That was last night, though. As for where he was going to stay *tonight*, Delmer had no clue. He was hoping he could find a woman of loose morals somewhere on the Strip and convince her to take him home, but he hadn't showered in nearly forty hours now, and he'd always been a, hm, a *fragrant* man at the best of times.

So, yeah, he could tell Fluck where to shove any number of things, from tangible objects to abstract concepts, and enjoy a flicker of satisfaction. Or he could knuckle under, struggle along until payday, then find somewhere, *anywhere* to lay his weary fucking head.

"Ok," Delmer said, as brightly as he could manage. "I'll be more engaged."

"Show me."

Delmer curled his lips back, baring his teeth. "Hello sir or madam! Might I please speak with the head of the household?"

"Why are you making a face? It's a phone."

"I don't know."

"Don't do that."

"Ok."

Fluck opened his mouth as though to deliver yet another bit of sage telemarketing advice, but came up short. He closed his mouth and stalked off to critique someone else.

Delmer watched him go with a scowl, then glanced through the opening of his cubical, across the little avenue between the cells, to the only person he could actually see from sitting.

The guy in the cubical across the way definitely looked like a musician. Probably a bassist if the ponytail was anything to go by. But hey, bassists were technically still musicians.

He tried to get the maybe-bassist's attention with a theatrical rolling of the eyes. A great introductory bonding experience, this would be. Sharing contempt for their boss. Classic coworker stuff.

The maybe-bassist, phone tucked between ear and shoulder, flitted his eyes towards Delmer.

Delmer nodded in the direction Fluck had gone, then pantomimed shooting himself in the head.

The maybe-bassist offered a half-smile and a nod, then turned his chair ninety degrees, to face the rear wall of his cubical.

Delmer sighed. He turned himself around, then took up his pencil and scraped its dull tip through the phone number that had belonged to that loquacious, blight-headed grouch. The line was getting to be so fat it was bleeding onto the other numbers, but the pencil sharpener was all the way over *there*.

Delmer's chest suddenly seized with a tectonic fury, burning red from the heart. He felt his fists clench until the skin beneath his nails broke. Lava poured from the wounds. His jaw cracked, his tongue became molten. Fire poured from his eyes, consuming all of West Hollywood, and then all of California. He observed this from space. He was in a satellite, high above a world consigned to flames. It was a red orb that blinked once, twice, three times. It was the call waiting button.

Delmer narrowed his eyes at it. It was Clutch. He was the only person who would be calling. Delmer was at *his* old station, after all, and Clutch knew that.

So Delmer answered it, said "fuck you," and then realized that it could also be Fluck calling, which it was.

"I put up with a lot of shit from you metallers," he growled, "but this is your last warning, got it?"

"Sorry."

"You keep saying that. I don't know if I buy it. *Shape up*. Quit flickin' your dick and *work the phone." Click*.

Delmer kept the phone pressed against the side of his head for a moment, then gently returned it to its cradle. "Fucker," he mumbled. Spinning once again, he checked to see if the maybe-bassist was still on his call.

He wasn't.

Delmer smiled, then spun the rest of the way around to face the maybe-bassist. "Hey," he called.

The maybe-bassist gave another grin-and-nod, then

turned back to his phone.

"I'm Delmer."

The maybe-bassist halted, sighed, and spun back towards Delmer. "Cody," he said.

"Nice to meet you, Cody."

"Yeah. Good luck on the calls, Delmer." Cody turned back to his phone.

"Do you play an instrument?"

Halt, sigh, spin. "What?"

"Do you play an instrument?" Delmer repeated. "Like, uh, bass? Or drums?"

"I took clarinet lessons when I was a kid."

"…okay. Do you know anyone who plays, like, rock instruments? I don't need a guitarist, but mayb-"

"Dude, I'm on day two without a sale." Cody pointed to his phone. "I gotta get back to it."

"Oh…yeah. Sure. Sorry."

Cody turned his back on Delmer and picked up his phone.

Delmer stared at the floor, then dragged his attention back to his own work station. He placed the tip of his left pointer finger under the next number on the list, and used his right pointer finger to dial it.

AW, G'S

ALL kinds of annoyances welcomed Isley back to Los Angeles. The first was an overwhelming urge to score some blow. Whence this came, and why now, she couldn't begin to imagine. But after weeks of *relative* chill *vis-à-vis* sniffysnow, here were the old urges carving their initials into her ribcage. Suffice it to say, she was already in a bad mood when Hollenbeck called. He demanded to know why Isley was once again calling Luca Colby, this time insisting the still-employed detective get a sketch artist up to some heavy metal burnout in San Francisco. "Excuse *me* for trying to solve a goddamned mystery!" Isley had quite reasonably replied. Hollenbeck did not excuse her, instead threatening her with all sorts of legal jibber-jabber that amounted to diddlyshit, because trying to help a cop do their job wasn't against the law. It was just annoying, apparently. "You can always reinstate me," Isley kept sprinkling into the conversation. Was she dreaming of the evidence locker, on some level, as she suggested that? Okay, sure. Maybe. It was possible. But mostly she just wanted the steady paycheck back. She had to assume, based on things other people had told her, that her credit card had a limit. No dice re: the sprinkles though. Sarge wasn't biting. Fine, ok.

So Isley called up Saacks and asked him to help her find some guy. Fortunately, she'd had the presence of mind to copy the name *Delmer Lippincott* onto a less fleshy surface before the rough and tumble of the drive home somehow smudged it from her arm. It occurred to her that her flesh might have simply absorbed the ink, and now the name *Delmer Lippincott* was floating around under her skin. More likely she'd just smudged it off, though.

Lippincott was easy enough to find. There weren't that many cornseeds bouncing around Tinseltown who hadn't changed their names to something sleeker, more likely to catch the eye of a casting director or whoever the fuck. "Grip" was a pretty shitty name, as far as single-syllable pseudonyms went, but it was definitely better than the boy's given. Indeed, it seemed life had given Delmer little cause to toot a horn. Saacks tracked him, with the greatest of ease and also the greatest of grumbling about not wanting to get in trouble (which Isley, through her ceaseless mockery of her friend's reticence, transformed into *truh-buhhhh),* to a drab apartment building on the western edge of Burbank that appeared to have been drawn by a toddler. It was a perfect sandy rectangle, with evenly spaced, single-pane windows and a level roof. A testament to whatever middling success Delmer had found, that he should live in an area with permit parking on the street. Saacks refused to actually go to the man's house, though, even in plainclothes and off duty, so Isley went on her own. Kind of a bummer, as it would have been fun to tell Saacks to wait in the car, so he didn't get in *truh-buhhhh*, but you can't win 'em all.

She headed into the building and found no legend to guide her. *Ugh.* Lippincott lived in apartment G. The fuck did that mean? What floor was that supposed to be on? How many units per story were there? G?! Isley tried the third floor first and discovered that she'd gone too far. Story of her life. Ha. She hustled back down a story to find units E through H. What a stupid way to label apartments. Anyway, here was G. Isl-E thumped on the door to G with the side of her F-I-S-T.

The door opened. A dull haircut in a suit greeted Isley. "Yes?" it said.

"Are you Mr. Lippincott?" Isley wondered.

"…yes?"

"I was talking to your old pal Brandon. Lamonica. He t-"

"Patch?" Delmer's demeanor instantly changed; it got, hee hee, denicer. "How's he doing?"

"Seemed chipper enough. Got a thrash band up in San Francisco. H-"

"Does he really?"

"Yeah, and do you wanna keep interrupting me or can

235

I finish a sentence?"

"Sorry, I d-"

"I'm gonna just stand in the hall too, I guess?"

Delmer made a fish face. "Sorry. Uh, come in." He stepped backwards and took the doorknob with him. Isley shouldered her way into his apartment. It was not a good apartment. Ok, well, it was a good apartment if your vision board was just cork with nothing tacked onto it. Put it this way: the place was fully furnished, yet somehow retained the breathless clutter of a life as yet unpacked. Put it this way: it was only upon close inspection that one realized the coffee table wasn't a cardboard box full of useless shit like watch straps or used tissues. Put it this way: Isley immediately turned around and said "I think I've got the wrong Delmer. The one I'm looking for plays rock."

The Delmer that turned out to be The Right Delmer twisted his lips like he was trying to wring them out. "That's me. Er, that *was* me."

"Jesus. What happened?"

"Nothing." Delmer tried to smile. "So I got a real job."

"You just gave up?"

"I didn't *just give up,*" he pouted. "I stuck at it for *years*. I just…I got a promotion, and then another, and pretty soon I either had to quit to make time for this music thing that wasn't gonna happen, and sure as hell didn't pay in the meantime…or keep doing what I was. Working for a living." He shrugged. "Keeps me dry and fed, at least."

"Why stay in LA? This place sucks. The music's all gone anyway."

"…the j-"

"The job, right, don't tell me. I know."

Delmer scrutinized her. A bit late to be scrutinizing somebody, once they were already in your house, but maybe better late than never? "So."

"So, yeah, anyway. I'm talking to Patches ab-"

"Patch."

"Brandon. I'm talking to Brandon about the Good Time Butcher, and he tells me I should…you feeling alright?"

A bit of color returned to Delmer's cheeks. "Ah, yeah. Great. Why were you talking about th-"

"I used to be a detective. I was on the Butcher case. Then I got fired because I threatened to kill someone over the phone, *by accident*, which doesn't even count. And also I did coke, which is *actually* why I got fired. Apparently."

Delmer tensed up. Like a spring that didn't know if it was strong enough to survive its next *boi-oi-oing*. "Is your name, like, Izzy, or something?"

"Isley Pultrock. Who the fuck wants to know?"

"…"

"Right, Delmer does. You. How do you know my name, just about?"

"I'm a shift supervisor at a call center. The same call center Gareth Kitchens works at."

"HA!" Isley clapped her hands together. "No shit!"

"…yeah, I was the one that reviewed the, uh, tape of

you and Gareth talking."

"Can I tell you what, it's a good thing for you I'm way over that and dry as a textbook, because otherwise I might think you were pretty fucking stupid telling me that, just sitting here, alone, in your apartment."

"…is that a threat?" Delmer asked it innocently, like a toddler pointing at a cat and asking *is that a dog?*

"No. I'm saying, *otherwise*. It's not otherwise though. It's *this* wise."

"…ok."

"Patches told me your sister got killed by the Butcher."

"…"

"Sorry if it's a sore subject, but, hey, I'm asking for justice. For justice's sake."

"I don't have a sister."

"Well not anymore, but you *did*. When'd the Butcher get her?"

"No, that's not…" Delmer sat on the arm of his boring sofa and looked down, maybe counting the pleats in his stupid pants. "I *never* had a sister."

"…how's that?"

Delmer lifted his gaze. "Patch doesn't know what he's talking about. This must be some weird little prank or something."

"When's the last time you talked to Patches?"

"Patch."

"When was that?"

"…years ago."

"Two? A hundred?"

238

"…maybe three or four. I think it was the end of '79. Over the phone. Last time I ever talked to him was over the phone."

"Some friend."

"We haven't been a part of each other's lives for a while."

"Three or four years, like? Since the end of '79?"

Delmer nodded, as though reluctantly conceding a point.

"So how does he get it into his head you've got a sister got killed by the Butcher?"

"I don't know."

"Do you know anybody whose sister got killed by the Butcher?"

"I don't, um…"

"When was the first time you ever heard about the Butcher?"

"You know…come to think of it. Huh. Wow, yeah. Now that I think of it, I *do* know someone."

Isley was ready with a pen *and* paper this time. "You know someone? Oh yeah? What kind of someone?"

"He's the one who told me about the Butcher. I think maybe he knew somebody who the Butcher killed."

"The name, gimme the name."

"Well, if he's still playing music, his stage name's Clutch. Or maybe just *was*. I don't know, I haven't spoken to him since '79 either."

Isley clenched her jaw. "So Patch tells me to see Grip tells me to see Clutch, huh? Any way I can skip Clutch and go straight to the next guy? Probably called Cinch or

Rivet or what?"

Delmer shrugged and smiled. Something about that smile was off. Isley didn't like it. But whatever. This was the job. Even if it wasn't *her* job anymore. It was *a* job. As long as it got done, it didn't matter who did it.

She considered calling Colby up, telling *her* to go back to Tower Records and endure Goofus and Gallant until they got around to rattling off who Clutch was and what bands he played with and maybe what's his real name, but who was she kidding. *Detective* Luca Colby wouldn't bother with that. Her heart wasn't in this case. Isley's was. And boy, did it get heavy as she climbed back in her car and scooted off to Tower Records. Maybe the guy's name would be Goose, the next guy Clutch told her to go find. It'd be fitting for the chase. It'd be a perfect fucking fit.

SEE WHAT I GOT

THERE was a bad thing to think about. Bub tried to only think of the good things first, that he wasn't the Good Time Butcher and that the teeth which were really just a tooth and a treat were gone (he hoped they got run over by a car, and that nobody else found them and picked them up and listened to them…but no, that was bad! Think good things!) and that there was always a new movie to see almost every week. These were all good things and Bub liked thinking about them. But there was a bad thing.

The bad thing was that he had been the Good Time Butcher at least once. And maybe he just regular Butchered Dominick. Bub thought those were probably the only two people he'd done but he had no idea. He wanted to ask the teeth but they were just a tooth and a treat. And they were gone, maybe run over or maybe picked up. Even if they were still here though, Bub didn't think they would have told him the tooth. Ha. It was still funny.

It wasn't right for him to walk around on Sunset and wave his arms and have a Good Time because even if he wasn't the Butcher, he had still done Bad Things. Because how did he know how to get the medicine bags that kept the guy on the bed alive? How did he know how to get him on the bed anyway? And Bub didn't even remember doing a Bad Thing to Dominick. But he probably had. It was not knowing all of this stuff that made Bub the most upset. He was pretty sure that if somebody could just tell him, oh, you did these Bad Things, he would be happier. He would say, oh, okay, please put me in jail. That was where you put people who did Bad Things. That was how the world worked. Bad people went to prison, and they stayed there until they were Good.

Queen were going to play a show in Inglewood. Actually, they were going to do four nights in a row at the Forum. They weren't coming to the Hollywood part of Los Angeles but Bub wanted to see them. They had a new album and it was a lot different from their other stuff. David Bowie was on it. Bub didn't think David Bowie would be at the concert, but anything can happen in rock and roll. So he tried to buy tickets for one of those shows in the middle of September. The first show was sold out, but then the second he ended up not buying the tickets for because he wasn't sure whether or not he would be in jail by the end of September. That was how he knew he was going to go to the police.

Bub went to the closest police station to his house, which was near the hospital where he probably got the bag of medicine from. He went inside and walked up to the front desk, because that seemed like a good place to go.

"Excuse me sir," he said to the guy behind the desk, "but I think I might be the Good Time Butcher."

The guy behind the desk just rolled his eyes and breathed really loud and pointed at a noisy part of the station and said "go talk to Pultrock."

"I don't know who that is. I'm sorry."

"Isley Pultrock. She'll be the one who's tweaking out of her fucking mind."

"Tweaking?"

"Uh-huh."

"I d-"

"Dude. Just go ask around. You'll find her. Or she'll find you – she can't get enough of you Butcher nuts."

"Okay. I'm sorry."

The guy didn't say anything else, so Bub walked around asking for the lady who was tweaking out of her fucking mind, and everybody pointed him to the same person. Once Bub saw her, he understood what tweaking meant. She was bouncing her leg up and down really fast and blinking strong like she was having a hard time belie-ving something. Bub wanted to know what she was look-ing at, but it was probably something only she could see.

243

"Excuse me," he said to her, "but the guy at the desk told me to talk to you."

Isley looked up at Bub, down to his feet, up to his face again, then down to his hand. "You got a tooth in that sweaty-ass mitt of yours? Don't tell me."

"Okay."

"Well?"

"I don't. I used to have one but I lost it."

"Ugh."

"I had another but it turned out to be a sweet treat. I think I'm the Good Time Bu-"

"The Butcher? You're the fourth fucking guy *today*. You got a tooth? So does everybody."

"I lost the too-"

"Everybody's got fucking teeth. Everybody's the fucking Butcher."

"I don't have the tooth anymore."

"Then what, guy? What the fuck?" She waved her hand and coughed.

"I'm sorry."

Isley relaxed a little and snaked her hand in the air over her right shoulder. "Go down the hall there. We've got a door with a big number five on it. Go through that door. That's the door, that's the fucking *door* you want."

"What's through the door?"

"*You*, soon. Soon as you get the fuck out of my face. Somebody'll come in and get your statement, all that shit. Put it in a file and shove it up my ass, that's about what'll happen with it."

"I'll try to keep my statement short, then."

The detective threw her head back and laughed. She kept throwing it back until she looked like she was near to tipping over. She didn't, though. "Keep it short! Funny. Good one. Good on you, buddy."

"Bub."

"Get the fuck out of my face."

So he did, walking down the hall until he found the door with the big number five on it. He went through and on the other side there was him, just like Isley said. Then there were also two other guys. He asked them if they had teeth in their pockets. They said yes. That was how Bub knew he was in the right place.

"I hate to break it to ya," one of the guys said, "but I'm the Good Time Butcher."

The other just rolled his eyes and said "he keeps saying that. That's what the other guy said too."

"They took his statement," the first guy told Bub.

"But the fact is, *I'm* the Good Time Butcher. I have the teeth to prove it."

Bub tried to whistle like in a TV show. But he didn't know how so he just blew some air out of his mouth. "Teeth like more than one tooth?"

"Four. I have four teeth."

"Oh."

The other guy leaned over his knees and fixed Bub with a face like he was trying to go to the bathroom but it just wasn't happening. "Four's nothing. I have seven."

The first guy frowned and said "that's funny, you've shown me two. Where'd the other five get to?"

"They're at *home.*"

"Uh-huh."

"I'm serious!"

"I used to have two," Bub informed them, "but one of them turned out to be a sweet treat. And then I lost them anyway." Both guys looked at Bub like he was crazy. Bub was used to people looking at him like he was crazy. It was less common for him to have other crazy people look at him like that. That was weird. "Oh," he suggested, "what if we're all the Good Time Butcher?"

Now they *really* looked at him, like he was *really* crazy.

"Really," he continued. "I'm pretty sure I Good Time Butchered a person, or maybe more, but there are some that I know I didn't Good Time Butcher that still got Good Time Butchered. So what if all of us Good Time Butchered a few people, but since we all do it the same everybody just thinks it's one person?"

The guys looked at each other, then back to Bub. The first one asked him, "then who was the *original* Good Time Butcher, smart guy?"

Bub shrugged. He remembered that one time his back hurt a while ago. "It might have been me."

"Oh, bull*shit*. It was me!"

"Nuh-uh!" the other said.

The two guys wanted to argue, so Bub stayed quiet and let them. Then the cops called the second guy in first, which maybe made him the actual first guy. The first guy who turned out to be the second guy tried to talk to Bub about a bunch of stuff like politics and the world, and Bub asked him if he had ever seen *The Thing*. The guy didn't understand the question, and then he got called in

246

by another cop so Bub never got to explain it.

About a half hour later a cop came in and told Bub to follow. So Bub did. They went back into the noisy part of the office. He saw Isley still tweaking at her desk. She was talking to the first guy who came in second. Bub waved to her but she didn't see him.

The cop who was going to listen to him was also a detective. She was named Colby, and she asked Bub for all his information. His name, age, where he lived, where he worked, all the regular questions you ask people if you have a clipboard. Then she asked him more unusual questions, like when he first suspected he was the Good Time Butcher, where and how he came by the tooth he'd since lost, how many people he thought he'd killed. Bub felt like he was failing the test because he kept having to say "I don't know." He didn't want to give them wrong information in case that ruined the, ha, case. But he also really felt like he was at least *a* Good Time Butcher, if not *the* one. Every time he said that though, the detective just nodded her head and asked another question. Bub was pretty sure she didn't believe him. He told her about how he thought maybe everybody, well not everybody but all of the crazy people, were all Good Time Butchers. She just nodded her head again. Bub didn't see her write down his idea.

Then it was done and she told Bub to go home, they would call him if they had any more questions. Bub asked her if he should go look for the tooth he'd lost. She looked at him like he was a dumb person.

"Here comes another!" cackled the guy from behind

the front desk, the first one Bub had talked to. There was another crazy person walking away from the desk guy, towards Bub. Actually towards the detective named Colby. The new crazy person asked where Isley Pultrock was.

Isley waved at him from across the room and shouted "hey! Over here!" Bub was a little bit sad that Isley hadn't returned his wave from when *he'd* waved, and now she was waving at this new guy who hadn't even waved to her, but also this wave wasn't a happy wave.

So three and a half hours after he'd walked into the station, Bub walked back out. Maybe he wouldn't go to jail. He didn't know if that was good or not. He didn't know if *he* was Good or not. But oh well.

He went to Inglewood and tried to buy a ticket for Queen, but two of the shows had been cancelled, and the other two were sold out.

A SUCKER IS BORN

AT the beginning of Delmer's third day at the call center, which was incidentally the third consecutive day of closing not a single sale, Fluck called him over to the water cooler and handed him a Dixie cup full of water that had, maybe at some point in the current century, been filtered. "Listen," the manager said, in the same tone prudish fathers had been using for generations to tell their sons about sex, "I don't enjoy firing people. I really don't. But the thing is, the *three days* policy is for everybody. I can't go around giving special privileges to new employees, or else everybody is gonna want them."

There was a voice in the furthest recesses of Delmer's head that was yodeling something witty into a bottomless pit. He was too tired to go fishing for that particular quip, though. He'd spent last night in the one-walled shelter of a bus stop, which was to say, he hadn't slept all that much. So sure, Fluck couldn't give special privileges. Fine by Delmer.

"So, I'll say this," Fluck did indeed say, "just, uh, you know. Close something today. Or I'll have to fire you."

"I already knew that," Delmer pointed out.

"Well, I just wanted to make sure you knew, there's no appeal. It's either you close a sale, and that three-day counter, uh, doesn't go away but it just resets, or you don't. And then the counter goes away, because you don't work here anymore."

"Got it." Which he did. Delmer slugged to his station, sat down, took up the phone, and got to work being hung up on. Most times the hangup came pretty much the moment he asked to speak to the head of the household – people were savvy to the script of the telemarketer these days. But that was how other, more successful phone jockeys opened fire, so Delmer didn't see any good reason to change up his approach there. A few times, he got as far as asking people about the depth of their emotional attachments, re: household appliances. A lot of hangups there. One time he got all the way to the end of a call, a *forty minute call*, only to discover that he was being goofed on. He discovered this when the person on the other end cackled "hey suck my fat *DICK*" and hung up. The goof, presumably, being that the guy had wasted Delmer's time. That seemed a pyrrhic goof to Delmer, but one of which the man, the grown adult man, could be proud. Said man had successfully wasted nearly an hour of Delmer's day. In another hour and a half, Delmer would be out of a job. No money, no hope of getting a goddamned place to live, no prospects for finding himself any new fucking bandmates. No future. Barely into his twenties, his best years already behind him.

God, what a fucking nightmare. This fucking city, and the fuckers who lived in it. Pennsylvania might have been boring, but it was predictable. For as little as it gave, it took even less. Los Angeles, meanwhile, was a magician, dazzling you with a good time while it took everything, picked your pocket, sucked you dry, and buried you at low tide.

Delmer would not be buried. He refused. This was just a compellingly bleak chapter in his story. The bit right before the big time. Brighter days right around the corner, goddamnit. Whether or not this was true…well, he would fucking *make* it true.

In an ever-thickening glaze of flopsweat, Delmer kept working the phone. The pencil guiding him further down the list, scratching off one number after another.

He barely looked up as someone else took Cody's cubical across the way. Because it had been three days since Cody's last sale. So Cody had been fired.

With less than an hour to go before his final shift ended, Delmer dialed a number that wasn't on the list. One he knew by heart.

The phone rang. And rang. Until it said "hello?" in his mother's voice.

Delmer's throat couldn't manage more than a dry *crick* sound.

"…Delmer?"

"Hi, Mom."

"Oh! Delmer, we've been so worried about you! How are y-"

"I'm okay." He took a deep breath. "Doing great. Making music."

"We haven't heard from you in so long."

"Um," Delmer replied. His voice cracked. Like he was about to cry. Like a fucking baby. So he said "gotta go, bye," and hung up.

He stared at the list of numbers in front of him. Then dialed another one that wasn't on it.

The phone rang twice, then said "hello?"

"Hey. It's Delmer."

"Oh…hey," Patch repied. "Uh…how's it going?"

"Toksick broke up. The album thing fell through."

"Damn, dude. I heard about that. That really sucks." Patch said this with a sincerity that Delmer hadn't heard from *any* human being in the past several weeks. He wasn't quite sure what to do with such unguarded, raw sentiment.

"Yeah, man," he concurred.

"…how are you doing otherwise?"

"Um…I mean…ugh…fine. Just trying to make it work like always, you know?"

"Totally."

"How about you? How's Bömerayñ?"

Patch laughed softly, like he was trying to not wake someone up. "If you have to ask, that's sort of the answer."

"Aw, come on. I thought I saw you guys on a poster

under Dokken, didn't I?"

"Yeah, like *way* under. But, yeah, we opened for 'em."

"That's awesome."

"It was pretty fun."

I wish you'd been there to play with us, that was what Patch was supposed to say now. Delmer waited to hear his best buddy, his lifelong friend, take the next step towards reconciliation. It had to be him now; it was into his back Delmer had plunged that hatchet, after all. But, also, anyway, that was way overdramatic. It wasn't like he'd *stabbed Patch in the back*. He hadn't done anything worth ending a friendship as old as time itself over, right?

I wish you'd been there to play with us, that was all Patch had to say, and Delmer would know everything was going to be alright.

"…"

"…"

"…it sounds like it," Delmer said. His voice caught on the space between the words "it" and "sounds."

"Mhm," Patch replied.

"Well, if you guys ever need another guitarist for live or whatever, I'm definitely still around."

"Yeah, maybe. So far we've been fine, with our new stuff we really only need one, but maybe someday."

"For sure. I'll be around."

"Cool. And I'm sure whatever band you land in, we'll probably play together at some point."

"Like a two, uh…or you just mean on the same bill?"

"On the same bill."

"Oh. Yeah. No doubt, at some point."

"Totally."

"…"

"…"

"…"

"…ok, well I'll let you go."

"Cool," Delmer gulped. "Yeah. Pretty busy over here. Gotta pay the bills somehow."

"Nice."

"I'm working at this call center. It's pretty lame, but you know. Everybody's got a day job. Until ya hit it big, anyway!"

"Mhm."

"I bet you probably know a few other people who work here. A bunch of rock guys work here."

"Oh, cool. Well, say hi to them for me."

"Which ones?"

"…whoever you see, I guess."

"Oh, right. Ok. I'll tell them you said 'hi'."

"Sounds good."

"…"

"…"

"…"

"…well," Patch drawled, "I don't want to eat up your whole work day, so w-"

"Oh, no worries! It's not a big deal."

"…anyway, I'll really let you go now."

"Do you wanna grab a drink anytime?"

"I mean…we're not old enough to go to a bar."

"I know a few that don't card. As long as you're cool."

"Well, I'm pretty slammed this week, to be honest."

"Doesn't have to be this week."

"…sure, yeah. We'll see if we can't find a time that works."

"I can do basically whenever. Flexible schedule. One of the perks of this place, I guess."

"…ok, good to know. Let me figure out my schedule and I'll get back to you."

"Ok. You'll wanna call me here, just make sure you hang up right away if somebody who isn't me picks up." Delmer gave him the number.

"Nice. Got it."

"Do you wanna read it back to me, just so I can make sure you got it right?"

"I'm pretty sure I got it."

"I can check though."

"I'm good, Delmer. It was great talking to you. I'll let you go now. Take it easy, buddy."

Click.

Delmer stared at the wall of his cubical, then slowly placed the phone back in its cradle.

And immediately picked it up again, to dial the next number on the list. When the other end engaged, Delmer tried to say "hello," but all the came out was a choked squawk.

"What?" asked the person on the other end of the line.

"Ahem…ah, sorry. Hello! Can I speak to the head of the household, please?"

"…are you a fucking telemarketer?"

"I'm calling to offer y-"

Click.

Without wasting a single moment, Delmer tapped the phone back into the cradle and returned it to his ear. He dialed the next number. He only realized that he was grinning when his cheeks started hurting. His head hurt too. Made sense; he was a volcano.

"Hello!" he erupted. "I'd like to speak to the head of the household, please!"

"I am she," some old lady responded.

So Delmer made his pitch, and the old lady listened dutifully. She was probably some lonely old biddie, sitting in a rocking chair, her living room lit only by the glow of a boob tube. He pictured her, painted the scene with enough detail to help him feel a little bit better about his own life. If he could imagine her in sufficiently miserable accommodations, he might well be glad of not having any of his own, miserable or otherwise. So all of her pictures were crooked, and there were water stains on her walls. Her walls *were* water stains, and the termites had nibbled a giant penis into them. Her drapes were on fire and the only thing on TV was commercials. Her teeth were in her lap and her husband's skeleton was still in his recliner. Her kids never called, and she always sat by the phone hoping they would. That was why she'd picked up so quickly. She had an awful life. Delmer was doing pretty well, in comparison.

"Well," she said at the end of Delmer's mindless spiel, "I'm sorry, sir, but I just don't see any need to buy any new s-"

"I need a win," he heard himself say. He didn't even

have the energy to be surprised by this. It wasn't as though his rogue tongue was wrong. "Please, ma'am. Just one thing. I'll put you down for a spatula."

"…you sell spatulas?"

"Um. No. Metaphorically."

"A metaphorical spatula."

"Yeah, I'm…uh."

"Are you high?" The sudden edge in the woman's voice kicked Delmer right in the ass.

"Huh?!"

"You sound like a young man. Young men are all high nowadays, that's what I hear. Did you call me up high?"

"No, I…I'm not, ma'am. I wish I was, to be honest."

With nary a care for the affective whiplash she was causing, the woman snapped into a sympathetic tone. "How come?"

"Because I'm…ah…I'm…sad." Delmer flinched at his own honesty.

"Why?"

She asked this, Delmer knew, with her eyes locked on her husband's skeleton. It was right next to her, after all. "Uh…someone…" He could feel more candor sliming up from the depths. Enough of the truth for one night, thank you much. "…they, ah, passed away."

"Who?"

"My friend. My best friend in the whole world."

"Oh. That's too bad."

Delmer could almost hear the *groan* of this old lady's hand on the transmission, cranking her sympathy into a lower gear. Luckily, inspiration struck: "My bro…sister.

257

My sister. My best friend in the whole world, who was my sister."

"Oh, *heavens.*" That was more like it! "I'm so sorry. I'm sorry if I wondered whether you were high. When did this happen? If I'm not prying?"

"Of course not." A smile flashed across Delmer's face. He didn't bother hiding it; oh, the joys of the telephone. "It was, uh, pretty recent."

"Oh, honey."

"Yeah…she was, um. Uh. She was sleeping at a bus stop. She'd had hard times, you know, not that she was… it's not like she'd bottomed out or anything, she was just on kind of a downswing. Which happens."

"No. Oh no. Did someone set upon her?"

"Pfft. *Did* they!" Delmer cleared his throat and adjusted his tone. "They did. It was a, a, a murder, yeah. She was murdered!" He couldn't hear the old biddie's response over his stifled laughter. It was, in fact, the hardest he'd laughed in quite some time. Sure! He had a sister, and she'd been murdered! And she had the head of a flamingo and the legs of a lobster! Why not? This was the first time he'd found a halfway productive outlet for his creativity since the *Brainface* recording session. Why not run with it?

"Yeah," Delmer finally managed to chortle, "actually, it was, you're never gonna believe this, it was a *serial killer* who got her."

"What? Lord Jesus."

"Yeah. She got serial killed."

"I don't mean to pry, but…"

258

"You wanna know which killer it was?"

"I just didn't know there was a murderer on the loose."

"Oh, don't worry. He only gets young people. He likes young, beautiful, talented people who just wanna play music and live their lives, who just want to have a good fucking time, they're not trying to hurt anybody, it shouldn't be this fucking hard to just *make something happen,* and every time they get close it gets…*snatched away.* It's not fair. It's not fucking fair."

"…"

"I'm sorry for swearing, ma'am, I just get so…when I think about it, I get s-"

"It's okay, sweetheart. I understand."

"It was the Good Time Killer that got her…no, *Butcher.* The Good Time Butcher. Kids are just having a good time, and maybe they sleep in the bus stop for a night or two, and he just…"

Forgetting he was on the phone, Delmer pantomimed cutting his own throat. He did so forcefully enough to actually scratch himself with the nail of his thumb.

"…cuts 'em open, and lets them bleed. Picks their pocket and sucks 'em dry."

"Oh, my God."

"Yeaaaah." Delmer searched his work station for a pen to pick up and click, but found nothing. "Anyway… sorry. I got worked up there."

"Like I said. It's okay."

"It's nasty stuff. The Good Time Butcher." A smile returned to his face. He pinched the roll of his belly through his shirt. "Anyway, I'm just trying to pay for my sister's funeral. She's just like a little toothless skeleton now, she's been sucked dry. We can probably get the casket half-price, maybe split it with another Butcher victim. They're easy to stack." He glanced across to Cody's replacement, to see if they were getting a load of what he was saying. Alas, his would-be audience was busy at their own phone. "Sorry," Delmer said, returning the receiver to his ear, "what was that?"

"If I…oh, Lord. Lord." She sighed. "Maybe I can spare something. I could…is there some sort of toaster I could buy? If that would, hmm, help?"

"I can put you down for a food processor. The commission on that would get me enough to have my dear old sis taxidermied."

"…what?"

"Made up to look normal in the casket, you know."

"Oh. Ok. Well, if you say so."

Delmer could hardly believe his luck. As he closed. A. Fucking. *Deal.*

After the deed was done, the old woman told Delmer she would pray for him.

"Sweet," he giggled as he slammed the phone down, lifted his hands in triumph, and choked on a *WHOO* before it left his throat.

Fluck was standing right behind him, hands crossed over his chest, mustache cranked to nearly vertical.

Delmer turned himself around with his feet, one futzy little kick at a time. "Hey boss. Uh, how long were you standing there?"

"Are you asking how much of that I heard?"

"Something like that."

"Oh, I'd say I heard pretty much the whole damn thing. And let me tell you, there's a word for what you just did." He leaned forward. *"Genius."*

Delmer didn't blink – he closed his eyes and opened them, very, very slowly. "What?"

"Everybody!" Fluck rose to his full height and clapped his hands. "Eyes up! Customers on hold!" He gave the operators time to comply, and then, once all eyes were on him, directed them towards Delmer. "Our newest recruit has proven to be the one with the most undeniable sense of initiative! I mean, holy shit! Tell them what you just told that person," he ordered Delmer.

"…" Delmer's brow fell across his eyes. "Seriously? I was just kind of…bullshitting, I didn't m-"

"Stand up!" someone called from the back.

"Speak up!" someone else shouted.

Fluck patted Delmer's shoulder. "Go on, tell 'em."

Delmer's mouth flapped open and closed. He glanced up at Fluck.

"You all," Fluck called across the call center, "listen up! This is official company policy going forward! If you're losing the client, then guess what?" He nudged Delmer. "Tell 'em."

Delmer cleared his throat. "You want me to tell them about…the…what am I telling them?"

"What?" a third someone shouted across the room.

Fluck sighed. "You've all got a sister, and she's been

killed by the Good Time Butcher!"

"What?"

"The who?"

"No I don't!"

"You sure as hell do, if it means making a sale! Tell 'em," Fluck enjoined Delmer, a bit less bounce in his voice.

With one last glance towards his boss, Delmer rose to his feet, cleared his throat again, and announced to the whole room, "well…he sucks ya dry."

THE WATER'S FINE

SOMEBODY was definitely fucking with Isley, which she didn't appreciate. The guy called Clutch, who was now singing with a band inexplicably called Clorbus, averred that he didn't know jack shit about the Good Time Butcher beyond what he'd read in the papers (Isley didn't believe he had much truck with papers that couldn't be rolled, but she took his point). "So who do you think I should talk to," Isley wondered, "who goes by one syllable and plays in a piece of shit band?" Clutch said what do you mean piece of shit band, and then they yelled at each other for a while, so Isley didn't get another recommendation. That was fine, though, because around then Saacks called and said "listen," he was whispering it

263

like it was past his bedtime, "listen, we got the sketch back, from that guy you found in San Fran. Colby thinks you should come have a look at it, but Sarge doesn't want you in the office."

"Tell her to bring it by my place."

"Well, uh, this is our only copy right now, and, um…"

"She doesn't trust me with it?"

"I don't think it's personal."

"Ok. So I can't come in to see it, and Colby won't bring it to me. You just calling to tell me about a sketch that exists, or do you got a way for me to see it?"

"Well," Saacks told her, "the solution is you just come in anyway. Colby was told she's not supposed to request your presence, but if you should happen to show up when the Sarge isn't in the office…"

"When's that, then?"

"He's got a court appearance at ten tomorrow morning."

So as ten tomorrow rolled in real slow, like a storm front, Isley got a call from someone at the statehouse who seemed to think Isley gave two shits about their opinion. They told her about how she hadn't done her community service hours yet, and how she had to start logging those or she'd be back in front of a Judge before she knew it.

"I heard about community service hours," Isley shot back, "I didn't hear anybody say, oh, you've gotta have 'em done by such and fucking such a time, did you?"

"Well, I wasn't at the sentencing, but i-"

"Then turns out you're not so fucking smart, huh?"

264

"You want to watch your tone."

"What I want's my own goddamn business and it happens to be blow, but life's not always cherries and bullshit, so fuck you!" She hung up the phone and went to sleep and then it was ten tomorrow.

She strode into the station like she owned the place, head high and shoulders thrown back, swinging one foot in front of the other. Kiss my boots, boys, you should be so lucky. "Alright," she thundered, "let's see this goddamned sketch!"

Colby flew across the room, crooning about what a fortuitous and unexpected turn of events was Isley's arrival. She presented the ex-detective the sketch and asked, "well?"

Isley didn't have to look at it for half a second before she said "motherfucker." She lifted her gaze to meet Colby's and repeated herself, adding "not you" for clarification.

"I'm not crazy, right?" Colby asked. "He was here?"

"Hell no and yes, respectively! No shit, whatever I was on back then gave me goddamned flashbulb recall. He was here. It was…"

"Summer of last year."

"Tell me we've got those fucking statements on file somewhere."

Colby replied by waving for Isley to follow, and leading her into a room in which two little paperwork grunts were gophering their way through filing cabinets. "I want to read you some names," the bearded one said as Colby entered. "Terry Heslov, Bryan Berry, Christopher Sim."

Colby shook her head. "None of those ring a bell." She turned to Isley. "I'm pretty sure it was me who took his statement, right?"

Isley nodded. Without a word, she dove into the fray, flitting through files with Colby's handwriting on them. At the top of each one was a hasty, almost glib addendum: TEETH, or NO TEETH.

"He had a tooth with him," Isley recalled.

"You're certain?"

"I sound like I'm not? I remember I had a goddamned headache, I think I'd seen Motörhead the night before but, I mean, I saw *somebody*, and it was a good show, so I don't exactly remember who it was I saw. You know."

Colby shrugged.

"He did *not* have a tooth with him," Isley amended with brio. "When I said he *did,* I meant he *didn't*. He said he *used* to have one but he lost it, or something. I'd seen Motörhead the night before."

"…so you're certain that he *didn't* have a too-"

"Yeah. So. I'm sitting there trying to keep my brain from getting squeezed out my goddamned ears, and I bet the kid on the front desk…who was on the desk back then?"

"I think that was Toomey."

"Toomey! Fuckin Looney Tooms, god he was an asshole. Yeah, he sends this guy over to me, probably because what I was saying was, he knew I was in a Russian way, and he was being a dick. So this nutbar comes up to me with a, *without* a tooth in his hand, and tells me…" Isley smacked her head, trying to get the slipped

266

gears to recatch. "…he tells me he had another one that turned out to be a tic tac or some shit."

"Oh my god," Colby marveled, "I remember that! I put that in the statement, I'm positive!"

The non-beardy gopher clicked his tongue and said "I don't remember seeing one that had anything like that on it."

"Well then keep fucking looking!" Isley shouted, as she led by example.

A uniformed officer swung his head in the door. "Sarge is coming back."

"Already?" Isley and Colby exclaimed in unison.

"I guess. The plaintiff had filed a motion to dismiss. Nobody told us."

Isley laughed. "Amazing."

"Not amazing," Colby scolded. "We've got a hell of a lot less time than we expected, then."

Isley shrugged, flipped through two more files, and paused. Colby's handwriting. NO TEETH written on top. Partway down the page, a reference to a lost tooth turning into candy. The name on the page: Bub Lawrence Bowersox. Beneath that, an address.

She fought the perfectly reasonable impulse to leap to her feet, click her heels, and spin around the room crowing about her success. More challenging was stifling the honking laugh she'd expelled with the force of a sneeze.

"What'd you find?" Colby asked, as reflexively as someone saying 'gablessyou' even though they knew full well nobody's soul was slipping out their nose.

"Nothing," Isley covered. "Just some of these wackjobs, you know? The stuff they say." She looked up to make sure everybody was nodding in assent, yes, these wackjobs, and the stuff they say. Because as long as they were nodding, they weren't likely to see Isley folding the Bowersox statement in half and slipping it into her pocket. It was only by biting her lip that she kept from giggling as she returned to fiddlefucking her way through the catalogue of small insanities.

She committed one of her own, nearly giving up the jig, as it were, when she attempted to excuse herself by saying "I better get out of here before Sarge gets back, he'll probably make me turn my pockets out, oops." Lucky for her Colby and the gophers had only one track to their minds, and it was full up with the prattlings of LA's goofiest losers. Colby just flapped her hand at Isley, which was good enough.

The ex-detective took her leave at a far less regal clip than the one that had marked her entrance, though the swell of her heart was damn near magisterial.

The triumph, alas, was short-lived. By the time she got home, Isley's answering machine already had a message from Luca Colby. "Hey," she wondered, "uh, this is a weird question, and I don't mean to offend you by asking it, but…did you take any files out of the records room? Just because, we looked through every single one, and the one from the candy tooth guy isn't there. Even though it would have to be, I think. We both remember-ed him, right? And it seems like all of the other files are here. So, uh, I'm just wondering, because I remembered what you said about Sarge making you turn out your pockets if he caught you, so, uh, this is really awkward for me, but I just wanted to make sure you didn't accidentally take a file. Like maybe you saw it and thought it was a possibility, so you just tucked it into your pocket and forgot about it, then you left and you forgot about it all the, on the way home. That might have been what happened? Anyway, please call me back. Otherwise, you know, nothing personal, but I might have to bring Sarge up to speed on, you know, what I've been up to. On this case."

Which meant Isley probably had a few hours to act on the information in Bowersox's file. That was her only option. It was what she had to do. What else could she do, turn it over? Lose the case? No. Unacceptable. It was a matter of pride. She was *so fucking close* – she probably had the Butcher's name and address here on this sheet! And she was gonna turn it over? No. This was *her* case. Even if it wasn't, because she wasn't a detective. Even if she was no longer legally supposed to have the gun in her closet, now her hand, now heavy in the pocket of her windbreaker. Even if the Butcher case didn't seem like it was as simple as one guy committing all of these crimes. She was too close. If she could bring Bowersox in, if they could connect him to just a few of the murders, then that would be the most dramatic lead in the case since, well, ever! Maybe they could start controlling for the Bowersox kills, and so drill down more carefully on the non-Bowersox ones.

But, Isley had to remind herself, Bub still wasn't a slam dunk. The kind of crazy that goes to the police station and takes credit for the crimes of a serial killer is actually a fairly common sort of crazy – more common, she had to imagine, than one that would try to turn himself in *and* go seek out a musician who happened to be singing about those same crimes just to say hi. It certainly wasn't outside the realm of possibility for one person to have both of those crazies, and not the sort of crazy that led to actually *committing* the crimes. The evidence was circumstantial, yes. But she had a hunch. Her hunches were generally pretty good. Of course, that necessarily meant that they sometimes weren't, because otherwise they'd just be pretty good full stop, but hey, if *generally* was an unsatisfactory basis for action, then why did they put *generals* in charge of armies, huh? Good question.

Granted, armies got stuff wrong too. *Generally*, though…well, actually, that might be a bad example.

BUB lived in a shitty apartment in a bad part of town. Kinda close to the Strip, certainly walking distance if you didn't have anything better to do. Circumstantial, again, but how much circumstance did a gal need, huh?

A lot less, Isley reminded herself, when she didn't have to worry about the fuddy-duddy bullshit of bureaucracy.

There were downsides to not having a badge to wave around, though. Chief among them was the question of approach. If you have a thick enough warrant, you don't have to scratch your knuckles on a guy's door if you don't want. Just grab the battering ram and knock it the fuck down. Isley didn't have that luxury, though, and she knew from experience that kicking doors in wasn't nearly as easy as the movies made it look. But if she knocked on the door, and this Bub fucker smelled something fishy…well, there were any number of ways the jump might be flipped, that this guy might get the upper hand. No way was Isley going to go out as the latest victim of the Butcher. She wasn't a notch on anybody's fucking belt.

Okay, easy to say. Harder to do. Harder, that was, unless she led with the gun, her teeny tiny .22. Not the most powerful firearm, but it was compact, easy to hide, and a killer at kissing distance. Over the threshold of a creak-hinged door? No question.

Question, though: Did she really want to lead with the gun? That was crossing a different sort of threshold. She was a private citizen. The moment she drew a gun on a man, in *his* place of residence, well, he was probably within his rights to defend himself. Boy, wouldn't that be rich, if she ended up getting hurt or worse by this guy, and the law vindicated *him!* It was conceivable. She recalled Bub with as much clarity as possible. Did he seem like the sort of man who could react quickly, who would pose enough of a threat to warrant her concerns of overturned tables? Or did he seem like the sort of guy who complied without question, who respected authority by whatever means it imposed itself?

Isley drew her gun.

The grip was cool, with diamond patterns punched into the plastic. She hadn't held this sucker in years. Nor, she realized with a start, had she fired it. Well, obviously.

She couldn't fire it without holding it. Nor could she clean it, which she also hadn't done. Furthermore…was this thing fucking loaded? Maybe that call from Colby had spooked her more than she'd realized. These were fairly basic oversights, of the sort Isley wasn't wont to make.

Whatever, though. What the fuck ever. Bub didn't need to know any of this, and she was already standing in front of his door, piece in her right hand, left raised into a fist and resting just below the peephole. It was too late to turn back. It had been too late for a while now.

She drew her hand back. *Knock, knock, knock.*

She tightened her grip on the gun. Slowly, with a pronounced tremble that shamed her as little else could, she lifted it to the space where Bub's self-professed five feet and nine inches of height would put his face.

She waited.

Footsteps on the other side of the door. They were light, tentative.

The doorknob rattled.

Isley rested her finger, gently, softly, ever so delicately, on the trigger.

She reminded herself to breathe.

The door creaked open.

"FREEZE!" Isley screamed, thrusting her gun into the empty space in front of her. She blinked, then looked down at the young, pigtailed Hispanic-looking girl who had opened the door. "Who the fuck are you?" Isley wondered aloud. The girl didn't appear distressed, at least not about anything happening in the apartment behind her. She *did* seem a little skeptical about being told to freeze by a gun-wielding stranger standing on her *COME ON IN* welcome mat, which, you know, fair play to her. "Uh…does Bub Bowersox live here?"

"DAAAAAAAD!" the girl screamed. "There's a lady with a gun here!"

"WHAT?!" a voice from the apartment cried.

Isley slipped the gun back into her pocket as a man who was, without a doubt, *not* Bub Bowersox appeared, at speed with a good running start.

"I'm LAPD!" Isley shouted, raising her now-empty palms. It occurred to her that there weren't many parts of this city in which a situation could be defused by shouting *I'm LAPD* with empty palms raised. Okay, so find a compromise: she reached back into her pocket and retrieved the gun, but let it point lazily to the ground.

The man charged towards the girl who was probably his daughter, then past her, then hard into Isley.

His shoulder caught her in the stomach and took her for a ride.

The last thing Isley heard before her unexpected early bedtime was a loud *crack*. It was either the gun going off, or her skull bouncing off the wall behind her. Impossible to say, before the dark closed in.

KNOWING AND THEN THE OPPOSITE

THE police hadn't heard what Bub wanted to say. Even though the nice lady had written it down, he was pretty sure she hadn't believed him. Her mouth had been twisted up in a funny way. Not funny like tee hee. Funny like how somebody hits their head and says they feel funny, and then they die.

The problem was that Bub still didn't feel Good. He didn't feel quite as Bad as he had before, because he really had tried his best to do a Good thing. But he hadn't been able to do it. What was between Good and Bad? Bub. That was what.

Did he want to go to jail? Maybe. He wasn't sure. Jail was how you became Good, but there were a lot of Good

275

people who hadn't gone to jail, so there had to be another way to do it. Unless all Good people who ever lived had gone to jail and just didn't tell anybody about it. If they didn't tell anybody about it, there was no way Bub could say it wasn't true. He was pretty sure he'd have heard about it, though. From somebody. And anyway, it wasn't like you went to jail and automatically got Good. Sometimes people went to jail and came out just as Bad as they went in, or maybe worse. And then sometimes people went in Good and came out Bad, like Bub's dad.

So then maybe jail didn't really matter. People went in one way and came out another, unless they didn't. So what? That was like anything. Sometimes Bub went into movies one way and came out another. He would be thinking about something in a way he didn't think of before. So what? It didn't mean anything. If it was like anything, it didn't mean anything. That, Bub felt, meant something.

There were other people he could talk to. People who weren't police officers. And Bub had a feeling they would listen to him, and believe what he told them, and then do something that reacted to what he said, all really quickly. Maybe at the same time, if that was possible. Anything was possible. What did *that* mean?

Bub took a walk up and down the Strip, for what he couldn't help but think of as the *last* time. The Last Good Time. That's what some people had right before they got Butchered. Bub figured that everybody had a Last Good Time. They had to. Even if the whole last twenty years of their life before they died, they never had one Good

Time, then that just meant their Last Good Time was twenty years ago. The only way to never have a Last Good Time was to never have a Good Time ever. Bub wondered what would be worse, never having a Good Time, or having a Good Time and then realizing that it was the Last one you would ever have. That was probably why being Butchered was so crummy. You knew. You knew you'd had your Last Good Time. Bub hoped he never found out when his Last Good Time would happen. He thought he was probably having it. That made him sad.

He saw Interesting Things for the last time. People porking on the yard out back of Gazzarri's. Except it seemed like maybe now they were porking there because other people had porked there before, and now it was just a Place People Porked. Like people woke up and said, hey, I think we should go pork on the yard out back of Gazzarri's. They planned it out, maybe. Bub felt like the first people who porked there, they did it because they were walking past the yard and said, hey, I think we should pork on that spot over there, because we want to pork *now* but we don't know where else to do it. He wondered if one was more of a Good Time than the other. To know it was coming, to say hey when you woke up, or to just walk past it and say hey. Bub didn't know. He didn't have anything to compare it to. He always just walked past things and said hey. He never woke up and said hey. Not like the people porking on the yard, or the people driving their very long cars slowly around corners, or having to add the letters S, O, L, D, another O,

U, and T to the marquee at the Whisky, or leaning over the hole beneath the crosswalk and yelling barf into it, or trying to walk on tall shoes and hurting their ankles and shouting ow ouch ouch, or driving a tiny little car like on a golf course down the sidewalk and making everybody jump out of the way and yelling watch it and motherfucker and goddamnit, or the one guy from the one band chasing the other guy from the other band down the street. They all had Good Times because they woke up and said hey. That didn't seem smart to Bub. Something might happen between saying hey and having the Good Time that meant you couldn't have the Good Time. Or something would happen after you had the Good Time that meant you could never say hey again.

Bub stopped walking and frowned. Something could even happen *during* the Good Time that made you stop having a Good Time. Something could always happen at any time. He didn't like that.

So he slouched his way above the Strip, wandering until he found who he was looking for. Ollie and Mike were having a grill with a bunch of other folks. Not on a roof. On the ground. Bub pointed to the grill and asked "is that the grill fro-"

"JESUS!" Mike shouted. He jumped up and all of the other folks laughed at him. Bub thought that was funny so he laughed too. Mike pointed his spatula at Bub. "You scared the shit out of me, man!"

"Oh. I'm sorry."

"The fuck are you sneaking around for?"

"I didn't think I was sneaking. I was just wondering if

278

that was the grill that you and Dominick put on your roof."

The mention of Dominick's name made Mike look sad. "Yeah."

"Why did you bring it down?"

"…because I wanted to. Wh-"

"Did someone help you?"

"The fuck do you care?"

"I was just wondering. I'm making a conversation."

Ollie stumbled over with a drink in his hand. It smelled very upsetting, even from as far away as Bub was. "Heeeey," he said. "Haven't seen you in ages! Where ya been?"

"I watch a lot of movies."

Ollie laughed like that was just about the funniest thing he ever did hear. Bub wished they were still laughing at Mike, because he'd understood what they were laughing about then.

Bub shifted his weight from foot to foot. "There's nothing funny about movies, unless they're supposed to be."

That only made Ollie laugh harder. Some of the other fellas who Bub had never met came over and they were already laughing. Bub didn't know why. He wanted to laugh but he didn't because he wanted to tell them something that you didn't laugh at when you talked about it.

"I think I killed Dominick," was what he wanted to say, and so did.

A few of the guys in the back laughed harder. Most of them stopped laughing though. Bub figured the people who kept laughing didn't know Dominick that well.

"That's not fucking funny," Ollie snapped.

Bub nodded in agreement. "That was why I wasn't laughing."

Mike came over and waved his spatula some more. Bub noticed that he wasn't wearing an apron. That was a weird thing to notice, he felt. There were a lot of things Mike wasn't wearing, like suspenders or a propeller beanie. Bub didn't notice that Mike wasn't wearing those things until he thought about things he wasn't noticing that Mike wasn't wearing. But no apron, he noticed. Did it make sense to say you noticed something that wasn't there? Anyway, Mike swung his arm and *whapped* Bub on the nose with the spatula. The pain smelled like hamburger. "THE FUCK YOU SAY?" Mike asked.

"Easy!" Ollie shouted.

Bub staggered backwards and rubbed his nose. "Ouch," he explained. Now the hamburger tasted like blood.

"Say that again, you fucking retard!" Mike demanded.

"Ouch," Bub repeated. He never saw somebody get so mad about their directions being followed.

Ollie stepped forward and put his shoulder in front of Mike's and said "he doesn't know what he's saying."

So Bub elaborated: "yes I do. I think I killed Dominick because I wanted to talk to him on a Ouija board, because I thought I was the Good Time Butcher and actually I don't think I was, but I think I did Good Time Butcher one guy, but that was kind of like an accident. I just got confused."

Mike and Ollie and all the folks just stood and looked at Bub for a long time. He thought they might be waiting for him to say something, but he didn't have anything else to say.

Except for: "I'm really sorry I did it. But I blinked one night and my tooth took over, then I woke up and it was tomorrow and I had a lot of blood on me, and then Dominick was dead. I think that was how it happened. That was the order of when they happened. Then I talked to him on the Ouija board and he said he was kind of mad but kind of glad. Only I think it was just the tooth talking to me. But the tooth was candy anyway."

The folks behind Mike mumbled a bit. A tall guy sitting on a pile of bricks said that Bub was crazy.

Bub just nodded. "I'm really sorry about that. I wouldn't have killed Do-"

"STOP SAYING THAT!" a lady in the back shouted.

"Oh. Sorry."

Ollie walked up to Bub and put his hand on his shoulder. He did it really hard. That was how Bub knew Ollie was just so mad, because Ollie knew that Bub didn't like being touched. He was usually the one telling other people, hey, don't touch Bub, he doesn't like it. "If you did what you're saying you did," Ollie's teeth growled, "then prove it to me. How'd you kill him? Where? Specifically?"

"Wherever the paper says."

He shook his head. "No. Fuck that." He jabbed his finger on the bottom of Bub's throat. "I'm asking *you*.

281

Tell me."

"I don't know."

"Then why do you think you killed him?"

"Because I thought about doing it, because he was the only person who would talk to me on the Ouija board. Then I woke up and it was tomorrow and he was dead. And I had a lot of blood on me. And then he talked to me on the Ouija board."

"But that was the tooth, right Bub? The candy tooth?"

"Right. Thank you for listening."

Ollie thumped Bub twice on the shoulder, *thump thump*, and then he sighed and shook his head and looked back at the folks and kind of waved at the others who were standing up and they sat back down. Then Ollie turned his head back to look at Bub and he said "you can't just walk up to…listen, some of the guys here, and me, we're still pretty fuckin' raw about Dominick. It's not been so long, you know? Some of us, we're tight with his family. Some of us feel like we just about *are* his family. So you sneak up outta the fucking shadows, saying about how you killed him…you can't do that."

"But I did. And also I'm telling the truth."

"Alright, lemme ask you this: how'd you think this was gonna go? Like, you walk up to some guys you last saw at a goddamned funeral service not too long ago, you see them grilling on the corner, and you sneak on up and cop to murdering the guy they're still fucking mourning. Is this…is…because, lemme tell you, I don't think you're appreciating that some of the guys here, those guys there who are wearing fucking sunglasses at night, they do more than just grill on the fucking corner. Or maybe you *do,* in whi-"

"I know that you do more than grill."

"Not me, *them.* And I want you to answer my question. Is this you trying to goad somebody into smoking you? Because that's super fucked up."

"I don't smoke."

"No...fucking killed. Are you trying to get killed, yes or no?"

"I don't know."

"Yes you do. You fucking do. Nobody doesn't know the answer to a question like that."

"I *don't* not know the answer. The answer is, 'I don't know.' I thought I wanted to go to jail, but the police wouldn't take me. They just wrote down what I told them and made me take a hike."

"...you went to the cops?"

"Yeah."

"You went to the cops," Ollie clarified, extending his hands with his wrists together, "and you told them you killed people, and *asked* them to arrest you?"

"Yeah."

"And they *didn't?!*"

"That's right. Otherwise I wouldn't be here."

Ollie looked like he wanted to laugh and scream at the same time. "That is the whitest fucking thing I ever... *fuck* man."

Bub shrugged.

Ollie sighed, then looked over his shoulder. Some of the folks were still glaring at Bub. Mostly the guys

283

wearing fucking sunglasses at night. Mike and a few others were walking closer, but not in a threatening way. In a way like Bub was a firework that they'd lit, but that hadn't blown up yet. Somebody pointed to the grill and said something. Mike went back to the grill to flip over meat.

"I just did some bad things," Bub said, "and I want…"

"To pay for them?"

"I don't k-"

"You don't know. Right. No fuckin' clue. Well, do you want to get the shit kicked out of you? Because you're gonna know that. That's what's gonna happen if you hang around here. But that's *all* that's gonna happen." Ollie lowered his voice, and drew closer. "I don't wanna see that happen. That's not gonna solve anybody's problem. Not theirs, not yours. So just go home, okay? I'll save you some food and bring it by tonight."

"Okay."

"Just go home and don't do anything…just relax. Just don't do anything you can't undo."

"Okay."

"You're not going to do anything, are you?"

"I don't know."

"…"

"I have to do *some* things."

"Are you trying to tell me something, or are you just being one of those fuckin' 'oh actually' guys?"

"I don't kn-"

"Yeah, you don't know. Alright. Just fuckin' go home,

take a breath. You'll know there. Home's where you know shit. And I'll be by with a plate, how's that?"

"…"

"Bub."

"See you," Bub said, before he turned around and walked back the way he came, down through the shadows, back onto the Strip, and then across it and beyond it, down on South Robertson, through Beverly Grove with its lazy palms, through Pico-Robertson and its sidewalks that ran every way but straight, through Culver Junction, around the park full of what looked like gravestones but who could be sure, past the Inglewood Oil Fields which were kind of pretty in a sad way, past Sunkist Park, through Fox Hills, onto South Sepulveda, through West Chester, past a baseball field that had all the lights on even though the sun was starting to come up, and even though it was early there was somebody driving a little car like on a golf course in circles on the pitcher's mound, and Bub wondered if maybe they were the people he'd seen on the Strip, or if you could have a Good Time anywhere as long as you had a car like on a golf course so lots of people had them, but anyway he didn't have one, he was just walking walking walking, for almost five hours now, but he was close, he knew where he was going even though he'd never been, there were so many signs, onto Vicksburg, and then into the lobby of LAX which was the brightest part of the city except for the Strip. Hey, it said, and it always said hey. It didn't have to wake up and say hey, or walk past something and say hey, because it never walked and it never slept so it never woke, it just always said hey. Maybe that was better. Maybe if you never stopped saying hey, nothing bad could ever happen. Because nothing ever happened that wasn't you saying hey.

He walked up to the Pan Am desk and its lady with the funny hat and said to her "I don't want to go anywhere."

She blinked at him and said "um."

"Because if I go somewhere," he told her, "then I won't know. I will just not know, somewhere else. But if I stay here then I will know pretty soon. I think."

The lady in the funny hat frowned at Bub and said "sir, if you're not going to buy a ticket, then I can't help you. I sell tickets."

"I don't want a ticket," he explained. "I want to know. So I'm going to go home now."

"Ok."

"I'm sorry I disturbed you."

"It's fine. Are you alright, sir?"

"I don't know. *YET!*"

The lady flinched.

Bub's scream echoed around the lobby. Everybody else got really quiet to listen to it. It was still bouncing around, and everybody else was still listening, as Bub walked back outside, up up up the way he came, and now he could really see where he was going and what he was passing and who there was in the city, and a lot of them seemed to be having Good Times even though they weren't porking on the yard out back of Gazzarri's or driving cars like on a golf course. They had Frisbees and dogs on leashes and hands they were holding or walkmen with headphones and some were just looking at trees and smiling. Bub looked at them and it was sort of a Good Time to just see them having Good Times. Something could happen to all of them but it hadn't yet, or maybe it already had but even still they had a Good Time after something had happened. It was hot and Bub was sweaty when he got back into his apartment. He was supposed to be watching a movie today, that was what he planned. Some airplanes had movies they played at you, and Bub thought it might have been cool to watch a movie in the sky. But that would have meant Bub was going away, and going away meant Bub wouldn't know. He hoped Ollie was right, that if he stayed here then pretty soon he would Know. He didn't know what he would Know, or what he wanted to Know, but he knew that he did. Want to Know. Because that would be something different, and he liked that. The same made him sad. Maybe different would make him happy.

So he sat on his bed, put his hands on his thighs, and looked at the door. He wondered if Ollie had come by with some food. He wondered if Ollie would be back again, to check on him. He wondered how long he would have to wait until he Knew. Probably at least until nighttime. That was enough time to watch a movie, maybe. But he didn't want to leave the apartment, because then he might miss whatever it was that would let him Know. So he stared at the door and tried to imagine a movie on it. The longest movie anybody had ever seen. It was exciting and had a lot of cool scenes with people having

Good Times and doing Interesting Things and no bad somethings that happened to make them be the Last Good Time, and it made you look at the world in a new and interesting way, and think interesting thoughts.

That was what he'd wanted to imagine. But all he could see was one about a guy who tried hard and mostly people were nice to him. But then Bad Things happened, and he was the one who did them. Then nobody would make a Bad Thing happen to him, because nobody believed the guy could do the Bad Thing. And he didn't know. So he decided that he had to make sure the Bad Thing happened, because people who did Bad Things deserved Bad Things. No, not Bad Things: Bad Times. Because Things passed, but Times kept going. Bad people deserved Bad Times. And that meant a Last Good Time. So the guy went to the Strip, where you could see the Interesting Things, and this time he didn't just watch. This time he didn't just pretend. He brought money and sold it for horrible things that he put into his body. Then the Interesting Things blurred together and became one Interesting Thing, and he didn't just Know what it looked sounded smelled like, but he Knew how it tasted, how it felt. And it wasn't as Good as everybody said. It was loud and fast and scary. That was why they were screaming. They weren't having a Good Time. They were trying to hold on. Screaming was something you could follow back into yourself. So the guy screamed into the blur, he screamed and screamed until even that couldn't lead him back, and then he listened as the blur swallowed the scream and dark gobbled up the Interesting Things and it ended on the yard out back of Gazzarri's laying in the sharp grass and listening to the people next to him porking each other, and watching their faces and seeing that they looked like he felt, looked like they were seeing what he saw, and what he was seeing looked like nothing. Bub was the guy and he didn't Know, but that was okay because neither did anybody, especially not on the yard out back of Gazzarri's.

Bub sat on his bed in his room and watched somebody throw beer on the two people porking next to him on the sharp grass. Some of it got on him, but he didn't flinch, he didn't blink, he didn't breathe. Bub watched this and then looked at his door. And then the door said

knock knock

KNOCK

DELMER beheld he who knocked upon the cubical wall: Fluck, for once deigning to smile at him.

"You're a natural," Fluck said, which made Delmer wonder if he was awake. "This whole Good Time Butcher gag?" He made a *whoosh* noise and angled a flat palm upwards, like a right-angle heil.

"Are those supposed to be sales?"

"Guilt's a hell of a lever. You just gotta lean on it a little, and suddenly everybody's saying, oh, let me buy a little thing. Just one little thing. End of day we're selling a hundred little things, *and* a few big things." Fluck leaned on the corner of Delmer's cubical. As a guitarist, the latter couldn't help but wince at the thought of how the former was compressing vital forearm nerves. But Fluck wasn't a guitarist. "Listen, son. I want to talk to you about your career ambitions."

Delmer laughed. He couldn't help it. He shunted his revolving chair around to face his boss, savoring every squeak and creak. "Now what do you mean by that?"

"I think you know."

"You want me here full-time?"

Fluck darkened ever-so-slightly, as though to hear the idea out loud convinced him of its absurdity. "And then some. I'm inquiring as to whether or not you might be amenable to a promoted position. There would be a pay raise, too."

"By how much?"

"That's negotiable."

Delmer leaned back and steepled his fingers. That was something he'd always wanted to do, lean back and steeple his fingers and press them to his lips, a double-barreled *shhh*, bidding his suitor to hold their peace while he considered their plaintive offer. Granted, he'd always imagined this scenario would play itself out in the aggressively windowed offices of some major record label, but beggars couldn't be…no, hang on, *he* wasn't the beggar here. He was the chooser.

"Delmer," the bossbeggar implored. "Don't jerk me around here. We're talking like a buck an hour, max."

Delmer leaned back further, but felt his equilibrium starting to lose confidence. So he tipped himself forward, hard, and ended up with his elbows on his knees. Rats! A deferential posture, *and* he was compressing vital forearm nerves! He returned to neutral and said "I don't know, man. I'm trying to make this music thing work. Some of the fellas here and I, we're gonna be starting a new band."

"Who?"

"…you wouldn't know them."

"I'm the manager. I know everyone who works here."

"…Cody."

"Cody who I fired?"

"…well, I'm gonna talk to some guys eventually who, I'll ask them about starting a new band. And then we'll be doing gigs and recording an alb-"

"They're not mutually exclusive," Fluck sighed. "I'm not asking you to run the company. You'd be a shift supervisor. You'd work the same hours, the only difference would be a few more responsibilities during your shift. A bit less time on the phones, more on organizational stuff. If you can pursue the music now, you can pursue the music with a promotion and a raise."

"Hmmm…" Delmer rebuilt the steeple.

"Gotta be honest here, I'm a little flummoxed as to why you would have any reaction other than 'cool, yes, thank you'."

"Well, I'm an *artist*. I have to safeguard my craft!"

Fluck sighed and dug the first knuckle of his thumb into his third eye. "Did you know I'm a sculptor?"

"Like…marble?"

"Wood. I've got pieces in a few smaller museums around town. I was part of a showcase last week." He dropped his hand. "I don't wanna astonish you so early in your shift, but I aspire to more than managing a goddamned call center hawking egg beaters and towel warmers."

Delmer couldn't help but be deeply, existentially horrified by the thought. Why that should be the case wasn't immediately clear to him, though laying awake all through the night as he would, the rationale for his terror would become clear: it had never quite occurred to him that ambition would be rewarded with anything other than success. Rocketed onward by the inexhaustible delusion of youth, Delmer had simply assumed that people who got ahead did so because they *wanted* it, while those who languished in obscurity did so as a consequence of their lassitude. After all, it wasn't like he'd heard all kinds of stories about people hustling hard and *not* coming out on top. The colossal obviousness of this was what would shake him awake each time he approached the sweet release of sleep that night: he hadn't heard these stories because…how would he? It was, he realized with an audible *gasp* into his darkened room, a replay of one of his more embarrassing middle school memories. One of his teachers, a vegetarian, was trying to talk shit about red meat. Why she'd hopped on this particular soapbox – as far as Delmer could remember, this had been Mrs. Arden, who was a history teacher, and what the hell was she doing talking about anything that didn't involve people saying "forsooth!" or whatever – was lost to the expanses of the can't-recall. What stuck firmly in Delmer's mind was that, as a kid from a farm that raised and processed livestock for the dinner table, he had taken this

294

one-comment crusade as a personal affront. Feeling quite confident he had an unappealable trump card in this particular discussion, he raised his hand, followed it up to his feet, and boldly asserted that he didn't know about her, but he'd "never met anybody who died from eating too much red meat."

Mrs. Arden, if that was who it was, had just smiled and said "well, you wouldn't have."

Everybody had laughed at Delmer for that one. He'd gone home and tried to write a song about the experience. And as young Delmer's artistic output had never lacked a thematic throughline, within two hours the song ended up being about titties.

Well, Delmer told himself, now well into a young adulthood made no brighter for having actually interfaced with live human titties, *I wouldn't have*. It didn't exactly strain credulity to imagine that he would try to make it in the music industry, try and try and try, and fail every single time. What he hated most of all was that this didn't make him want to stop trying – it simply braced him for misfortune in a way he hadn't been before. The natural corollary of that was to start imagining contingencies. Ok, well, if *this* thing doesn't pan out, I can do *that* to make ends meet. And if I'm doing *that*, maybe I'll have to go about *this* in a different way.

It was, in other words, a way of thinking diametrically opposed to the one that had ferried him into a U-Haul, and kept him sane in the convection of that conveyance as they sweat their way westward, allowed him to sleep on the floor of the basement of some stank-ass factory, given him the liberty to hit the Strip and blow all of his money on booze and babes and, uh, blow. How could he have managed any of that, if he'd entertained the sorts of doubts which might be described as, well, healthy?

There was no guarantee that his new band – which was definitely going to exist, and that he'd already decided should be called Donkey Hotay until he thought of something better – would hit the big time, or even the medium time. Fuck, even the *small* time. They could write and record the greatest album ever, and then some deep-vibrato dipshit could join Scorpions or some other band with a following, and *poof*, there goes everything again. Donkey Hotay up in smoke. The insult to injury, of course, was that Delmer had resolved to join this band with the stage name of Grip. Get it? Grip, Clutch? He was going to beat that bastard to the big time, and with a synonym for his pseudonym, no less. Oh fuck, that was a song title, wasn't it? Synonym for a Pseudonym? The challenge would be to write it without allowing it to be hijacked by titties. Old habits died hard.

But hey. Even if the song did get away from him a bit, that'd be cool. Because it'd be a song, and having a song meant he was that much closer to an album. And an album meant a tour, and a tour meant publicity, and publicity meant global domination. It wasn't that hard. A pretty logical progression, actually, albeit one along which progress was far from guaranteed; after all, the straight line to success he'd imagined himself to be foll-owing was nearer to a tightrope, and beneath his feet yawned a depthless chasm.

And here he was, afraid of heights.

Morning came, but the light did little to penetrate the darkness over which he teetered and trembled. What it *did* do was brighten the line that would carry him across, wherever that far side lay. Yes, there was a fall, but there was also a path. Yes, the path was narrow and the fall beckoned, but he could resist. He could do this. He could make it across. Great things lay ahead for him, he knew, and even if the way to reach them was through that damned call center, it was *through* it. To the other side. He would take this little promotion and as much of a raise as he could finagle, and he would stay in the job no longer than a year. At that point, even if the music thing hadn't taken off yet, he would move on, keep himself vibrant, throttle complacency in the cradle.

Yes, by the time 1980 came, he would be out of there, and onto greener pastures. Not literally, of course – he'd been *born* in green pastures, and headed west in search of a foothold amongst, uh, greyer ones? Come to think of it, that didn't sound so great. It was a dumb metaphor anyway.

Whatever. He had plenty of time to refine his poetic imagery.

"Ok," he told Fluck the next day, "I'll be your damn shift supervisor. But I'm telling you, I'm giving you my one-year notice right now."

Fluck just smiled and nodded.

"I'm serious."

"Oh," his manager said, "I believe that you are."

Delmer glared, then walked back to his station, picked

up the phone, dialed the next number on the list, and asked to speak to the head of the household.

THE LAST GOOD TIME, LIVED AND GONE

IT was, to put it mildly, not a good time to be Isley Pultrock.

The guy who had tackled her into the wall was named Sandor Cardozo. He was the son of a well-respected Portuguese poet, and when Isley wondered aloud what the hell he was doing in a shitty apartment in LA, then, if his dad was such hot shit, Sergeant Hollenbeck informed her that Sandor was in America after fleeing the Chatalenango province of El Salvador in the wake of a military-led murder campaign. When Isley wondered what the hell a Portuguese fellow was doing in El Salvador, since last she checked there was a whole big ocean between those two places, Sarge explained to her that Sandor was married to a Salvadorian woman, and he had made the impossible decision to leave his daughter at home in the US, risk life and limb by sneaking into El Salvador with his wife, and do everything he could to smuggle *her* family to safety in America. His wife, and her extended family, perished in the effort. Sandor was left to recross the southern border of Texas on his own. The subsequent months had been a tale of woe and ultimately triumph, his life having arrived at a kind of equilibrium. Right up until Isley showed up, banged on his door, and pointed a gun at his daughter.

"I didn't point it *at* her," Isley corrected him snidely. "I pointed it *above* her." She tried to demonstrate, but it was hard with her hands cuffed to the table.

Sarge just shook his head. He further made clear that he was being ordered, in no uncertain terms, by people an indeterminate ways up the food chain, that Isley was to be treated as if she had never had the slightest connection with the LAPD, and, more to the point, she was to conduct herself as though this were the case. Any attempt to curry favor with the jury by talking about Bub Bowersox and the address she'd culled, *illegally*, from the station's records, were strictly forbidden.

"Or what," Isley scoffed, as that was the easiest way to cover the tremble in her voice, "you'll put me in prison for *two* hundred years instead of one?"

Another shake of the head. "I don't think you understand what I'm telling you. This comes from *up the food chain.*" That Sarge left it there had a more profound chilling effect on Isley than if he'd tried to hit the point more forcefully.

This was, it turned out, also not a good time to be any sort of American anything-enforcement agency sharing headlines with anything vaguely Central Amercian. Isley wondered if this was some kind of fucking joke, that she was being bullied into falling on somebody else's sword so the LAPD didn't have to be associated with El Salvador. When Time did that cover, and Reagan did that speech, he was talking more about, like, Nicaragua, right? One of those other ones.

"Most people don't know the difference," Sarge sighed. Isley certainly didn't disagree – she couldn't have pointed to any of the places she'd just listed on a map. She knew that Portugal and Spain were in Europe; beyond that, the provenance of Spanish speakers was a mystery to her. She had enough problems of her own, she felt, without bringing geography into it.

"So no fault of my fucking own," Isley scoffed again, "and I'm done. Like that."

"...did you seriously just say you're in this situation *through no fault of your own?!*"

"I mean, not *here* here," Isley clarified, rattling the chains of her cuffs, "but like, here as in how was I supposed to know I was knocking on the door of a fucking PR problem?"

"BY LETTING US DO IT!" Sarge thundered as he slammed the desk with an open palm. "Can I tell you how fucking stupid you are?"

"...name-calling's beneath you, Sarge."

He quite literally ducked that rebuke, leaning down and regaining the upright with a folder in his hand. He tossed it towards Isley.

She reached for it. The links of the cuffs pulled taut.

Sarge just watched her reaching vainly for the file. He laughed, threw his head back, and made an exasperated *aaaaah* noise. "That," he told her, "is the autopsy report of Bub Bowersox."

Isley stared at it. Maybe, she felt, if she stared hard enough, she might light it on fire, and so make it untrue.

"What you'd have *known*, if you'd allowed Colby to run your hunch instead of going vigilante, what you *could* have known in a fraction of the time it took you to drive to the apartment in which Mr. Bowersox used to live… was that he didn't live there anymore. Because he doesn't live *anywhere*. Just a few days after he gave us his statement, he was found dead outside one of those skeevy clubs on Sunset. Overdose. Apparently he'd been laying there for two days before anybody even noticed he was any further gone than the other wastoids down there. So you got what you wanted years before you knew you wanted it. How about that, huh? Isn't that fucking something?"

"What do you mean, *got what I wanted?"*

"You had your gun drawn."

"Because the guy…" Isley frowned. "I didn't want to shoot him. I wanted to bring him in."

"The coroner did that. Which you would have known, if you hadn't been high out of your mind."

"Now shut your goddamned mouth one second. I wasn't high. I w-"

"Then how was it that two kilos, two *kilos* of coke

vanished from the evidence locker at just about the same time you popped in and stole the Bowersox statement? Coincidence?"

"Oh, bullshit! I didn't take any fucking coke! You ask anybody if they saw me with two goddamned bricks un-der my ar-"

"Nobody saw you take the statement from the file!"

"I could fit that in my pocket!"

"How do I know how big your goddamned pockets are?!"

"No." Isley adjusted herself into a more upright pos-ture and wagged her finger at Hollenbeck. "No, no, fuck no. I took the file, I knocked on the door with the gun, I *used* to take coke from evidence, whatever. All true. I've fucked up, and I've maybe done some fucked up shit. But somebody saw me come in, saw me leave, and that fucker goes, hey, I can take the coke and pin it on her, and everybody'll believe it! You want me to take the fall for stuff I've done, well, I was gonna say I'll do it but fuck you, I'm dragging whoever I can down with me."

"Don't y-"

"BUT! I'm not gonna be railroaded on some shit I didn't do! No fucking way! I'm clean, I got clean on force of fucking *will!*" She slammed her right forefinger down on the table with enough force of a more literal sort, she would later discover, to fracture it below the second knuckle. "Ow. You do a drug test on me, toxicology, what the fuck. Try me. If I've got a microscopic fucking *granule* of coke in me right now, you call CBS and we'll do a live execution. I'll sign a waiver and we'll fucking do it. I'm *clean*."

Sarge kneaded his unibrow. "No. Ok. Listen. Here's the deal. This is all from up the food chain, yes, so *you* keep *your* fucking mouth shut and let me say this." He sighed, dug his knuckles into his brow, then met Isley's gaze with an intensity she had never seen from him. "Bub Bowersox was the Good Time Butcher. We're going to announce as much. And, thanks to the tireless efforts of Luca C-"

"Are you fucking kidding me? The Good Time Butcher could st-"

"QUIET!"

"NO, *YOU* QUIET! Who killed Bub, huh? One of th-"

Sarge laughed. "He O.D'd, you fucking fruitcake!"

"Right after he came to confess?! Somebody was trying to s-"

"As I was saying, thanks to the tirel-"

"One of the other Butchers silenced him! This is a conspiracy of Butch-"

"JESUS, PULTROCK, LISTEN TO YOURSELF!"

"A CONSPIRACY OF BUTCHERS, AND THEY DIDN'T WANT ONE OF THEIR OWN TALKING!"

Sarge kicked his chair out from under him on his way to standing.

Isley flinched. Felt her chin burrowing into her neck.

"I'm done," Sarge growled. "I'm done with you."

"NO! GET THE FUCK BACK HERE!" Isley tried to stand, but her cuffs yanked her back into her seat. She missed, glancing the armrest with her hip. It plopped her down at an angle that tweaked her low back. She wouldn't notice until about the time she became aware of her fractured finger. "I'M NOT FOLLOWING THE GODDAMNED PARTY LINE, YOU ASSHOLE! I'M GONNA SAY I GOT A CALL FROM THE FUCK-ING PRESIDENT HIMSELF TELLING ME TO GO KILL THAT CARBOZO MOTHERFUCKER! I'M… I'M GONNA SAY EVERYTHING I EVER KNEW ABOUT WHAT THIS FUCKING DEPARTMENT DOES WRONG! I'M GONNA… Sarge! SARGE!" her voice caught in her throat. She tried to power through, but couldn't generate much more than a ragged cough. Besides, the door was closed. That didn't mean Sarge couldn't hear her though – she had no doubt he'd de-camped to the far side of that one-way mirror.

She turned to the mirror, trying to imagine she was looking at Sarge, and not herself. "Sarge, please! It's like you said, if I'm in jail…I can't go to jail! I busted some of these people, probably! I swear to fucking, whoever you want, I was trying to help! I was just trying to catch a…I was…"

Without meaning to, she made eye contact with her reflection.

She slumped down in her chair, allowing her shoulders to drop by their own weight for the first time in, hell, who knew how long. It didn't feel good, or relaxing, or restful. It felt like surrender.

She tried to hike them back up, but found it more than she could manage just then. She was so, so tired.

THE DARK ON SUNSET

MOVIES tended to put Delmer to sleep nowadays. They were just getting so damn long, the big blockbuster ones, and it had been quite some time since he'd managed to sleep straight through the night without having to get up for at least *one* bladder evacuation. That was what his wife Katrina called them. "Bladder evacuation?" she'd mumble on those nights his rising roused her, and he'd just pat her shoulder and smile. Chances were, in the morning she wouldn't remember having said it. She was a heavy sleeper, which granted her vibrancy during the day. This evoked in Delmer the shade of envy one can only feel for the love of one's life. Not that it had been a love uninterrupted. Delmer had met her during the early eighties, which had proven challenging to him for a number of reasons. Not the least of them was the way the Good Time Butcher, a gilb, off-the-cuff invention of his, had clawed its way into reality and racked up a body count. It was impossibly surreal, that his, what, just some bullshit sales technique, that that should become a rumor, and then by the hands of some copycat chucklefucks as deficient in imagination as they were in empathy (but really, what was the difference), a reality. And then, at a certain point, a legend. Before long that detective had found him, after which he'd had a genuine nervous breakdown. Certainly, he thought, she'd catch on to his rather lame attempt at deflection. Clutch must have heard from somebody that Delmer had made the Good Time Butcher up. He'd tell the cop, she'd come back with cuffs. That'd be it for poor Delmer Lippincott. So fearful had he become after that, so *paranoid*, that he'd fled the City of Angels and moved north to San Francisco. The thrash scene was just hitting its stride when he arrived, and even as his glam dreams had faded, he'd kept up his disciplined, daily guitar practice regimen, and so preserved what modest chops he had on the ol' six string (that he thought of it as *the ol' six string* ought perhaps have been a sign that he wasn't cut from the same cloth as the thrash community). Was there a tearful reunion with his childhood friend Patch? Yes, but not immediately. That would come years later. In the interim, Delmer met Katrina. He'd been out wandering Haight-Ashbury, trying to imagine what it must have been like nearly two decades earlier, before its counterculture became culture, and stopped in a dinky little bakery for lunch. Katrina took his order, a floating head behind a tall counter. Luckily for him, she also brought him his meal, which if memory served (quite a big *if*) was some formulation of eggs and potatoes. The moment he looked up to his incoming meal, he noticed two things, in the following order: the woman bussing it over was wearing a Black Sabbath T-Shirt, and she was beautiful. Beautiful enough to overwhelm the frustration Delmer still felt towards Black Sabbath, and towards Ronnie James Dio and his stupid, majestic voice…but no, he was over that. Which was why, when she put his food down, Delmer asked her out, and now, nearly forty years later, through highs and lows and even a dismal year-and-a-half long separation, there they were, Katrina lying heavy on their regal memory foam, mumbling about Delmer's piss-filled bladder.

But that was neither here nor…well, it was *there*, actually. *Here* was that darkened movie theater, in which Delmer had, with a trepidation he hadn't felt since the night after discovering that his old boss Fluck was a failed woodworker, plunked down fifteen bucks to see a movie called *The Dark on Sunset*. If it wasn't quite star-studded, it was at least star-speckled, the razzle-dazzle of names like J.K. Simmons and Jessica Chastain obscured by the cloud cover of B-listers like Brydon Plyst. Most movies made Delmer sleepy, yes, but this one commanded his full attention, to such an extent that as the studio logos rolled out over the opening riff of Mötley Crüe's "Wild Side," Delmer felt as though his ticker was fit to spring a gear. He was able to still his nerves somewhat by chuckl-

ing to himself about the anachronistic song choice –
"Wild Side" was off *Girls, Girls, Girls*, which didn't drop
until 1987, years after the era in which the events of *The
Dark on Sunset* took place. Jessica Chastain played detective Luca Colby. Simmons was Sergeant Hollenbeck.
And Brydon Plyst played Bub Bowersox, known to
history as the Good Time Butcher.

This was all astonishing enough to Delmer, and in a
way slightly galling. The film was apparently based on a
nonfiction book about 'the Butcher' that Delmer had
never heard of, not that he was much of a reader. So
plenty of people not on screen were seeing royalties off
this project. Delmer couldn't help but feel like he was
entitled to some – not much, just enough to pad out the
piddling pension that had been his prize for decades of
serving as third-in-command for a consultancy firm that
liased with countless vineyards in and around the Napa
Valley (how that had come to pass, boy, that was a whole
different story). He clung to that rather childish sense of
frustration like driftwood, to keep his head above the roil
and toil of his benthic terror. Here was his fiction that
had become nonfiction, presented as nonfiction re-
enacted as fiction.

The Good Time Butcher was, he recognized with
existential indigestion, the sole creative output of his life
that had ever seen anything approaching a large-scale
release.

The moment that damn near gave him an aneurysm,
though, was when Anne Hathaway showed up in something between a minor supporting role and a glorified

cameo. She was buried under subtle and unflattering prosthetics, presumably because nobody wanted the vaguely villainous comic relief to challenge the heroine in the looks department…and at the same time, nobody wanted to cast an actor who couldn't look good on the press trail.

Hathaway sneered and snarled through her scenes, chewing the scenery as aggressively as she chewed whatever was in her mouth at any given moment; someone, either Anne or the director or whoever, had decided that Detective Isley Pultrock should be eating something – like, *aggressively* eating – for literally every single second of her screentime.

At first, the character's appearance stirred little more than a vague loathing in Delmer. He'd never had any particular distaste for Hathaway – in as much as he could remember seeing her before, he'd thought her swell enough – but his granddaughters all said she was so *out,* or whatever words kids were using this month to off-handedly dismiss people they'd never met. So maybe this was the feeling to which they were responding.

It wasn't until nearly three quarters of the way through the film that a spaceship landed on Delmer's head.

Jesus Fuck: Isley Pultrock was the detective who had tracked him down all those years ago.

For the remainder of the film, Delmer wrestled with one of the most absurd, and yet acute terrors he had ever known: was he going to be in this movie too? Was some young, not-terribly-attractive up-and-comer going to snort and sniff his way into frame and announce himself as Delmer Lippincott, the man who'd created the Good Time Butcher as a goof?

Oh, goddamnit, if only he'd read the book first!

This fear, of course, proved foolish. No one answering to his name appeared on screen. What unraveled, instead, was a fairly straightforward little potboiler about a harried detective with a flaw (apparently the real Colby had kept her nose clean, because the worst 'flaw' the scriptwriters could come up with for her character was that she had OCD and, if Delmer was reading the subtext correctly, IBS) tracking down one of LA's most notorious serial killers. Isley Pultrock, Delmer discovered through the film, sought at multiple turns to obstruct Colby's investigation, motivated by petty jealousy and a selfish desire for the limelight. Our heroine triumphs, though: Pultrock goes to jail, and Bowersox is killed.

The film was rather vague on the mechanics of that last point – they had him dying off-screen, but it was all too happy to plant a flag on his grave. The film concluded with Chastain-as-Colby watching the sunrise over, ugh, Sunset Boulevard (that little flourish was fairly indicative of the quality of the film's script, as it happened). Fade to black, that's all folks. Roll credits.

But wait! Not before the perfunctory 'where are they now' text crawl. Luca Colby had hung her own shingle as a private detective in 1994, then retired in 2005. She lived with her husband in Ojai. Sergeant Hollenbeck received a special commendation in 1983 for leading the investigation, and then died in 1992. His wife was still kicking in Cali, as were three little Hollenbeck kids who probably had broods of their own by now. Isley Pultrock, it turned out, died in prison. Hung by the neck, with bedsheets tied first around her neck, and then the handle of a doorknob. Delmer's first thought was, *I didn't think they let prisoners have bedsheets. Or doorknobs.* He supposed it depended on the prison, though.

His second thought was that Isley Pultrock hadn't seemed the suicide type to him. He knew a few people who'd ended up offing themselves. Mad Mick, Delmer's old Bömerayñ bandmate, he'd shot himself around '89. One guy Delmer met in San Fran, during his brief attempt to enter the thrash scene, he jumped off the Golden Gate once one of those big festivals back east dropped his band in favor of a grunge act. In both of those cases, Delmer had heard about their suicides and been horrified, but not shocked. When he called their faces up before him, there was a desperation to the sadness in their eyes. In as much as suicide could make sense, Delmer found something coherent in their having done what they did.

Pultrock, though? He'd only met her once, but she'd seemed too…agitated, to kill herself. If that made sense. If such an act could ever make sense.

Ah, well.

Delmer put his small soda in his popcorn bag and ferried it out to the lobby. He tossed it in the trash can by the door and wished the usher, or whatever you called the people who stood at the podium and took tickets, he wished her a goodnight.

"Did you like the movie?" she called to him.

Delmer paused, caught off guard by the question. He read nothing sinister into it, as he might have a few hours ago. If he wasn't in the movie about the Good Time Butcher, then he wasn't a part of that, for lack of a better term, *history*. It existed independently of him. It was, he was happy to note, not his problem anymore.

"I did," he replied.

"Me too," said the ticket taker. "I think Anne Hathaway should get an Oscar for that." Then she turned to engage in the act that conferred her her title.

Delmer stepped outside and shivered. He tried to enjoy the way the night ran its finger up and down his spine, doinking each vertebrae in turn. Tried, but didn't quite succeed.

He felt the ticket stub in his pocket, a little paper rectangle, soft at the edges from being fiddled into oblivion. He listened to the voices of theatergoers filing out onto the sidewalk, trying to sound insightful about the film, but…not quite succeeding.

Delmer let go of the ticket stub and smiled.

Whether or not anybody won anything for that movie, or made any money off of it, well, he didn't much care.

It had nothing to do with him.

Also by Jud Widing

Novels
Down The High Tomb
Go Figure
Jairzinho's Curbside Giants
The Little King of Crooked Things
A Middling Sort
Patience, Ambrose
Westmore and More!
The Year of Uh

Stories
Identical Pigs

Made in the USA
Middletown, DE
05 November 2022

14063769R00189